BIG THAW

A MIAMI JONES FLORIDA MYSTERY

A.J. STEWART

Jacaranda Drive Publishing

Los Angeles, California

www.jacarandadrive.com

This ebook is a work of fiction. Names, characters, places and incidents are either products of the author's imagination or are used fictitiously, and any resemblance to actual persons, living or dead, business establishments or locales is entirely coincidental.

The Heisman Memorial Trophy is a registered trademark of the Heisman Trust. The author and publisher are in no way affiliated with the Heisman Trust and no affiliation is implied.

Cover artwork by Streetlight Graphics

ISBN-13: 978-1-945741-36-4

Copyright © 2021 Jacaranda Drive

No part of this book may be reproduced, scanned or distributed in any printed or electronic form without permission from the publisher.

To Heather.
There is but one adventure, and I'm lucky to share mine with you.

CHAPTER ONE

My body stiffened as the cutthroat razor made contact with my neck. I really only had myself to blame for the predicament I was in, and the grins on the faces of those watching did nothing for my mood. To top it all off, when the girl holding the blade saw the look in my eye, she gave me a wink.

"Don't worry, Mr. Jones, I know what I'm doing."

I nodded using my eyelids. Motioning with my entire head felt a foolhardy thing to do given the sharpness of the blade beneath my chin.

"If this doesn't pan out, Miami, I've got dibs on your car," said Ron.

He was looking way too relaxed, leaning back in his stool at Longboard Kelly's with a cold one in his hand. From the corner of my eye, I could see Muriel watching intently from behind the bar.

I was in a chair previously unknown to me, one of the plastic numbers that sat under the beer-labeled umbrellas in the courtyard. My face was covered in white shaving foam, and the paving stones beneath my feet were littered with the offcuts of my formerly ragged hairdo.

Keisha, the one holding the blade, began moving it smoothly along my skin, giving me a shave that was closer than normal and too close for comfort. She had recently finished a stint at the West Palm Beach School of Hairdressing and Cosmetology. Apparently that gave her the credentials to offer a haircut *and* a shave.

I had met Keisha during a recent case. She was a kid who on the outside was nothing like me, but whose fears and desires I understood intimately. When we had come upon each other she had been standing at the fork in the road, not so much weighing one choice over the other, but rather being dragged down the potholed gravel track paved with poor choices and bad outcomes.

I was familiar with the kinds of life choices being thrust upon her. But, unlike her, I was also familiar with the good luck associated with someone pointing me down a better path—in my case, Coach Dunbar, my high school football coach, and Lenny Cox, who had taught me everything outside baseball that every man needed to know. For reasons I was only just now beginning to understand, I had felt the need to point Keisha in such a way. While I knew I couldn't make someone do something they didn't want to do, and it wasn't my place to try, sometimes you saw in another's eyes the desire without the means.

Keisha had helped me get to the bottom of a case, and I had given Keisha the means to attend hairdressing school—her goal—by providing a loan to cover the tuition that would have otherwise been beyond her. Now that she had graduated and found work in a salon in nearby Riviera Beach, she had begun to pay back the loan.

In haircuts and shaves.

She had already given Ron a little trim—anything more than that seemed sacrilegious to his fantastic silvery-gray mane. She had even taken care of Mick, the owner of Longboard Kelly's, with a buzz cut that would have done the Marines proud.

In my infinite wisdom I had agreed to the full two bits, and I could feel my balled fists cramping as she swept the sharp blade up along my throat and over my jawline. But the West Palm Beach School of Hairdressing and Cosmetology had taught her well, and not only did I come away with no nicks or cuts, but my haircut had elicited a positive comment from Muriel.

"Looks good," she said.

"Too much?" I asked.

Muriel smiled and passed a beer across the bar as I retook my stool.

"Not at all," she said. "You still look scruffy, but Danielle will approve."

I was about to make some witty retort about not needing my wife's approval for my haircut, but I saw Ron's subtle headshake just in time.

We sat in the fall sunshine and watched the locals get cheap haircuts. Those weren't on me. Once Keisha had covered her tuition payment by getting Ron and me spruced up, and she had covered her chair rental by shearing most of the hair clean off Mick's head, she then settled in to make a little cash. I was fairly certain that the Department of Health would frown upon such a thing, but the Department of Health only made occasional rounds at Longboard Kelly's. It wasn't like the place was in poor shape. Anyone who knew Mick knew he ran a tight ship. It was more that the health inspectors liked to do regular passes at the places with better views and nicer-looking clientele.

I was wiping the tiny hairs off the back of my neck when Ron's phone went off. I figured if it was Lizzy calling in from the office to tell us our extended lunch break was over, then Ron would have quietly slipped the phone back in his pocket. Instead he quietly slipped from his barstool and wandered to the back of the courtyard, near where the surfboard with the shark bite out of it hung on the wall, where the cell phone reception was best. He paced back and forth, gently nodding, and I spun back to face Muriel and enjoy my beer.

When Ron returned to the bar, he wore no expression on his face. It was as if the call had been neither good nor bad. The color beige came to mind. He sipped his beer before glancing at me.

"That was about a job," he said.

Getting work was usually a good thing, so I suspected there was more.

"An insurance client," he said. "Here in West Palm."

Insurance clients were like yin and yang to me. I didn't love the work—it was more often than not boring and vacuous—but it paid well, or at least it paid. But it still didn't explain Ron's face. He generally took on the insurance work, and claimed to not mind doing so. So I waited.

Ron took another small sip of his beer. "They'd like a meeting this afternoon."

And there it was. A gorgeous, sunny South Florida afternoon with no work on the books and nothing dragging us away from the bar at Longboard Kelly's. Until now. I almost felt sorry for Ron. Almost.

I nodded slowly, giving sufficient weight to the gravity of his situation. Ron liked fewer things worse than being dragged away from a half-finished beer. "I'll keep the home fires burning here," I said. "Perhaps you can drop by again later."

Ron shrugged and put his beer down. "I think you might want to be at this one."

I glanced around the courtyard and up into the clear blue sky. I couldn't imagine wanting to trade that in for an insurance company boardroom. I was going to say so but felt a simple shake of the head conveyed the message just as well.

"It's about the new sports arena in Mangonia Park," he said.

I was sure that Ron was hoping the word *sports* would pique my interest, and to be fair it almost did. I hadn't had a chance to visit the new arena, and Ron well knew of my somewhat unnatural attachment to sports arenas. Some people visited churches, and not just for service. For me there was no greater joy than the pulsing and heaving mass of a full sports arena. But there was also no greater peace to be found than in an empty one. Despite the fine afternoon, I could feel my better angels dragging me from my barstool. A paying job and a visit to a previously unseen cathedral of sports. There was no doubt in my mind that Ron was playing me, but I consoled myself with the knowledge that he was playing me well.

"This afternoon?" I asked.

"Half an hour," he said. "If we're available."

I looked at Muriel behind the bar, all tanned skin and strong arms. I'd never seen her do a workout, other than lifting heavy kegs of beer, but I knew she must have one heck of a routine. I gave her a look like I'd lost my puppy, and she simply answered with a lifting of the shoulders.

"We're here all week," she said.

CHAPTER TWO

The insurance company was located in one of the new office complexes in Rosemary Square. Being well acquainted with the joys of parking in that particular facility, Ron decided we should drive back to the office and make the rest of the journey on foot.

As we walked along South Dixie Highway, he passed me a stick of gum. Despite my long history with baseball, I'd never become a fan of chewing gum. It seemed utterly pointless to me. It wasn't a great look and it provided me no sustenance, but it would do the job of covering up any beer breath we might have from our respite at Longboards, and insurance guys could be sticklers for things like that.

Rosemary Square was the kind of downtown area that liked to proclaim itself the heart of the city. It was originally known as CityPlace, but the name had changed during renovations, for reasons that eluded almost everyone. I had read that the architecture was considered Mediterranean or Venetian, but I was fairly confident that anyone from Venice who saw Rosemary Square would have called the design "American shopping mall."

It was a somewhat soulless place, but I had to admit, it was a decent step up from the desolate non-downtown hub of crime and decay it had replaced around the turn of the millennium. As was the case with so many cities and towns in South Florida, there had been no *there* there—no hub, no town square. In Europe a visitor might find a town square designed for public use where it was perfectly acceptable to go and do nothing more than people-watch. Rosemary Square, on the other hand, was available for people to visit but designed specifically for them to spend plenty of cash while there. And as I had learned in philosophy class back in college, being a good consumer was what life was all about.

As we entered the office building, Ron took a tissue from his pocket and deposited his gum in it, then offered for me to do the same. By the time we reached the reception desk we were minty fresh.

Ron told the young guy at the desk who we were, and who we were there to see. We didn't even have time to take a seat on one of the flat, uncomfortable-looking sofas before our prospective client came out to greet us.

He looked like a New York banker, with short, neat hair, graying at the temples, and an immaculate pinstripe suit that for reasons I couldn't explain made me think of a penny-farthing bicycle. I noted that he was shaven as smooth as a baby's cheeks, and I wondered, for the first time in my life, whether he had noticed that I was the same. I caught a whiff of orange blossom. He nodded quickly several times as he shook Ron's hand, the serious expression on his face never wavering. He reminded me of J. Jonah Jameson, editor of the *Daily Bugle* in the *Spider-Man* comics.

"Thank you for coming so promptly," he said to Ron, then turned his stern face to me and pumped my hand with the same vigor.

"I'm Peter Parker," he said. "Let's talk in my office."

He spun on his heel and led us into the throng of open-plan desks. I gave Ron a sideways glance, and he shook his head in return. There was no way he could have known that I had framed the guy as a comic book character in my head, but there was no doubt that he already knew the guy's name was Peter Parker, and how much joy that would bring me.

Parker's office was planted in the center of the building. His only window gave us a great view of the desks. People seemed to be busy doing things that involved headsets and computer screens and the kinds of postures that kept chiropractors in Ferraris and Lamborghinis. His office was as neat and tidy as his haircut but littered with the usual tchotchkes of a white-collar executive: small plaques for achieving sales goals or teamwork objectives, family photos, and a framed picture of Parker with various semi-important people, including the city mayor twice removed.

He pointed us to two chairs in front of his gleaming desk, and as he closed the office door behind us, the hubbub of clicking computer keys and whispers into headsets went silent. Parker rounded his desk and took a seat. He didn't offer us coffee or water, but I wasn't thirsty for either of those anyway.

Ron took the lead. These were his people. Both in the sense that he himself had once worked in insurance but also because he was well-connected to the executive set in the Palm Beaches.

"So, Mr. Parker, how can we help?"

"You were recommended to me by John Kramer. You know John?"

"I do," said Ron. "We play golf occasionally."

"He said you were good with delicate insurance matters."

Ron was far too classy to say *yes, we are,* so he just gave a gentle nod. "What is the nature of your matter?"

"It's regarding a policy we've issued," said Parker. He leaned forward as if we were about to share state secrets. "You know the new hockey team in town?"

"Yes," said Ron, without a great deal of confidence.

"The West Palm Beach Chill," I said.

Parker shifted his eyes to me. "That's right. We insure them. They're playing out of the brand-new sports arena up on Forty-Fifth Street. You know the one?"

"Yes," I said. "Haven't had the chance to visit yet though."

"But obviously you understand it's a very new facility."

"I'm sure the paint is barely dry," I said.

"You could say that." Parker pushed off his desk and leaned back in his chair. "See, we've written a policy to cover losses for the Chill." He shook his head a little, as if the movement was involuntary, possibly reflecting his distaste for the name. It was clearly the work of a genius marketing department: juxtaposing the idea of chills and ice with the heat of South Florida. Like I said, pure genius.

"What kind of losses?" asked Ron.

"Losses not related to competition," said Parker. He leaned forward onto his desk again, and I wondered if he had piles. "To give you an example, if the team doesn't perform and is unable to build a following, and as a result, they lose ticket revenue—well, that would be competition related." He wiped his pointer finger across his eyebrows as if the mild office was unbearably hot and causing him to sweat, and for a moment I was sure he was going to cross himself.

"But, for example, if the arena burned down and they had to play somewhere else and incurred additional costs with that, or the alternate venue was unable to hold as many fans, we would cover those losses."

"Do they really think that's likely to happen?" I asked.

"No, but that's the nature of insurance," said Parker. "See, it's like shorting a stock. When you buy stock in a company, you expect it to go up, but big investors, like mutual funds, want to cover the risk in case it doesn't, in case it declines in value. In that instance they would short a stock future, meaning they'd purchase a contract to buy the stock at a lower price sometime in the future, an option they would only exercise if the price fell. It's a form of insurance. A hockey team can't short itself, so they take out insurance to cover things that might damage their brand or hurt their bottom line that they can't otherwise control."

"You can insure for that?" I asked.

"You can insure for anything. It's all just a balance between risk and premium. Actuarial tables are simply probabilities—the likelihood of something happening during the term of the coverage. If something is more likely to happen, or more expensive to cover, then the premium is higher. If something is less likely to happen or costs much less to cover, then obviously the premium is lower."

"So has the arena burned down?" I asked.

"No. But there are some strange things happening."

"What sorts of things?"

"The sorts of things that a policy like ours might have to pay out on. Computer glitches that affect the ticketing system. Scoreboard malfunctions that might have affected the result of a game, had they been during one. There was a gas leak only a couple of days ago, and then last night, when the basketball court had to be re-laid, the workers couldn't access the floorboards because somebody had changed the locks to the storage area."

"Somebody changed the locks?" said Ron. "Surely that would have to be approved by someone."

"I'm sure it would," said Parker. "I just don't know who that someone was."

"It sounds a little weird, to be sure," I said. "But like you say, it's a new facility. You would expect hiccups, wouldn't you? Wouldn't your actuarial tables account for that?"

"We do account for things like that. And any one of those things might be written off, but all together? They seem beyond the likelihood of probability."

"So you're saying it's a math problem," I said.

Parker nodded. "In a manner of speaking, yes. It's the math that drew our attention."

"I'm not sure math is our forte."

"I don't want to hire you for your math skills, Mr. Jones. What I need is someone on the ground. Someone independent of the team and the facility. Someone who knows what questions to ask, and who to ask them of, and when to ask them in order to get the answers that we need. I need someone to find out if these things really are just random chance or if someone is throwing a deliberate monkey wrench in the works."

Now it was my turn to lean back in my chair. I glanced at Ron and let him move the discussion forward. Talking terms and contracts about jobs was *his* forte. My strengths lay elsewhere: in the knowing who to talk to, and when, and how, in order to find out who was doing what and to whom.

And I knew a little bit about monkey wrenches—deliberate and otherwise—and how to find them, and how to use them too.

CHAPTER THREE

So it was that Ron and I found ourselves cruising back up Route 1 in the general direction of Longboard Kelly's, but sadly turning away on Forty-Fifth Street and heading around Lake Mangonia.

Ron slowed as we came upon the new arena. The facility itself sat at the far rear of the property, backed up against the Mangonia Park train station. In the foreground was a massive parking lot laid in cracked, sun-bleached blacktop that, unlike the arena, was anything but new.

The entire space had been home to a jai alai fronton back in the day. But, like so many things that were huge in the eighties, by the nineties the fronton had been boarded up and had fallen into disrepair. It would spend decades in that state, the parcel being bought and sold by various property developers with grand plans for housing and retail and all manner of other schemes that never saw the light of day. Eventually it found its way into the hands of a developer who juggled one too many plates at a time and ran afoul of the Internal Revenue Service. I hadn't followed the politics of it all too closely, but my understanding was that the county had bought the land for a song, and then, in some kind of public–private partnership, developed the arena into what was supposed to be a new hub for sports and entertainment in the Palm Beaches.

Ron pulled in past the gate and drove the long open expanse to the front of the arena. We got out and stood in the warm sunshine for a moment, taking in the monolith before us. The whole thing had been designed to within an inch of its life. The exterior was a mess of curves and sharp edges that pushed the limits of modern architecture and good taste. There was a spire of sorts that looked like a sliver of honeycomb spiked on top of a crème brûlée. I remember some politician on the six o'clock news telling me that the silhouette of the arena spire would become a Palm Beach icon. I didn't see it myself—but then I would have said building a theme park in the baking pastures and swamps outside Orlando was a fool's errand, so what did I know. After all, folks willingly flocked to Rosemary Square, seeing some kind of event destination where I saw a line of stores selling the kinds of things humanity would gladly leave behind when the apocalypse began.

There were only a handful of cars parked in the lot, which told me there was no event happening that evening. We walked up the concrete steps toward the glass and marble frontage of the arena. Up close it looked like an Italian bank—very classy and utterly impenetrable.

We followed the building around until we reached a series of ticket stalls, all shuttered and sleeping, beyond which we found a solitary open door.

The security guy standing out front of the entrance gave every impression of competence: a sharply pressed uniform and a gun belt pinched tight around an athletic waist. He would have been an intimidating sight if not for the broad smile on his face.

"Help you, gentlemen?"

I could always tell a new transplant to Florida. Even one stacking the shelves in a grocery store or mopping the floors at a high school wore a look on their face that said *why would you want to be anywhere else but here?* Of course it wasn't always about the job, but when you're in a place that you really want to be in, and that place seemed to want you in return, then almost everything else was details.

When I offered my hand to the security guard, he seemed somewhat taken aback but quickly recovered and shook it.

"I'm Miami Jones," I said, glancing at the nameplate on his uniform. "And you're Devon?"

"Yes sir, that's me, Mr. Jones."

I jinked my head in Ron's direction. "This is Ron Bennett. We have an appointment with Mr. Gelphert."

"Mr. Gelphert, yes, sirs. If I could have you jot your details down in the visitor log here," he said, gesturing to a clipboard on a small table by the door.

As usual, I let Ron take care of the paperwork. Devon wrote out a visitor name badge, slipped it into a plastic sleeve with a clip on it, and handed it to me. *Mr. Jones*, it said in black marker. I kept it in my hand rather than wearing it. It wasn't that I thought the clip might damage my shirt—an old tollbooth worker's shirt with pictures of beaches and sailfish and flamingos along with Florida destination names like Alligator Alley, Yee Haw Junction, and Florida's Turnpike—I just preferred to fly as far under the radar as possible for as long as I could.

Devon handed Ron his name tag. Ron clipped it to his shirt pocket, a plain blue Oxford. His tag simply said *Ron*, rather than Mr. Bennett. Devon had no idea how apt that was.

He announced into his walkie-talkie that Mr. Gelphert's visitors were at entry one. He got some kind of garbled response, then motioned toward a couple of the plastic chairs inside the dim concourse.

"I prefer to wait out here in the sunshine, if it's all the same with you, Devon," I said.

Once again he appeared somewhat taken aback by me. "Of course, sir. I prefer the sunshine myself."

"Where you from, Devon?" I asked.

"Originally? Wilmington, Delaware. You?"

I wasn't sure that I still wore the glow of a recent transplant to Florida, but I hoped it was so. "New Haven, Connecticut."

Devon nodded and offered me what was becoming in my mind his trademark smile. "How long you been here?"

"More or less since college," I said.

He looked me up and down. "So it don't wear off?"

I didn't ask for clarification of what *it* was. Devon and I were decades apart in our discovery, but we had both arrived at the same conclusion.

"No," I said. "It doesn't wear off."

"Mr. Bennett, Mr. Jones."

The three of us turned at the sound of the voice coming from the doorway.

A woman who couldn't have been much north of five feet tall stepped out into the sunshine, shielding her eyes from the glare. She was probably in her early thirties, with short blond hair. She wore a tan skirt below a blue Oxford shirt that matched Ron's, except for the arena logo embroidered on her chest.

"That's us," said Ron.

We introduced ourselves to her and with a firmer grip than I would have given her credit for, she told us that her name was Amanda Swaggert, VP of public relations and media for the arena.

We said goodbye to Devon and followed Ms. Swaggert. On the inside, the arena looked like every other semimodern sports facility I'd ever been in. There was lots of concrete and wide-open spaces to move masses of people in and out as fast as possible. There were signs pointing us in all directions using a code of numbers and letters that seemed to be half modeled on a Broadway theater and half on the Dewey decimal system. We walked past concession stand after concession stand, all unlit and unstaffed. I was offered the concept of cold beers and hot dogs and nachos with cheese, and Polish sausages with onions, and churros and donuts and French fries. I resolved that there were few things sadder in life than the sight of an empty popcorn dispenser. As we walked by a dormant bar that proclaimed itself to be a microbrewery with twenty-seven different beers, our host gave us the abridged history of the arena.

She restated that which we knew, about the jai alai, the long dormancy and fresh renewal, and the new hub of sports and entertainment. She told us about the state-of-the-art nature of the facility, how it was the greenest sports arena this side of the Mississippi, or south of the Mason-Dixon Line, or some such nonsense. I had switched off on the spiel as my attention drifted, inevitably, from the concourse to the bleachers.

Without speaking I dropped off the back of our little group and wandered down the short corridor that led out into the stands, where I came to a stop.

It truly was a new arena. The plastic seats, each with their own cupholder, still wore their factory shine, yet to be worn down by a thousand backsides rising and falling with the cheers of the baying crowd. A humongous screen hung from the rafters in the center, playing video of long golden beaches and rolling coils of foaming Atlantic Ocean. I'm not sure for whose benefit, but I took it as mine.

Down on the floor a team of people worked like little ants moving things a hundred times their body weight, either pulling apart or putting together an ice rink. One half was white and the other black, as if there were no floor there at all. I took in a deep breath, in through the nose, out through the mouth. The place even had that new arena smell.

I sensed someone at my shoulder and turned to see Amanda Swaggert standing behind me, watching me like a proud parent.

"The view's even better from the CEO suite," she said. "I'll take you there now."

"Thank you, Ms. Swaggert," I said.

"It's Amanda. And you're quite welcome."

She took us across and used a magnetic key card clipped to her hip to summon the elevator. When we got out, it was like we had landed on a new planet. Gone were the concrete and neon and the merchandise stands. This level was all engineered wood flooring, freshly painted walls, and chandelier lighting.

We followed Amanda past a series of doors marked as suites that bore the logos of companies that I assumed had rented the spaces out for the kinds of boondoggles that executives liked to call networking.

Rather than slip into one of the suites, Amanda opened a door that seemed like it would lead out of the arena, three or four levels above the parking lot. Beyond it was like a secret staircase leading us up to a mezzanine area.

Amanda said, "The executive level."

The wall-to-wall carpet smelled like it had been laid that morning. There was an unstaffed reception desk and a series of doors that appeared to lead to spaces directly above the company suites below.

Amanda rapped her knuckle on one of the doors, then opened it up and stuck her head in. I heard her say, "Mr. Bennett and Mr. Jones," to whoever was inside, and she must have received an affirmative response because she stepped back and ushered us in with a sweep of her arm.

There was nothing special about the office. It was a decent size, bigger than Peter Parker's at Rosemary Square, large enough for a messy desk and a couple of small sofas around a coffee table in the corner, where Amanda gestured that we should take a seat.

My eyes, however, were on the floor-to-ceiling windows overlooking the arena. The windows were designed in a way that gave the view a sort of fisheye effect, offering a panorama of the arena. In another context it might have been a bit creepy, the boss man with a view over his domain and all who worked below. But all I could think was that this guy had the best seat in the house. If he had a bar fridge and a john in here, he'd never have to leave.

The guy behind the desk was on a call, so Ron and I sat on the sofas and Amanda stood at ease, hands behind her back, smile on her face. When he finished his call, he swung around his desk and clapped his hands as he came toward us.

"Sorry about that, gentlemen," he said.

Having just sat, Ron and I stood up again. It felt like one of those quadricep workouts Danielle loved to have me do.

"Con Gelphert," he said offering his hand.

We introduced ourselves as I looked him over. He was the kind of guy who would have been all that and more back in college. Broad shouldered and big chinned. He wore suit pants and a well-pressed button-up shirt but no jacket or tie. Florida business casual, or some such. I was glad I hadn't worn shorts. As with Amanda, I pegged him in his early thirties, and the years since college hadn't done him any harm. He had the kind of muscles pushing at the fabric of his shirt that suggested he was into CrossFit or some other similar crazy business.

"Sit, sit," said Gelphert. "Can I offer you a beverage?"

I waited for Ron to say *beer* as a reflex, but instead he asked for water. Gelphert nodded and looked at me, and I returned his nod with another.

Having deciphered the kind of code that couldn't have been broken by the enigma machine, Amanda said, "Three ice waters coming up."

Gelphert did indeed have a bar fridge that I noted was stocked full of bottled water and Diet Coke. She cracked open three waters, poured half of each into a glass and then carried the entire arrangement back to us on a silver tray, which she placed on the coffee table. Then she stood back.

"I'll leave you gentlemen to it."

"Thank you, Amanda," I said.

"You're very welcome," she said, taking her smile out the door.

I took a sip of my water and focused my attention back on Gelphert. His shave wasn't as close as mine. Perhaps it had been a day since his last, or maybe he was one of those guys who got a five o'clock shadow at two in the afternoon.

"So Spider-Man's got his panties in a bunch," said Gelphert with a wide toothsome smile.

It was a bold opening gambit. Gelphert had no way of knowing if we were golfing buddies, best friends, or even blood brothers of the team's insurance agent. But then I recalled that the big man on campus rarely played the percentages. He had one game. Full-on charm and over-the-top personality.

"Spider-Man?" said Ron.

"Yeah, Spider-Man," said Gelphert. "Peter Parker, you get it? With great power comes great responsibility." Gelphert slapped himself on the thigh, then picked up his water and took a long slug like he was Jerry Seinfeld doing a set in New York.

Ron looked at me like he still didn't get it, and my return glance told him I'd explain it later. I knew I wasn't going to be telling him about the J. Jonah Jameson thing if he had trouble getting as far as Peter Parker. Perhaps he hadn't been a comic kind of kid growing up. Perhaps they didn't have cartoons on television when he was growing up in Jamaica. Perhaps he'd never seen a movie.

"Mr. Parker has some concerns," I said.

"You know how it is," said Gelphert, his arms open wide. "We're a brand-new facility. There are always going to be teething problems. To be honest I've seen much worse. If he didn't anticipate that sort of thing, he's in the wrong business."

"So you're not concerned about all the things going wrong?" asked Ron.

"I'm concerned about anything less than perfection, Mr. Bennett, but I am also aware that facilities need to work out the kinks. People need to learn their roles. As long as the public is unaware and they enjoy the show, then we move on and the team learns from their mistakes."

I asked, "Who approved the changing of the locks on the storeroom yesterday?"

Gelphert frowned. "How do you know about that?"

"It's our job to know things like that."

"That would be the facility manager. A miscommunication. It was worked out, and I'm confident that it won't happen again."

It was a plausible story, as the best tall tales often are. I didn't see anything so wrong here, but the view from the CEO suite was often different from that down in the trenches.

"Perhaps we could take a little look around," I said, "to settle Mr. Parker's concerns."

"Of course," said Gelphert, like he was a realtor agreeing to the showing of a listed home. "Although Parker's policy is with our tenant, not with us, I'd hate for him to not sleep well at night. I'll have the PR girl show you around."

CHAPTER FOUR

Gelphert got up to call the PR girl, and I excused myself to make my own. I went back to the vacant reception area and called my office manager, Lizzy, to do some digging and put together a dossier on Gelphert, the arena ownership and management, and how all the pieces fit together.

"A dossier?" she said.

"Yeah. Isn't that what you call it?"

"If you're a hit man or a spy. Neither of which you are."

"What would you call it?"

"A file."

"That sounds like the same thing."

"It is. If you're not a hit man or a spy."

Amanda and Ron found me sitting on the reception desk, staring at my phone, wondering what kind of bee had gotten into Lizzy's bonnet. We took the stairs down to the suite level, and Amanda opened up one of the corporate boxes. It was a plush space, lots of blond wood and beige seating. A marble-topped serving area and glass-fronted refrigerators, all sadly empty. There was plenty of seating for guests to spend the evening ignoring whatever was going on out in the arena. I noted a framed print on the wall that read *Feel the Chill*, with the word *chill* stylized in the hockey team's logo.

"The suites have flatscreens with closed-circuit vision of all events, plus cable. Full-service food and beverage. The lighting is environmentally friendly LED, powered by our state-of-the-art solar panel array on the roof."

She led us toward the floor-to-ceiling glass. I could see the people working on the arena floor. It felt strange that it was only half finished. I would have thought the playing surface was one of the first things you'd get done in a new arena.

When we were done, Amanda took us down in the elevator to the maintenance level, one below the public concourse. The concrete reappeared. There were the same wide spaces as in the public concourse but no natural light. Everything was lit by some modern version of a fluorescent tube, the new ones that made everything look blue. It served to make the space feel even colder than it was, and it was a good few degrees cooler than the level above.

We walked past large doors with prosaic nameplates on them: *Storage Room 6* or *Machine Room 2*. There was an electric golf cart parked to one side but no sign of its driver.

Amanda talked the whole way about innovation and community, and she must have used the phrase *state of the art* at least half a dozen times. She stopped at one door and turned to look at us. "This is the bit most fans want to see but never get to."

She pushed the door open, and we stepped into an anteroom with a concrete floor and painted walls, and then through another wide door into a room the variety of which I was intimately familiar.

It was a locker room. It looked like pretty much every other locker room I'd ever been in, in one way or another. Rows of lockers around the perimeter, each with a wooden door and a number printed on the front. Below was empty open shelving. A wooden bench ringed the room in front of the lockers. The space resembled the changing rooms at one of those national chain gyms rather than any baseball or football locker room I had used in my life. But there was also something different, something slightly off.

I stood in the middle of the room and looked around. Amanda was watching me with a smile as if I was starstruck by getting to visit the sacred territory of a locker room. But I wasn't starstruck at all. I was just trying to figure out what felt so wrong.

Then it hit me, or in another way it didn't. Locker rooms have a fragrance all their own. Somewhere between the sweet tang of sweat and the stench of a decaying body. Usually overlaid by the spicy scent of rubbing oil or Tiger Balm. That clean-but-not-so-clean sense one gets when antiseptic and gym socks frequent the same space. This room had none of that. We could have been the first human life forms to ever step through the doors if the lack of aroma was anything to go by. But I did pick up something on the air, and it took me a moment to recognize it.

Rubber.

The entire floor was laid with rubber matting. I realized that the room was designed to be used by big guys wearing ice skates, and the rubber was not only for the protection of the floors, but also to protect the blades on the skates.

I nodded at Amanda as if to suggest I was very impressed, and she told us that our next stop on the tour would be the greenroom.

"It's a lot like this room, to be honest," she said. "But fewer lockers and with carpet rather than rubber flooring. It's more for the bands and other artists who perform here."

She led us back out into the concrete corridor and headed toward the greenroom. But I stopped. I didn't want to see a greenroom. I didn't feel the need to do the fan tour of an arena that had barely seen any fans and housed teams that I could hardly name. What I wanted to see were the bowels of the facility, behind the scenes, the dark parts that even the diehard fans weren't interested in. I wanted to see where things were going wrong.

Ron glanced beside him and then slowed when he found I wasn't there. Amanda must have sensed it because she stopped and looked back at me.

"Is there a problem?"

I was about to tell her what I really wanted to look at when the aforementioned golf cart snuck up behind me. A short, stocky guy with a serious face and furrows in his tanned forehead that rivaled my own was sitting in the driver's seat. He had black hair and the kind of leathery features that suggested he had spent most of his life outdoors. The man nodded at Amanda and touched the brim of a tattered ball cap that bore the orange *SF* logo of the San Francisco Giants baseball team.

"Miss Amanda," said the man.

She took a step toward the golf cart. "Cisco, I'm just doing a quick tour for our guests here, Mr. Bennett and Mr. Jones."

"Aha."

"Gentlemen," said Amanda. "This is Francisco Monaro, our facility manager."

"Facility manager?" I said, stepping over to the cart and shaking Francisco's hand.

"Hey," he said. "Nice to meet you, but if you'll excuse me, I got lots to do."

"Of course," said Amanda. "Don't let us keep you."

He touched the peak of his cap once more and then buzzed away in his little ninja vehicle. We watched him go, then Amanda turned back with a smile.

"I don't know how this place would run without him."

I was sure she didn't. I had met people like Francisco Monaro before. Sometimes they looked after ballparks, or gyms, or they were equipment managers or bus drivers or concierges in hotels. They were the people who got things done, the people who did the real work while the CEOs sat in their fancy offices. They were like sergeants in the Marines. My friend and mentor Lenny Cox had always told me that officers won medals, but sergeants won wars.

I let Amanda finish her tour. We saw the greenroom, which was not much more than a storeroom with nice carpet and a sofa. She asked if we would like to see the room where they operate the video scoreboard.

"They have all kinds of special effects tools," she said. "It's state of the art."

I told her that we had enjoyed the tour, but I was sure that we both had more important work to get to. She said she would direct us back to the exit. I told her not to bother, that I had a couple of calls to make before we left.

"We'll just take a seat in the stands for a few minutes and get that done," I said. "We're happy to show ourselves out."

"I don't mind waiting," she said, again with the smile. I wasn't sure if she was flirting with me, just ultrafriendly, or under orders to not let us out of her sight. I suspected that the first option was me having delusions, but the other two felt pretty close to on the money.

"No, I'm sure you've got things to do," I said. "Don't worry, we're from the insurance company."

It felt a little bit like telling the folks from Bedford Falls that I was from the bank, but it got the desired result. She slowly retreated, shaking both of our hands before she left and reminding us to hand our visitor tags in to Devon upon exit.

I led Ron out through an opening in the stands into the arena proper. We were on the floor level and could have walked straight onto the half-finished ice. But we didn't.

I turned up an aisle, walked up into the stands, and took a seat about a quarter of the way up the first section. I generally preferred to sit much higher, not only during a game but also during my times of stadium contemplation, but I wasn't there to watch my team play or to ponder life's great mysteries. I wasn't even there to make a phone call. What I wanted was some alone time with someone who really knew what the heck was going on in this place.

CHAPTER FIVE

Ron and I sat and watched the guys work on the ice. I wasn't sure if my eyes were deceiving me, because the patch of white seemed to be getting smaller, not larger, as if they were taking the ice away. I watched one man wheel in a movable stand with a stack of what looked like black rubber matting on it. When he got to the edge of where the black floor met the ice he stopped, and he and another guy set about placing the first piece of rubber on top of the ice.

I had grown up in New England and seen more than my fair share of frozen winters. I'd ice-skated on frozen ponds and even played the odd bit of hockey, just for hits and giggles, nothing serious. But I'd never learned anything about ice rink maintenance. These guys seemed to be covering the ice up, not installing it, as if the blanket of rubber would help keep it frozen or something.

I saw the golf cart appear from underneath the arena seating. Francisco Monaro jumped out and walked up onto the rubber flooring where he spoke to one of his workers. For a moment I contemplated wandering down to chat with him, but I was conscious of Big Brother up in his fancy suite, watching everything like a hawk.

When I saw that their conversation was over and Monaro

turned to walk back to his golf cart, I dashed down the steps to intercept him.

He stood in the large breezeway that led from the playing surface into the maintenance concourse, next to what looked like a movable stand of seating that was pushed aside to make it easier for the workers to move in and out of wherever it was they stored all that rubber.

Monaro was watching the work proceed when I walked up beside him.

"What's with the rubber?" I asked. "Does it keep the ice frozen?"

"No," he said. "It's to keep everything else dry."

I wasn't sure what everything else constituted, but I let it go. He didn't strike me as the most talkative guy, so I looked for an in, some common ground to help establish our relationship, to get him to trust me.

"You a Giants fan?" I asked.

"Huh?"

"Your ball cap."

"Oh. No, not really. Don't really follow baseball."

"It just goes with your name, huh?"

He shrugged his solid shoulders. "Yeah, I guess. I was named after San Francisco. I was born there, but I don't remember it."

"How long you been in Florida?"

"Couple years."

"And before that?"

"Why? You writing a book or something?"

I shrugged. "Just curious how a guy from the Bay Area learns how to build an ice rink."

"We moved to Michigan. I learned there."

"The weather is a good deal better here," I said.

"Got that right." He glanced back at the workers on the arena floor and then looked me up and down. "So what was your name again?"

"Miami Jones."

"And what is it you're here for, Mr. Jones?"

"My friends call me Miami. And we're here on behalf of the insurance company that covers the West Palm Beach Chill. They're concerned about some of the issues the arena is having."

Monaro crossed his arms over his barrel-like chest. For a moment I thought he was going to clam up, as if we would hold him personally responsible for everything that was going on. It wasn't outside the realms of possibility.

"What can you tell me about all these freak accidents and so-called teething problems?" I asked.

One side of his lip curled up in a facsimile of a smile. "Teething problems," he said. "Is that what they're calling it?"

"According to your CEO. Why? You think something different's going on?"

"What I think don't matter," said Monaro. "But I'll tell you one thing: it ain't my fault."

"No one's suggesting it is," I said.

"But somebody will," he said. "Guys in the corporate suites never take the rap for anything."

"That's because the guys in the corporate suites never really know what the hell's going on. But you do. Don't you, Francisco?"

He stood silent for a moment and then slowly nodded. "You really want to know what I think's going on?"

"I do."

"I think this place is cursed."

"You mean like unlucky? Or *Curse of the Bambino* cursed?"

"You remember when they first started building this place?" he said. "When all the local dignitaries and whatever had the groundbreaking ceremony?"

"Vaguely. What of it?"

"They were all standing out front of the old fronton, celebrating how it was going to get knocked down and rebuilt. Standing there with their shovels so shiny you could comb your hair in the reflection."

"So?"

"An old woman came out of the crowd and laid a voodoo curse on the place."

"Seriously? An old woman?"

"Yep. Even before it was built. She cursed the developers, and the mayor, and the whole damn thing."

"And you think that's got something to do with what's going on?" I tried to keep the incredulity out of my voice.

"All I can tell you is this. Just after that, the mayor lost his election. And during construction it was just one problem after another, injuries and whatnot. The power guys and the stonemasons went on strike. And ever since it opened, all this strange stuff just keeps happening. I don't think the curse is done."

"So you're telling me that gas leaks and ticketing system failures are the result of a curse?"

"You got a better idea?"

I did not. But I wasn't going back to my client with a curse as my only explanation. I decided to change tack. "Who authorized the locks to be changed on the storage unit?"

"Who do you think?"

"It was a curse."

Monaro shrugged.

"That isn't something that you would take care of?"

"If I had authorized it, my guys wouldn't have been stuck for hours waiting for the damned door to be opened. They wouldn't have had to work overtime to get the floor laid."

"So you're saying it wasn't you, and yet it doesn't seem to be anyone else. So who then?"

"Search me," he said as he glanced up into the rafters toward the executive level.

I figured at that point he had said all he had to say on it, because he slipped into the seat of his golf cart.

I bent down and handed him one of my business cards. "You're right about one thing. It's guys like you who always get left holding the bag. I don't like that, and I don't think it's fair that you get caught in the middle of something you had nothing to do with. So if you see anything strange happening, give me a call."

He took the card, looked at it, then shoved it into his shirt pocket, right behind the arena logo. He didn't say he'd call, but he didn't say he wouldn't. He just flicked the lever to kick his cart into reverse and backed down into the maintenance concourse. Then he flicked it again and sped away.

CHAPTER SIX

Ron and I headed back to the office. We parked in the lot between our building and the monolithic county courthouse and eschewed the elevator for the stairs to get some semblance of exercise in.

Lizzy was sitting at her desk typing at a pace faster than I could speak. She must have reached the end of a sentence as Ron closed the door, because she stopped and looked up at us.

"So you've been working this afternoon?" Her tone suggested she found the concept difficult to believe.

"We have," I said. "A new insurance case. Ron has all the details."

"You're working an insurance case?"

She glanced at Ron, and I saw the grin on his face as he nodded.

"Did you find out anything?" I asked.

"I found out plenty," she said. "Not that it means anything to me."

"Why don't you come in and give us the rundown."

I opened the door to my office, and we assumed our regular positions. I sat behind the desk and kicked off my shoes, keeping my feet off the desk. Lizzy took the seat on the other side and wouldn't take kindly to having my pinkies waved in her face. Ron flopped down on the sofa, opened the bar fridge, and pulled out a bottle of water.

"So what's the context?" asked Lizzy.

She had already made it clear that we were neither hit men nor spies, and if we were, we might have chosen to keep her out of the loop. But we didn't run our office that way. Generally speaking, the more we all knew, the more value we had as a group. I gave Lizzy a brief rundown on the case, such as it was, and the little we had learned at the arena.

"Can you fill in any of the gaps?" I asked her.

She rustled some papers then licked her thumb through vermilion lips and flicked to the page that she wanted.

"So you're asking about this guy, Con Gelphert, and how he fits into everything."

"Yes," I said. "We were told the whole thing was some kind of public–private enterprise."

"It is. So here's how it seems to fit together. The facility itself is co-owned by the County of Palm Beach and a private company called *Provents*. The joint venture then hires Provents to manage the day-to-day running of the arena."

"So this Provents owns half the arena and then gets paid to manage it?" I asked.

"Exactly."

"Nice gig."

"It gets better," she said, then sort of wobbled her head. "Or worse, depending on your point of view. See, it seems this management company, Provents, is itself owned by another company called JTX Holdings."

"Okay."

"JTX Holdings, in turn, is also the owner of another company called Chill Sporting Brands. This company owns the arena's number one tenant, the West Palm Beach Chill hockey team."

"So you're saying the company that owns half the arena also owns the team?"

"Once removed, but, yes."

Ron sat up from his supine position on the sofa. "And it's the team that our client is insuring."

"But it seems like it's the arena as much as anything that they're insuring against," I said. "Weird." I looked back to Lizzy. "Is there more?"

"Oh, there's more. As owner of the team, this JTX Holdings is a stakeholder in the overall league, the Southern Sunshine Hockey League LLC."

"How does that work?"

"The league is essentially a pass-through entity," said Lizzy. "It's not designed to keep any profit. The way it works is, any operating surplus from the league is passed through to the stakeholders, which appear to be each of the teams in equal share. It's the teams themselves, or their owning companies, that then get taxed on any profits."

"And are there any profits?"

"Not yet." She flipped to another page. "According to the *Palm Beach Post*, all three entities are massively leveraged at this point: the league, the team, and the venue. They seem to imply that it's all expected, but it will take several years to build the fan base to the point of profitability."

"So it looks like all roads lead back to this JTX Holdings?" I asked.

"They do," said Lizzy. "But it doesn't stop there. JTX Holdings is itself owned by a company called JTX Systems, which is based in Bermuda."

I glanced at Ron, and he raised his eyebrows. "Tax haven," he said.

"And then where does the trail go?" I asked.

"Don't know," said Lizzy. "The Bermudian authorities don't like to share much information about private companies based there."

"So that's the dead end?"

"More or less. But I did find a common link." She flipped to another page in her notes. "There's a common name on most of these company records. Provents, Chill Sporting Brands, even the league. Plus JTX Holdings."

"What's the name?"

"Trainor. John Trainor. It seems he's a local Palm Beach boy, grew up here before going to boarding school in the Northeast, and then college in New York. I looked him up on the *Palm Beach Post* website and found a few bits and bobs. He worked in banking in New York City for a few years before returning to Palm Beach. He's one of those guys."

I didn't need to ask her what she meant by that. Lizzy had a particular way of looking at the world. She didn't much care for rich people in general, but particularly bankers and those investment types who moved money around in great quantities and got horrendously wealthy from it but never seemed to produce anything of value.

"And what about our CEO, Con Gelphert?" I asked.

"There's not so much about him," she said. "But I can tell you this. He reports back to the co-owners of the arena—Provents and the county—but his salary is paid by Provents, as part of their role as manager of the facility. All the other employees I could get info on appear to be paid by the joint venture, the holding company."

"So Gelphert answers to this Trainor guy?"

"I haven't seen an organizational chart or anything, but you could make that assumption, at least on the management company side."

"And on the county side?"

"The county side of the arena is handled by a unit called Palm Beach Events, based out of the county office downtown. They seem to be tasked with bringing events to the area—you know, concerts, conferences, that sort of thing. The unit is run by a general manager called Jessica Prior."

"What do we know about Ms. Prior?"

"At this point, nothing," said Lizzy. "I was focused more on the corporate side. You want me to make a file on her?"

I looked at my watch then at Ron, who gave me an almost imperceptible nod.

"No, don't bother. She's in the neighborhood. Why don't we just pay her a visit."

CHAPTER SEVEN

Palm Beach Events was housed in the Palm Beach County Robert Weisman Governmental Center, a laboriously named building right around the corner from our office. I could have chipped a pitching wedge out my window and landed it through a window there. At least I would have made that shot in my dreams.

Ron and I took to the streets and walked along Olive Avenue into the main foyer. An information board pointed us in the direction we needed to go.

The home of Palm Beach Events was nothing elaborate. Displayed in the window was a small sign with a logo that looked as if it had been printed by an inkjet machine. I opened the door and stuck my head in. Like at the arena, there was an empty reception desk, no computer either. We moved inside, and I glanced around, looking for signs of life.

There was a small open-plan area beyond reception, so I wandered until I found a human being. A guy in a crisp white button-up shirt with a Palm Beach Events logo sat staring at a computer screen. I made a mental note to talk to Lizzy about whether we needed polo shirts with our logo. I made a further note to talk to Lizzy about whether we needed a logo.

"Excuse me," I said.

"Huh?" The guy looked up like I had just woken him.

"We're here to see Jessica Prior."

He looked toward the reception desk as if perplexed how someone had breached their security, then fumbled his reply: "I, um, do you have, um, an appointment?"

"No, I don't need one. I'm from the insurance company." I said it with my most serious tone of voice, all the gravitas that I could muster. I was well aware such gravitas was limited while I was wearing a tollbooth worker's shirt.

"I don't think she's here."

"Let's hope you're wrong about that," I said. "I'd hate for the new arena to have to be shut down because of safety violations, and then have the insurance company sue the county for losses. Not sure the taxpayers will be happy about that."

The guy frowned and then glanced at a closed door nearby. I wouldn't have minded playing poker against him. It was as big a tell as you're ever likely to see outside of Vegas.

"Um, just wait here," he said.

"Sure thing."

He almost tripped out of his chair as it rolled away from him. He stumbled toward the door, knocked softly, and stepped inside, closing it behind him.

We waited about sixty seconds. Then he reappeared and ushered us into a different office. It was set up like one of those corporate boardrooms, with a long table ringed by high-backed chairs and a large screen on the wall. But the room was far too small for the purpose, and we had to edge around chairs just to get in through the door.

The guy offered us water, which we declined, and told us that Ms. Prior would be with us momentarily.

Momentarily turned out to be about five minutes, the lower end of what I had expected. When the door finally opened, two women came in who couldn't have been more different if they had agreed on their look beforehand. The second woman, dressed in a plain gray skirt and jacket, entered with a bowed head, almost in deference to the first. She carried a notepad, a large binder, and two cell phones. I couldn't see any makeup around her eyes or on her brown skin.

The other woman was the polar opposite. She had the kind of skin that burned like paper under a magnifying glass in the Florida sun. She compensated for her alabaster tone by plastering herself in makeup. It was all well applied and designed to accentuate her cheekbones and eyes, but it was certainly on the heavy side. Her jacket and skirt were the color of a fire engine, the kind of outfit you could wear out to sea in case you capsized and needed to be spotted from the air. This woman carried nothing in her hands.

"I'm Jessica Prior," said the woman in red. "I'm the general manager of Palm Beach Events. What is this about safety violations?"

"We're working on behalf of Stone Strong Insurance," I said. "We've come from the arena. There are a lot of unusual things happening there."

Prior looked at me for a moment—not up and down, the way some people do, but right into my eyes as if she had read a book on ESP and was trying it out. She glanced at Ron, then pulled out a chair and sat.

"I haven't heard of anything strange going on," she said. "I'm sure it's nothing. But why don't you tell me about it?"

The woman in gray took a seat on the same side as Prior but was not introduced.

I went over the issues that Peter Parker had outlined to us. I didn't mention the curse. The response I got was more or less the same story we had received from Con Gelphert: teething problems. But Prior added a disclaimer.

"It's not the county's fault. Even new NFL stadiums have these issues."

"How many NFL stadiums have you operated?" I asked.

She closed her eyelids very slowly and opened them again, seemingly brushing away the stupidity of my question.

"Look, Mr. . . ."

"Jones. Miami Jones."

"Mr. Jones. I'm aware of everything you've mentioned, but nothing you've said is out of the ordinary. As I'm sure Mr. Gelphert explained to you, new facilities like this take time to bed down. Everyone is working very hard to make the arena the success I know it will be. Having people like you go around town casting aspersions on our team only serves to hurt the good people of Palm Beach County."

I wondered how often she had practiced that little speech in the bathroom mirror at home.

"All I can tell you, Mr. Jones, is that Stone Strong Insurance is not a partner in this facility, nor are we or the management company a client of theirs. If they have written a policy on behalf of the team regarding the use of a brand-new arena, they should've known the potential pitfalls before they did so. If they didn't, they are incompetent and shouldn't be in that business."

Prior stood up, pushing her chair back into the wall. Her unnamed assistant followed suit slowly, without the furniture hitting anything.

"Now if you will excuse me, I have an event to attend." Prior turned to leave but found her way obstructed by her assistant, who for a moment didn't appear to know what to do. Her instinct seemed to be to step aside and allow Prior to leave the room first, but the tight squeeze made that impossible, unless one of them was prepared to climb up onto the boardroom table. Prior jinked her head with a wide-eyed look to the woman in gray, who gathered up her files and folder and phones and stumbled out of the room, followed by a flash of red.

Once they were gone, I turned to Ron: "That was different."

"Your tax dollars at work," he said.

"What do you think?" I asked.

"I think they all have good reason to play down any funny stuff. But beyond the curse, I don't see any evidence of anything untoward."

"You want to go down to Rosemary Square, talk to Parker?"

Ron shook his head. "It's five o'clock. He won't be there. Let's drop by in the morning."

"Okay. So what do we do now?"

"Are you driving back to Miami tonight?"

"Not if we're planning on visiting Parker first thing. Danielle is working late anyway."

"Then you'll stay with me," he said. "Cassandra and I have a dinner thing, so you've got the place to yourself."

"I don't know," I said. "I feel like I should be paying rent or something."

"I'll have none of that crazy talk. You're just a little like driftwood on the ocean right now. You're trying to find the right current. And you will. Then that current will bring you back to shore."

I looked at him, all silvery-gray hair and blotchy sun-speckled skin. There wasn't anything that I wouldn't do for him, but I still felt uneasy when the shoe was on the other foot.

"You're starting to sound like Lenny," I said.

Ron stood up, easing his chair back slowly. He laid his hand on my shoulder and winked. "I should be so lucky."

We looked at each other for a moment, knowing exactly what the other was feeling. Even after all these years, we both shared a Lenny Cox-shaped void in our souls. Lenny had been more a father to me than to Ron, but he had saved us both in different ways. Since he had died, we had both come to realize that we needed to be there for each other, even if we rarely put that sentiment into words.

"Come on," said Ron. "If we leave now, we'll have time for a quick one at Longboard's."

I said nothing. I just stood up and followed his lead.

CHAPTER EIGHT

I woke up the next morning feeling more refreshed than I had in a long time. Perhaps it was the lack of alcohol in my body, or maybe just the benefit of an early night. Ron and Cassandra had gotten dolled up and headed out to some mansion or other for a charity dinner, leaving me alone in their apartment overlooking the water on South Ocean Boulevard.

I had become restless, so I took a walk along Australian Avenue looking for something to eat or drink but found nothing that suited my mood. I felt like I needed to be wearing wedding attire to even wander into most of the places I passed by. I got as far as Cocoanut Row then wandered back up Worth Avenue toward the ocean.

Worth Avenue was one of those places that had the power to make you feel worthless, unable to afford any of the designer goods displayed in the storefront windows. I ended up walking back to the apartment and making myself a grilled cheese, which I drowned with a can of Coke, sitting on the beach beneath the old clock tower at the end of Worth.

After a coffee breakfast, Ron drove us back to the parking lot by our office, and we walked over to Rosemary Square. This time we waited a few minutes for Peter Parker to arrive. He got out of the elevator with a takeout coffee in his hand but didn't seem overly surprised to see us sitting in reception. He told us to follow him back to his office.

"So what's the report?" he asked. His face was serious, but not overly so, as if being in the insurance business put a guy in a perpetual state of moderate concern.

I told him about our visit to the arena, and our meeting with the CEO, and our chat with the facility manager, and finally our brief interlude with the general manager of Palm Beach Events, Jessica Prior. I told him that yes, it did seem that strange things were happening but that we had uncovered no sense that it was anything more than typical operational issues.

"I can tell you that everyone we spoke to seemed pretty intent on protecting their backside," I said, "but I'm afraid no one seemed to be particularly incompetent."

Parker absorbed this information without any change in his expression.

"There was one thing that I found odd," I said. "But it wasn't specific to the arena itself."

"That being?" Parker asked.

"The whole ownership situation. It all felt very incestuous. I mean, the county being in bed with a private enterprise—that bit I can see. But the management company seems to be owned by the guy who also owns the team. And because he owns the team, that guy is one of the main stakeholders of the league."

"John Trainor, you mean?"

"You know him?"

"Of course, he's our client. Or more specifically, it's the corporate entity that owns the team who is our client. Chill Sporting Brands. But Mr. Trainor is the chairman of both the company and the team."

"And yet it's his company that runs the arena," I said. "Doesn't that seem a little strange to you?"

Parker shook his head. "Not really. Lots of professional sports teams own stakes in their home arenas or stadia through various corporate structures. The Bruins, Philly, Denver—it's not that unusual."

"And that's your problem," I said. "If the insurance policy you wrote covers the team, and the same guy who owns the team owns the private share of the arena, then there's no logic to allowing the arena management to intentionally or unintentionally sabotage the arena's operation."

"I'm not sure unintentional sabotage is a thing, but I see your point."

"So, correct me if I'm mistaken, but if something in the arena goes wrong and you have to pay out to the team, your payment would only cover any actual losses, right?"

"Yes."

"In the example you gave us yesterday, about ticket sales at an alternative venue, you wouldn't just take their word for it that they could achieve a full house every game at the arena?"

"No."

"They would have to prove past ticket sales to claim future losses. Am I right?"

"Of course."

"So at this point, everyone is suggesting that these issues are teething problems because everything—the arena, the team, and even the league, for that matter—are all so new. Which means they couldn't have established any decent level of ticket sales to claim against."

"I suppose not. What's your point?"

"My point is, this doesn't seem to be anyone's first rodeo. So having these incidents continue, if they are freak occurrences, seems unlikely. And if they're being done intentionally, I can see no gain in that. It seems like a zero-sum game."

"It may be a zero-sum game for those making a claim," said Parker, "but not for us. My concern is the likelihood of losses on our policy."

Ron gave me his *I have nothing further to add* face, and we both turned back to Parker. I wasn't sure there was a whole lot more we could do for him, other than go through the motions to pad our invoice. And even with an insurance company, that kind of thing never sat right with me.

Parker opened his mouth to say something, but his phone rang. He stuck a finger in the air to put a pin in the conversation while he took the call.

It sounded like a one-way conversation—lots of information from the other end and lots of *ums* and *ahs* and *okays* from Parker. For the first time, I saw the creases in his forehead deepen, as if his normal sedimentary layer of worry had been overlaid by something new and closer to the surface. He finished the call, put his phone back in its cradle, and then steepled his fingers on his desk.

"So much for your zero-sum game," said Parker.

"Why?" I asked.

"That was my man at the arena. Apparently they've just lost all power."

CHAPTER NINE

When we arrived back at the arena, the place reminded me of a kicker looking to boot the winning field goal in a Super Bowl. On the outside it was all calm and business as usual, but the inside was utter mayhem.

We wandered up to the security door and found Devon standing sentry. When I asked him what was going on, he vigorously shook his head.

"I don't know," he said. "But nothing good."

Ron stepped over to the small table to log us back into the facility as I peered inside. It didn't immediately look chaotic—there were no people around—and the only sound I heard was the soft whisper of breeze slowly channeling its way around the concourse.

Then Amanda Swaggert came running down the concourse. She wasn't sprinting—she looked like she could have taken it up another notch if she needed to—but she was moving quicker than the average PR professional usually did. I noticed she was wearing running shoes with her skirt. I wasn't sure if that was how she arrived at work, before changing into something less practical, or whether she'd been wearing them the previous day and I'd simply failed to notice.

She saw me standing by the door and slowed her gait but didn't stop.

"Mr. Jones," she said, not seeming to be out of breath at all. "What are you doing here?"

"We heard something's gone wrong?"

She jogged past me. "Not at all. But Mr. Gelphert's off-site right now."

She left it at that, then turned away from me and picked up her pace, bouncing down the concourse, her running shoes squeaking on concrete.

I turned back toward the sunshine to find Devon looking over my shoulder.

"Does that look like nothing do you?" I asked.

He just shrugged his ample shoulders. Then his radio squawked, and he pulled it from his hip. This time I was close enough to understand the message.

"Secure all exits," said the voice.

Devon rolled his eyes at the radio. "I did a full sweep about an hour ago. Everything was locked down."

"Do it again," said the voice. "Right now."

This time Devon scanned the parking lot and the arena forecourt, then came back to the radio. "I'm on entrance duty."

"Then close the damn door, and get it done."

"What happens if someone comes—"

"Get it done. Out."

For a moment Devon stared at the silent radio. Then he hooked it back onto his belt. He looked like a man in turmoil—like the guy who guards the gate at Fort Knox but has been called away to put out a fire in the basement.

"You sure all the other doors are locked?" I asked.

"Yes," he said. "I did the rounds not even an hour ago. I always check everything is locked, and everything was, unless it was unlocked from the inside."

"If everything's already secure, then it won't take you long to do a quick double check, will it?"

"No, but what if someone important needs to get in?"

"I'll tell you what," I said. "You do your rounds. Be quick about it. Ron and I will stay here at the entrance and won't let anyone in. If they seem important, we'll come up with a story to hold them until you return."

"I don't know," said Devon. "You don't have training for this."

"You're right, Devon, but I know how to handle myself, and I know how to stop someone from walking in a door. Ron and I won't go inside either. Unless you've got a better idea?"

He paused, offered me a definitive nod, and dashed off around the building.

I wasn't sure how long it would take to run a lap around the arena without stopping, but Devon couldn't have been much short of the record. He came sprinting at us from the opposite direction within a few minutes, and even when he saw us standing there alone, he didn't stop running hard until he reached his post.

"Everything okay?" he asked, puffing lightly.

"Everything is peachy," I said. "No one in or out."

"Okay, thanks."

"Don't mention it. Now if you don't mind, we need to go and find out what's going on inside."

"Sure, no problem." He gestured toward the entrance then suddenly stopped. "Did you sign in?"

Ron held up two visitor tags. On one he had written Ron, and on the other, Mr. Jones. "All signed in and accounted for."

Devon stood tall, and for a moment, I thought he was going to salute us. "Remember, Mr. Gelphert isn't on-site."

"That's okay," I said. "He's not the one I need to see. Do you know where the facility manager is right now?"

Devon jumped on his radio and, after a couple of garbled squawks, reported that he had checked all perimeter entry and exit points and that the facility was on lockdown. Then he asked where Francisco Monaro was.

"Why?" asked the voice.

Devon glanced at me. "A car alarm went off in the parking lot.

Maybe it was just the wind or something, but I think it was Mr. Monaro's car. Just wanted to let him know." The radio voice offered a short response that I didn't quite catch, except for the word *out*. Then Devon clipped his radio back on his hip.

"He's in the control room."

CHAPTER TEN

We found Francisco Monaro in a room that from the outside looked like every other room around the maintenance concourse. The simple door had a small plaque that read *Control Room*. I knocked, stepped inside, and found Monaro and one other guy looking at their laptops. I guess in my mind's eye I saw something more akin to mission control at Houston than two guys with laptops and a table that could have come from IKEA. Perhaps it was a testament to the fact that computing power had come so far that you could almost run a major sporting facility from your living room, sitting in your jammies.

I was reminded of a guy that I had met at a bar who had worked his entire life up the road at Cape Canaveral. He said there was more computing power in my cell phone than was available to all of NASA during the Apollo 11 mission. Was I more impressed that people were able to land astronauts on a celestial body using such limited computers, or that we could now pack so much into such a tight little glass-and-aluminum container? The guy clarified that NASA's machines made the calculations slowly compared to today's computers, but those machines were backed by the finest minds on the planet, whereas the average lightning-fast cell phone was often operated by some moron whose intelligence extended to screaming down I-95, no hands on the wheel, with the phone plastered to his ear.

When Francisco Monaro saw me, he simply shook his head.

"You see," he said, "it is a curse."

"What's up now?"

"The power's been cut," he said.

I surveyed the small room. "So how are the lights still on?"

"Different system. I'm talking about the system that powers the floor heat."

"Floor heat? Why on earth does anyone in Florida need underfloor heating?"

Monaro looked at me like I was the dullest tool in the shed. "It's not for the fans. It's for the ice rink."

"Okay, now you've lost me completely."

"It doesn't seem that hard," said Monaro. He asked the other guy with the laptop to check some numbers.

"Seriously," I said. "Did you say a heating system for the ice?"

"I did. Look, the ice for the rink is built on top of a concrete slab that sits on a base layer of gravel, and underneath that is earth. The heating system sits under that concrete slab to prevent the freezing temperatures above it from damaging the substructure. If we crack the ground down there, we can crack the concrete, and the whole thing would have to be ripped out."

"Doesn't that melt the ice?"

"No, it doesn't heat up that much. Just enough. But now, for some reason, we can't get the backup power to kick in. And if we can't get that going, then we can't get the heating system restarted. We'll have to turn off the cooling system for the ice, or it might crack the ground and cause a lot of damage."

"What sort of damage?"

"A million dollars' worth of damage."

Their laptop screens showed various graphs and numbers but no flashing red warnings or sirens going off. I had seen more panic when the internet went down at Starbucks.

"What happens if you turn off the cooling system?" I asked.

Monaro's stress was written across his face. "A big thaw."

That didn't sound good. Then a radio on the table between them squawked, and a voice told Monaro to get down to Machine Room 2.

Monaro was standing before he picked up the radio and asked what the situation was.

The voice simply said, "It's bad."

We jumped in Monaro's golf cart and zoomed along the maintenance concourse around the arena until we reached a set of double doors, each twice the width of a regular door. A small truck or large forklift could have easily passed through had the doors been open.

The brakes on golf carts are always surprisingly good, and when Monaro hit them, I had to brace myself to ensure I didn't go flying out the front of the cart. He slipped out and pulled open one of the doors. Ron and I followed him inside.

The room was much larger than the doors suggested—a massive space with a vaulted ceiling that ran upward, like upside-down steps—and I realized I was probably looking at the underside of the stands.

The room was stuffed full of hulking machines and snaking pipes and guys standing around looking like the losing team on election night.

One of the men, his hands and arms covered in black goop, turned to Monaro: "The backup generator still hasn't fired."

"Why not?" asked Monaro.

"Looks like it's full of sludge." The guy held up his dirty arms to illustrate the point.

Monaro shook his head.

"How can it be full of sludge?" I asked. "I thought everything was new."

The guy looked at me. "It *is* new."

"What does it run on?"

"Diesel oil."

"Could the oil be dirty?"

"Not this dirty."

"Can you clean it?" I asked.

"Like I say, it's diesel oil. We need a tanker to get it out before we can clean anything," said Monaro, not taking his eyes off the large drum that must have held the diesel. It looked like one of those massive steel containers industrial wineries use to hold their cheap wine before they throw in the wood chips that imitate the taste of an oak barrel.

"What does that mean?"

"It means there's no power to the heat systems." Monaro was looking in my general direction, but his gaze seemed a million miles away.

Then he took off out of the room like a keg-shaped greyhound.

CHAPTER ELEVEN

Monaro jumped into his golf cart and hit the gas, or the battery for want of a better term. I barely managed to grab a bar on the rear-facing seat and drag myself up into it.

Monaro whizzed around the constant bend. He turned savagely, almost pulling a Tokyo drift as the rubber wheels skidded across the concrete, and we sped out of the dim maintenance concourse into the bright lights of the arena floor.

Monaro hit the brakes hard again, but this time I was merely pressed into the seat back. I made a note to use that seat in the future.

I jumped out and followed him down the concrete path to the edge of the playing surface. No sign of ice. Half the surface was black rubber, and the other half a basketball court, the large pieces fitting together like a jigsaw puzzle.

Monaro called one of the guys over and, before he got halfway to us, yelled, "Get it up, get it all up."

The guy coming toward us held his palms to the ceiling as if to say, *What the—?*

Monaro yelled loud enough for anyone on the floor to hear. "The boards. Get them all up, get them off the ice."

The guys laying the basketball court looked like a pretty

unflappable bunch. There was a shrugging of shoulders, then they set about removing the large, heavy pieces of wood and placing them back on the trolley racks from which they came. A man in a forklift truck who was delivering the racks full of wood pieces simply turned on a dime to return the boards.

As we watched them dismantle the jigsaw, I asked Monaro why he wanted it pulled up.

"We have an underlay between the ice and the boards," he said. "That does protect the wood from the ice, but it's more about stability and soundproofing than anything. It's not a water barrier. If the ice melts, it will destroy the basketball overlay, and that's worth a couple hundred thousand dollars."

"So you don't take the ice out after each game?"

"No. It would cost more to do that, but the important factor is time. See, for these arenas to be profitable—hell, even for them to not take a loss—they need to be multipurpose. You can see it here. We host hockey at the same time of year we host basketball. But we also have concerts and other large events on the slate. We need to move fast to change the configuration from day to day. In any given week we could have a hockey game on Monday, a basketball game on Tuesday, a down day on Wednesday, a concert on Thursday, and then another hockey game on Friday. Melting the ice takes too long, and refreezing it even longer. If you want good-quality ice, that is."

"So how on earth do you keep the ice frozen under there?"

"There's a series of pipes in the concrete base underneath. We use an indirect cooling system to make the ice. It's less efficient, but, hey. We basically run a calcium chloride brine through the pipes, below thirty-two degrees Fahrenheit. The brine doesn't freeze, but the water on top does. Then the brine flows into another machine room where we have the cooling system."

"You say it's less efficient? I thought this arena was supposed to be superefficient."

"It is, but like everything in life, there's a trade-off. It would be better to run the refrigerant itself through the pipes, in the same way as your household refrigerator. Problem is, with a system this large, that's a lot of refrigerant, and the refrigerant is both highly toxic and bad as far as greenhouse emissions are concerned. So it's safer and more environmentally friendly to keep it contained to one small area and use less of it."

We stood for a moment watching the men removing the basketball court. It was a much more manual job than I thought it would be. But they had a system and appeared to know it well. I figured it would only take them several hours to complete the job.

"How does this happen?"

"What do you mean?" said Monaro. "You're looking at it."

"A blockage in a new generator, I mean. Was it secondhand?"

"No. It was nine months old."

"So how?"

Monaro glanced at me with his typically serious-looking face.

"And don't give me that voodoo-curse business," I said. "I mean seriously, is it a maintenance thing?"

"No," said Monaro tersely.

"So you test everything?"

"When we're allowed."

"What does that mean?"

"Look, the county wanted this place to be green. Like everything has to be super environmentally friendly these days, whatever that means. So there's all kinds of new technology in the building. They pushed pretty hard for the backup power systems to be an electric UPS, like the kind of thing you might attach to a computer server."

I had no idea what someone might attach to a computer server, but I had seen electric-battery backup systems before.

"Problem is, an electric UPS and melting ice don't mix. So after a lot of arguments, they went with diesel, but they don't ever want it really running because it's bad press. So ordinarily you test the backup system on a regular maintenance schedule, maybe every two weeks, monthly tops."

"And how often do you test it now?"

"We were allowed to test it when it was put in, but we haven't done it since. Five months."

"But if it's never been used and it doesn't get tested, how does it get clogged?"

"Search me. Even if you weren't testing, you'd want to turn over the oil periodically, just to keep it fresh. But this stuff has just been sitting there."

"So either it's always been faulty, or someone cut the power and then sabotaged the backup."

Monaro frowned. "Sabotage?"

"Are there any cameras in the machine room where the generator is?"

"Not in the machine rooms, but there are in the maintenance concourse."

"So you would know who's been in and out of that room today?"

Monaro looked to the maintenance concourse. "You assume if it happened that way, that it happened today. But like I said, it never gets used, so if someone wanted to tinker with it, they could've done it months ago."

He had a point. But that point would have meant some serious planning. Sabotaging the backup ahead of time and hoping that it wouldn't get checked or tested and then cutting the power later meant considerable forethought. But something about this whole thing felt more ad hoc.

"So where did the power go out?"

"What do you mean?"

"We're talking here about the backup system, but the backup is only relevant if the actual power goes out. I'm asking, where was it cut?"

Monaro shrugged. "Could have been anywhere. Somewhere between our electrical panel and the power station."

"So somewhere on the grid?"

"I guess."

"But all the lights are still on, and your computers are working. You said something about a separate system?"

"Yes. We have a zero-carbon system for things like lighting and power outlets. That all comes from a solar panel array on the roof, via a bank of batteries in a room on the other side of the arena. But that's separate from the ice-making system. A solar system simply can't generate the power we need to create ice in South Florida. We need as much as two million kilowatts a year."

I barely even looked at my power bill. Rightly or wrongly, I just assumed they got it right. So I didn't know a kilowatt-hour from a mile per hour. But two million still sounded like a lot.

Monaro pointed back in the direction of the concourse. "We have a dedicated power service for the rink. It comes directly from the local substation."

"So you called Florida Power & Light?"

"The boss man did." Monaro nodded in the general direction of the CEO's office upstairs.

"How? He's not here."

"Before he left."

"He called in a power emergency and then left the building?"

Monaro shrugged. The movement again made me think of Lenny Cox, and of all the sergeants in all the military units in all the world who had shrugged their shoulders at decisions made or not made by their superior officers.

"What time did all this happen?"

"The power went out at eight fifty-five in the morning. The boss left about ten minutes after that."

"So where are they? The FPL guys?"

"Somewhere between here and the power station."

"Can you narrow it down?"

"The substation?"

"Do you know where the substation is?"

CHAPTER TWELVE

I caught Ron on the way out, telling him to stay put and let me know if things escalated. As I ran out toward the parking lot, he called to me.

"You want these?" he said, dangling his car keys.

I jumped in Ron's car and followed the directions to the electrical substation that Monaro had given me.

It wasn't more than a few minutes' walk from the back of the arena, but to drive there took a good ten. I cut back down Forty-Fifth Street to Australian Avenue then had to wind my way through surface streets back toward the train line on the other side of the tracks.

Located on a street corner in a light industrial section of town—lots of outlets for truck parts and factory supplies—the substation itself was surrounded by a high cinder-block wall whose dull taupe color had faded and peeled in sections, leaving it a mottled tan and gray, like a sick leopard. There was a tight mesh gate, the kind of thing even a monkey would struggle to climb, with a decent coil of razor wire running the entire perimeter.

The level of security designed for a nuclear silo suggested this was a priority facility, but I suspected it was just cheaper to install a mile of barbed wire than it was to keep a guard on duty.

I pulled into a gas station on the opposite corner. One of the international petroleum companies had owned the place, but that was a long time ago. Signage had either been painted over, covered by silver duct tape, or wrapped in canvas. If some Hollywood hotshot wanted to film a scene for an apocalypse movie, where our hero finds the last drops of gasoline available on the planet, they could do worse than scouting this location. A reasonable person would question how such a place stayed in business, but reasonable people were not so well acquainted with money laundering.

I parked in a slot next to the stout building that housed the cashier and what was surely a selection of junk food long past its sell-by date. I sat for a moment and watched the comings and goings across the street—that is to say, I watched nothing happen at all. So I ambled over to get a closer look.

Traffic was almost nonexistent, which was no surprise given the street ran along the rail line and dead-ended in some kind of stone yard.

I heard the prickly hum of electricity as I looked through the mesh gate and saw a small trailer, the kind a construction company might dump on a large building site as the foreman's office, its windows covered in grime. No vehicles anywhere. Opposite the trailer I could see rows of electrical transformers and other equipment. I really didn't know a lot about electrical power supply, other than the basics we learned back in school. The idea that electrons moved from one place hundreds of miles away through a filthy, half-abandoned yard like this one and then into my refrigerator to keep my drinks cold was akin to black magic as far as I was concerned.

I spotted a silver box on the wall by the gate with a keypad but no visible speaker. I stood with my hands on my hips looking up at the top of the gate, wondering if some kind of vault onto the other side might be possible, but the razor wire gave discretion victory over valor.

Seeing nothing of interest, I wandered back over to the gas station. It felt like a long shot, the idea that such a business might bother having security video, but I knew from experience that such looks could be deceptive. Often the business owners who were too tightfisted to keep their stores clean opened their wallets just enough to spring for a second-grade video system to deter would-be gasoline thieves.

I pushed in through the door of the gas station. There was no electronic ding-dong or the rattle of a bell, but the hinges creaked so loudly there was no sneaking in. My instincts on the quality of the merchandise seemed vindicated. The end cap closest to the door held a selection of potato chips, each bag topped with a greasy sheen.

The cashier sat behind a glass pane that offered nothing but the veneer of protection. For reasons I couldn't begin to fathom, several dollar bills were taped to the glass along with a hand-written note that said this location had sold the winning ticket in Powerball. The printing on the note was faded so badly I wondered in what decade that windfall had occurred.

I nodded to the cashier as I approached and got so little response that I was afraid for a moment I'd stumbled upon a guy who had died weeks earlier. But I noticed him blink ever so slowly, like a chameleon.

"Morning," I said.

He cocked his head like a parrot.

I found that the best way to elicit a positive response from such a person was to use either hollow threats against the guy's health or his employment, or to ingratiate myself by buying something. He looked like he could do with a good blood transfusion, and getting him fired might be a positive career move. I went with the latter option.

"You got any gas?" I considered asking for a hot dog but feared that once seen, the state of the so-called foodstuff might linger in the memory.

"We're a gas station, ain't we?"

"Can you give me twenty bucks' worth?"

The guy squinted out the window at the four vacant gas pumps then looked back at me. "You don't got no car?"

"It's parked on the side. I thought I might need some air in the tires."

"That thing don't work."

"Figures. Just the gas, then."

"I don't know which pump you gonna stop at."

I took a deep breath in through my nose and out through my mouth then pointed at the closest pump. "That one."

"That's number two," said the guy as if this was vital information.

He rang up the charge on an ancient cash register, and I paid cash.

As I slipped my twenty through the hole in the glass, I said, "You got security video here?"

His eyes pinched some, and he glanced underneath the counter, perhaps at a shotgun or a baseball bat.

"I'm not going to knock you over," I said, holding my palms up in peace. "I just wondered if you had any video outside. Maybe something that looks across at the substation over there."

The guy peered through the window again, but only a small warehouse with a hand-painted sign reading *Sinks* was visible.

"It's on the other corner," I said, pointing.

He looked across the sordid collection of merchandise in the store, toward the back wall, as if he had X-ray vision. "Hardly anyone goes in or out of there, and they never buy gas."

"There is another twenty for you if you've got video."

He didn't bother locking the front door as he led me into a back room. It wouldn't have been impolite to call it a closet. There was a monitor sitting on a dirty desk, and a desktop computer covered in a heavy layer of grease and dust.

"When did you want to see?" asked the guy.

"This morning, around eight fifty-five."

He turned the computer on, and we waited for a good five minutes as the thing booted up. I used to have a car like that, once upon a time; you had to start it five minutes before you ever went anywhere, or you might get nowhere at all.

The guy brought up a screen and typed some stuff in. It was that blocky type, DOS, I think they called it. It looked like that old Matthew Broderick movie about the computer starting World War III. Ancient.

"You're lucky," he said. "This thing only keeps twenty-four hours of video."

He opened up the footage where the timecode said 8:32 a.m. The picture quality was poor—not so much black-and-white as blue-and-white, and grainy as a breakfast cereal.

We watched the video as the time crept forward. The camera must have been mounted on the canopy over the forecourt, positioned to the side the cashier couldn't see from his post, designed to snap the license plate of any ne'er-do-well who dared to pump gas and not pay. The notion that this was a pay-before-you-pump kind of place crossed my mind, so I couldn't help but think that the security system was somewhat redundant. Yet I was glad it was there.

At 8:46 a white truck slowed at the top of the frame and pulled in front of the gate at the substation. The picture was too blurry to make out the license plate, but whoever was driving knew the key code: the gate opened, and the truck drove in.

We kept watching as the timecode crept up and passed the 8:55 mark, when Monaro had told me the power outage occurred. At 8:59 the gate opened once more, and we saw the truck pull out and drive away.

I could make out the FPL logo on the side of the vehicle. It was one of those maintenance trucks, the kind that looks like a pickup with a canopy over the truck bed, where the workers keep their tools and wire and whatever else it is they use to keep our electricity flowing. What I couldn't make out was any kind of identifying feature. All FPL maintenance trucks looked pretty much the same.

I asked him to run the video back so we could see the truck

again, and when it turned I got him to pause the shot. But the frozen picture was so fuzzy it was difficult to even confirm it was a vehicle.

I was about to give up when the guy said, "Hang on," and punched some keys to bring up a different camera angle. This one had more or less the same view as the cashier himself, across the forecourt to the street that led away from the tracks. "If he's not going to the place with all the rocks and stuff, then he's going out this way."

He was right. We watched as the FPL truck drove by the other side of the gas station, clearly having turned the corner offscreen. Again he paused the video, but once more I couldn't make out much.

"Thanks for trying," I said.

"Hang on," he said again. He rewound the video, and as the truck drove by for a second time, he pointed to the rear side of the truck bed. "There," he said, his finger following the vehicle across the screen. "That's a unit number."

I leaned in. "Can you read it?"

He rewound and we watched the truck for a third time.

"The first thing is a pound sign," said the guy.

"Like a hashtag," I said.

"Whatever."

It took a few more minutes of rewinding and replaying to get the whole number. We pieced it together one number at a time. After the eighth pass, we had something.

"Number 14646," I said.

"That's his unit number. That's your man." Then he frowned. "This guy owe you money or something?"

"Not me, not exactly."

CHAPTER THIRTEEN

I sent Ron a text message to let him know that I was returning, and then I wound my way back to the arena. When I arrived there was no one at the front entrance. Not Devon, the security guard, nor anyone else. The tinted glass door that we had previously entered through was closed, so I gave it a yank, to no avail.

I stepped back and pulled out my phone. With a shudder the door flung open, and Ron stuck his head out into the sunshine.

"Fancy meeting you here," he said.

I put my hand against the door to hold it open and asked Ron what was going on.

"They locked the place down completely. Even old Devon has been called inside. I'm afraid that young man might wilt without the sunshine."

"And Monaro?"

"He's zooming around on his Club Car like a drunk man on a golf course. Not sure what's going on exactly. I've been waiting here to let you in."

There was movement in the dim light behind Ron that I couldn't quite make out from my sunny position outside. But I heard the voice.

"Shut that damn door," he said. "We need to keep the damn humidity out."

I took a couple of quick steps in and let the door close behind me with a bang. As my eyes adjusted, I saw a man in coveralls watching us. He shook his head like he was looking at the dumbest tumbleweeds ever to roll into his neighborhood, and then he strode off along the concourse.

Ron and I looked at each other, and he shrugged.

"We could just stand here and wait for the Club Car to come zipping by," he said with a grin.

"I get the distinct impression he keeps the golf cart down on the maintenance level. But I have a better idea."

"Into the bowels?"

"Something like that."

I led Ron to the control room, where I had previously left Monaro. I tried the door and found it locked, but my attempt must have roused someone because it almost instantly snapped open. Monaro stood there with the radio to his mouth. He gave me his customary stern face and added a shake of the head for good measure. Then he turned and continued barking orders into the radio.

Ron and I stepped inside. The other guy was still in his seat, looking at his laptop. There were still no red warnings on the screens or sirens blaring, but the mood seemed to be even more tense.

Monaro dropped the radio from his mouth and looked at me.

"There's no one at the substation," I said. "They don't appear to be fixing anything."

I was about to tell him about the FPL truck in the video when he waved his hand in the air as if to brush my information away.

"That's not my concern right now," he said. "The arena AC system is down."

"Obviously," I said, "since the power's out."

"No, no. You don't get it. I told you, the refrigeration system for the rink is on a dedicated line, from the grid. But the ambient

AC is handled by our internal system. Solar panels, the battery panel."

"So if the power to the AC is still on, why do you say it's off? It's not that warm in here."

"Not yet it's not. And heat is not the problem. The problem is humidity." Monaro pointed to bar charts on his screen, the kind of thing you see on the news to help explain how the national debt keeps rising day after day.

I gave Monaro a blank look.

"It's the humidity reading," he said. "It's going up. Fast."

"Why is humidity such a big deal? This is Florida, it's always humid."

A crackle on the radio drew Monaro's attention, and he told whoever was listening to call the rental place and get the loader on standby. The voice at the other end said the loader was already on the truck, awaiting his order.

It all sounded vaguely military to me, like a call to arms.

Monaro clipped his radio onto his hip and opened the door.

"Follow me," he said as he strode away.

CHAPTER FOURTEEN

We got in Monaro's golf cart again. I let Ron take the front seat, and I jumped on the rear-facing bench at the back. We zipped around the maintenance concourse then out toward the arena floor. Monaro hit the brakes hard, like he was stopping for a bunny on the road, and I pressed back into my seat, hoping Ron hadn't flown out the front.

The basketball court floorboards were all gone, as were most sections of the black underlay. The last of the insulating rubber was being removed at the other end, suggesting it was stored on the opposite side of the arena from the floorboards.

We followed Monaro to the very edge of the ice rink, where a low fog had formed all the way across, making the whole thing look like an eighties disco.

"Is this normal?"

"No," said Monaro. "This is not normal."

"So how? Why?"

"What do you know about humidity and dew points?"

"I grew up in Connecticut," I said. "The ice just made itself."

"Sure, but did you ever notice in the winter that your throat would get dry, or your nose might bleed for no reason?"

"Yeah, because the air was dry."

"Exactly. Up there you get both extremes. Summer brings heat and high humidity, but winter is the exact opposite—cold with low humidity, often around thirty percent. That's ideal for making hard, dry ice. But we never get that kind of humidity here in Florida. A dry air day here might be sixty percent, and then tomorrow it could be close to a hundred percent."

"So you're saying humidity is causing this fog?"

"It's really got to do with dew point," said Monaro. "But I don't want to explode your brain, so, yeah, let's call it humidity. And it's death to good ice. See, we can keep it frozen by dropping the temperature, but that creates an ice pack with air bubbles, and that means poor-quality ice and a bad surface."

As we watched the soft fog roll across the arena floor, the radio squawked again.

"Monaro," he replied.

"Boss, you're needed in the AC machine room, like now."

We all clambered back into Monaro's golf cart, and he explained as he drove.

"See, in order to keep the ambient air comfortable for the patrons while also keeping the humidity low enough for good ice, we have to precool the air that goes into the AC system, to bring the humidity down. It's called a dehumidification system. Basically it's a series of pipes that use cold water to cool the incoming air, before going through to the AC system proper, which then further cools the air and drops the humidity. It drops the temperature so low we actually have to warm it before putting it back out into the arena."

"You heat the air in a Florida arena?" I asked.

"Yes. The same water that precools on the front end then goes around as warmer water on the back to slightly warm the air. But the system allows us to produce the temperature we need in the ambient air while keeping the dew point—your humidity—artificially low. If we didn't, then people would have to dress like they were in a Minnesota winter during a game. Most Floridians I know don't even own those kinds of clothes, and the snowbirds who come down sure as hell don't bring their winter coats with them."

"So you're like your own little ecosystem in here," I said.

Monaro nodded. "Now you're getting it. See, if the dew point increases, then we get fog, just like you do on a cool Connecticut morning, before the sun burns it off. In reality, it's not burning anything; it's just raising the temperature, and so raising the dew point. But for us the problem is that fog means the ice is melting slightly, just like on a frozen pond in New England. But freezing, thawing, and then refreezing ice over and over produces poor-quality ice and a dangerous surface."

"Don't you have a Zamboni?" asked Ron. "Isn't that what they use for ice hockey?"

"Yeah, we've got a Zamboni," said Monaro. "And it's not ice hockey; it's just hockey."

"We played hockey at my school growing up," said Ron. "And it was played on grass. Didn't get a lot of snow in Jamaica."

"That's field hockey," said Monaro.

"It's just hockey where I come from," said Ron. "So what about the Zamboni?"

"The Zamboni is like a Band-Aid on a bullet wound. The players' skates rough up the surface, and a Zamboni is designed to take care of the ice quickly but temporarily. It shaves a thin layer off and pulls that ice up into a waste tank. Then it deposits clean water back onto the ice and spreads it out evenly and smooths it down using the conditioner. The layer of water is so thin that it freezes almost instantly, leaving a smooth surface. But it's so thin and so new that the ice doesn't stay in good condition for long. That's why you see the Zamboni come out during every break in a hockey game. Either way, if the humidity stays up, the Zamboni fights a losing battle."

Monaro stopped with a jolt, a good way short of the machine room. We jumped out of the golf cart, and I instantly wished I had some of that Minnesota winter gear that Monaro had been talking about. Water was spewing out of the AC machine room into the concourse. Monaro strode right on in, splashing through the water and into the room.

Ron shook his head—I'm sure ruining a perfectly good pair of shoes was not on his agenda. I, on the other hand, was wearing deck shoes. For the most part they were affectation. I didn't sail, at least not enough to justify specialist footwear, and not usually without Ron. I just found them comfortable, and they looked good without socks. I figured they were designed to get wet, so I really had no excuse.

I sloshed my way through the water and into the machine room. A guy in damp coveralls was explaining to Monaro that the dehumidification system was leaking.

"Obviously," said Monaro.

I could feel the warm humid air filling the room, as if I'd hit a southerly in a sailboat on the Gulf Stream. I felt a sensation in my ears like they wanted to pop.

"Is it turned off?" said Monaro.

"Yes, boss," said the guy in coveralls.

Monaro sloshed out of the room and into the concourse. He spoke into his radio: "Let's get the loader in here, right now, and tell the floor gang to get ready."

"We'll need the whole team," said the voice on the radio.

"I'll call them in. I'll call them all in." Monaro turned back to the guy in coveralls. "Get a sump pump in here. Let's get this water out."

I stepped over to Monaro and said, "What's happening?"

Monaro took a long slow breath deep into his guts and let it out slowly.

"We're losing the ice."

CHAPTER FIFTEEN

THE NEXT HOUR WAS ORGANIZED CHAOS. THE GUYS AT THE FAR END OF the arena floor doubled their efforts and pulled the remaining black insulation off the ice. I watched a bank of bleachers get rolled back into the maintenance concourse and out of the way to make a wide path from the ice rink floor to the large external doors of the arena. The huge space looked like a missing tooth in a boxer's mouth.

I was sitting in the stands with Ron, watching the ice steam like a New England morning, when I heard a loud bang. A glow of light came up from the gap in the stands. I leaned over the opening and looked back and saw that the wide doors had been thrown open. Then I heard a deep mechanical rumble. The silhouette of a massive front-end loader filled the doorway, like a gunslinger coming into a saloon.

It chugged its way in, drove straight up onto the ice, dropped its front bucket down, and scraped the rink into large chunks. It was like watching an act of vandalism as the front-end loader tore up the ice, then swept up large scoops of it and moved it outside. It returned and continued smashing and unloading ice.

Between trips I walked outside and stood next to Francisco Monaro. The driver deposited the load into a large dumpster, where the chunks started melting in the sun. Perhaps the dumpster was just to keep the mess contained. It seemed a crude way to break down an ice rink.

"You can't just let it all melt inside?" I asked Monaro.

"No, it's too slow and too messy. Water is hard to control, ice not so much, as you can see. We can get this ice out in an hour and cleaned up in two. It gives us at least a fighting chance of getting the boards back in place before tonight's game."

"There's a game tonight?"

Monaro nodded.

"You can do it that quick?"

"We're about to find out."

"How do you hold a game if there's no air-conditioning?"

"We can't. But as soon as we get the water cleaned up, we should be able to route the air around the dehumidification system. It won't be super cool, not enough to lower the dew point, but it won't be too uncomfortable for Floridians."

We went back inside and watched as Monaro's team scraped the smaller and wetter bits of ice off the concrete surface below. Then a guy in an FPL uniform finally turned up.

"It's like getting a beer delivery after the bar has burned down," I said.

The guy gave me a look like he'd eaten a bad pickle, or maybe he just didn't get my sense of humor. Either way, it felt like he was at least a day late.

Monaro said he'd take him to the electrical room, so they walked back down into the dim light of the maintenance concourse. I had nothing better to do, so I followed.

When we reached the door labeled *Electrical Room 1*, Monaro handed his keys to the FPL guy, who unlocked the door. I noticed a small pink flamingo hanging from a chain on the key ring. The colorful bird seemed at odds with Monaro's serious demeanor. Perhaps it was a gift from a child. Sometimes you just can't read people.

We passed a series of five-foot-tall free-standing electrical units.

The man headed for the back wall, where he unlocked a series of cabinets, each housing panels of switches and buttons and fuses. He took his sweet time, methodically checking each fuse, switch, and button. Perhaps it was the kind of diligence required in the situation, but it just felt slow.

We were watching the guy checking the fuse boxes in the second cabinet when Amanda Swaggert rushed in, out of breath.

"Cisco," she said, "what on earth is going on?"

"He's checking the electrics," said Monaro.

"Not in here," she said, panic rising in her voice. "Out there." She gestured with both hands toward the stadium interior.

"The AC system is down. We gotta get the ice out," he said.

"You need Mr. Gelphert's permission to remove the ice."

"Is Mr. Gelphert here?" I asked, knowing the answer.

Amanda frowned at me. "No, but that's not the point."

"Does Mr. Gelphert know anything about building ice rinks?" I asked.

"I don't know. But, Cisco, you still need permission."

"Look, Miss Amanda," said Monaro, "I left him a voicemail, but he's not bothering to call back. I need to get this ice out of here now. Otherwise, we won't just be canceling tonight's game. We'll be dealing with hundreds of thousands of dollars in damage. You gonna cover that? Is he?"

Amanda didn't seem to have an answer for that, so she glanced back down the concourse then returned her gaze to Monaro.

"I'm going to call Mr. Gelphert," she said.

"You do what you gotta do," said Monaro.

CHAPTER SIXTEEN

AFTER AMANDA HAD DASHED AWAY, I TOLD MONARO THAT I WOULD be in the stands with Ron if he needed anything. I had no idea what he might require of me, and the expression on his face suggested that neither did he, but I was bored watching the guy from Florida Power & Light examining what looked to be perfectly fine electrical fuses.

Monaro was right. It took them just under an hour to get the bulk of the ice removed with the front-end loader. Then men appeared from parts unknown to scrape and sweep and clean up the rest. The concrete base was clear of ice by the time Monaro walked out to the edge of the playing surface. He looked tired as he glanced at his watch. I wandered down from my perch in the stands.

"Why do you have to rent the front-end loader?" I asked.

"To get the ice out," he said.

"Yeah, I can see that. What I'm saying is, why don't you have your own loader?"

"Because we're only supposed to need it once a year."

"And you don't ever take the ice out the rest of the time?"

Monaro shook his head. "We build the ice up over a few weeks before the season. Then during the year we just cover it in the thermal underlay, then put the basketball boards over the top."

"So why don't you take it out?" I asked. "I mean, you've done this pretty quick."

"Because, like everything, it's about time and money. We can rip it out fast enough, but laying it again takes time. It's not just one big block of ice. It's done in a series of sheets, layer upon layer. Building and smoothing and then letting it set, then laying another sheet on top. Even the week or two at the start of the season is pretty quick."

"I didn't realize it took that long."

"People don't. But the thing is, we're not just trying to freeze water; we're trying to create a strong, sturdy, smooth playing surface. It's not the same as making ice cubes in your freezer. Did you know that for the Sochi Olympics, the ice maker in the speed-skating arena put the ice down eighteen months before it started?"

"Eighteen months?"

"Yep. Like hockey, speed skaters want a solid, hard surface. It's different from the ice dancing events, where they want things just a little softer on top. The guy in Sochi even played classical music to the ice."

"Was he a kook?"

"I don't know," Monaro said with a shrug. "Never done it myself, but he said the vibrations of the music helped get the air bubbles out of the ice. Air bubbles are the enemy in our game. That's the risk we run when we have to re-lay the rink quickly. That and the cash."

"What about the cash?" I was thinking about my client's policy.

"To get the ice in and out fast, with the loader and the extra manpower, you're looking at about twenty-five thousand dollars to remove it and replace it. But we can cover the ice with the underlay and floorboards for only about four."

"That explains why Amanda was flipping out."

"I wouldn't do it that way if I had another option. But this thing melts and damages the court? That's hundreds of thousands. You gotta pick your poison."

The guy in the FPL uniform emerged from the concourse and called Monaro over. I stood by the rink, which was now nothing but a large concrete space, and watched the guy hand Monaro his keys with the pink flamingo. The guy offered him a nod then walked away, and Monaro headed over to me.

"They've got the rink's cooling system back online," he said.

"So all this work was just a waste?"

"No, we can't do anything without the AC. Right now the humidity just keeps rising, remember?"

The guy in the damp coveralls, who had been in the AC machine room, appeared on the other side of the arena and walked slowly across the concrete playing surface, leaving damp footprints in his wake.

"So, boss. The precool pipes have been damaged."

"Tell me something I don't know," said Monaro.

"No, I mean they've been cut."

"Cut?" Monaro and I said at the same time.

"What about diverting around the dehumidifier?" asked Monaro.

The guy nodded. "As soon as the sump pump gets the surface water out, we can get that done. But someone's gonna need to fix the damaged pipes."

"I'll call the dehumidification guys to get them out and repair them."

The guy in the coveralls shrugged like he didn't care either way, then turned around and walked back across the concrete floor.

I thought about how things had definitively moved from a curse or a series of random but disconnected events into sabotage territory. I still wasn't sure why anyone would want to do what they were plainly doing, and I was equally unsure if there were any ramifications for my client. I was mulling all this over when I heard the bellow come from above.

"What in God's green earth is going on here?" screamed Con Gelphert.

CHAPTER SEVENTEEN

Gelphert stood on the public walkway that separated the lower tiers of seats from the upper tiers, his face crimson, as if he had spent too much time on the beach in Fort Lauderdale. He came charging down the steps toward us at the arena floor, ranting all the way.

"Are you crazy?" he yelled.

I assumed he was talking to Monaro but couldn't be a hundred percent sure.

"What have you done? Do you know how much this is going to cost? Are you trying to shut us down?" By the time he got to us, he was panting like a thirsty Labrador.

"The AC system went out," said Monaro, not bothering to raise his voice a single decibel.

"Are you insane?" said Gelphert.

"Do you know what a high dew point does to the crystallization of ice?" asked Monaro, with a look that suggested he was well aware of what Gelphert knew about making hockey ice.

"I don't care about that," said Gelphert. "You have just cost us tens of thousands of dollars."

"No," said Monaro. "I've just saved you hundreds of thousands of dollars by not having to replace the basketball floor."

Gelphert looked at the expanse of concrete. "What basketball floor? There *is* no basketball floor."

"That's because we pulled it up when the AC system went down. If we didn't, the ice would've melted and warped all the floorboards."

"We have backups for all those systems."

"You know full well that the backup generator failed yesterday."

"Yes, I do. Another maintenance failure by you and your team, so called. You can't hide your incompetence anymore."

I thought Monaro might slug him one, because the thought had crossed my mind, and I wasn't even involved. But Monaro seemed to be one of those truly unflappable guys, the kind for whom the phrase *water off a duck's back* doesn't even begin to explain the even keel under which they sail.

"My team and I know exactly what we're doing. But you ignored the curse at your peril."

"Curse?" said Gelphert. He let out a deep and throaty laugh that sounded somewhat forced. "You are all excuses." He dropped the faux mirth on his face and got serious: "And you're fired."

If Monaro was going to go off like a firecracker, I figured this was the moment. But all he did was slowly shake his head.

"My contract is with the management company and the county. You can't fire me without county approval."

"Oh, I assure you that will be my next call." Gelphert turned on his heel and headed for the maintenance concourse. He suddenly stopped and looked around—perhaps he didn't know the way back up to his lofty perch from down here, where all the work seemed to get done. He turned around and stormed back past us, then up the steps in the stand. At the top of the first section he met Amanda and fired a few quick but inaudible words her way. The two looked back in our direction for a moment before Gelphert marched away. Even at that distance I could see sadness in her face, like a child who realizes that her family is breaking apart and there's nothing she can do. Then she, too, turned and walked away.

Monaro refocused his attention on the concrete surface, where the team was bringing out the thermal underlay sections on their racks. I watched him for a moment. He wasn't even breathing heavily.

"Will he get what he wants?" I said. "Will he get the okay to fire you?"

"Maybe." He took a step forward and yelled across the arena. "Start from both ends. Two teams, double time." Then he said directly to me, "But I won't get fired because I don't know my stuff. I've been doing this a long time, well before this place was even some politician's dream. I know what I'm doing, my boys know what they're doing." He glanced back up in the direction of Gelphert's office. "Not everyone can say the same."

More men appeared and started putting down the underlay from both ends of the floor. I figured Monaro must have a list of freelance workers he could call on in a crunch. Or maybe he just did a drive-by of the parking lot at the local big-box hardware outlet and picked up a truck full of day workers.

I heard Ron quietly call out my name, and when I turned, he directed my attention to the walkway where Gelphert had first appeared. I saw Devon, the security guard, standing there. He didn't look his usual chipper self. Perhaps Ron had been right that Devon suffered from being cooped up inside the arena, like a sunflower. But I could see a slackness to his shoulders, slumped like he had something to do that he didn't want to. He just stayed there, his radio in his hand, as if awaiting word from the king that the execution should proceed, that the pardon was not coming.

I noticed that Monaro had seen him too.

"What will you do?" I asked.

"Until I hear different, I'll do my job."

It didn't take long. Devon got a message on his radio, which he then clipped onto his belt as he slowly made his way down the stairs. He ambled up next to us and, in a voice I can imagine him using with his grandmother, said to Monaro, "I've been told to escort you out of the building."

Monaro, still serious but a little less confident, looked to me. His eyes seemed to be asking me what he should do.

"You should go," I said. "Making a scene just gives them ammunition. Do the right thing, and as soon as you're out of here call an attorney. Fight them."

Monaro yelled out some final orders to his crew and nodded to Devon. Together the three of us walked back up the steps, out through the public concourse, and outside. It was a spectacular day, warm but not blistering, the kind of picture-postcard day the tourism folks in South Florida love so much. The kind of day that just didn't fit with what was actually happening.

Devon and I stood by the entrance door and watched Monaro walk to his car.

"This isn't right," said Devon.

"I know what you mean," I said. "But a lot of things have gone wrong. Things that Francisco was responsible for preventing."

Devon shook his head. "It's not his fault."

"You're not talking about this damn curse, are you?"

"No, but something about this whole thing don't smell right."

"Like what?"

"I don't know," he said. Then he turned and looked at me. "You hunt?"

"You mean like out in the wild, with a gun?"

"Yeah."

"Not really. Why?"

"I used to hunt, with my dad. And you learn something when you take an animal down. Sometimes out there in the woods an animal might already be sick. It might have a disease or a wound or something. You don't know what it is exactly, you just know there's something wrong. Like something just don't smell right."

It wasn't exactly the way I would have put it, but I knew exactly what he meant.

Monaro drove away across the never-ending parking lot. Then

another vehicle pulled out from the side of the arena and tailed him. I recognized the outline instantly and the color of the logo on the door: an FPL truck. But I couldn't see the unit number on the side as it sped through the vacant lot.

I wanted to jump in Ron's car, but I had given him back his keys. I figured the truck had too much of a head start anyway, so I stood there in the bright sunshine and watched it drive away.

CHAPTER EIGHTEEN

After the chaos of the afternoon, the rear courtyard at Longboard Kelly's was pure serenity. The sun was sinking into the horizon, and a handful of streaky clouds had wafted across to give it a canvas on which to paint its pink and purple hues. The party lights were on, offering a colorful glow across the tables, their umbrellas closed up for another day.

Ron and I walked to the outside bar and saw that our favorite stools were taken. Normally this would be cause to speak with the management, but when they were occupied by our favorite people in the world, it was nothing but a source of joy.

Ron's wife, the Lady Cassandra, was wearing a long blue dress with a white cardigan, a casual look yet sophisticated enough for any of the fine restaurants in Palm Beach. She had come from money, I think, but had certainly married into it with her first husband. After his passing, she had settled into the single life of a lady of a certain age. Then she had the good luck to meet Ron.

I had all the time in the world for the Lady Cassandra. It would be enough that she made Ron infinitely happy, but there was more to her than that. One of those people who was equally comfortable in her finest pearls at the opera or playing pool at the local dive bar, she seemed to have the capacity to talk to anyone about anything and be genuinely interested in what they had to say, regardless of their so-called station in life. It had become my learned opinion that too many people were narrowing down the choices of who fit as their kind of people. Cassandra wasn't like that at all. She didn't tend toward pigeonholing anyone, taking each human as she found them and drawing out their positive traits as she went. It spoke of a level of character that I wasn't sure I possessed.

On my stool sat someone equally classy, although less likely to be found at the opera. Danielle was wearing a white T-shirt and a pair of jeans, and as I walked toward her, she offered me that half smile that turned my gut upside down.

The ladies were drinking white wine, the provenance and variety of which was a mystery to mankind. Mick generally stocked three kinds: white, red, and something bubbly. Muriel didn't reach for the wine bottle for us, instead pouring two cold beers as if we were the creatures of habit that, in fact, we were.

Ron regaled Danielle and Cassandra with the goings-on of our latest case. He was a natural raconteur, the kind of guy who could describe a chess match in a way that made you want to cheer queen to rook five.

"So who do you think is behind it?" asked Cassandra.

"If you believe the facility manager, it's a curse," said Ron.

"You running with that?" said Danielle.

I took a sip of my beer and shook my head. "Curses don't tend to cut cooling pipes with a hacksaw."

"So who's on your list?"

"It's long, and getting longer. There's the CEO, who seems more interested in the razzle and dazzle than the minutiae of actually running the place; the facility manager, who seems to be the one to have his finger on the pulse, until he got fired today. There's also the county manager, who was more focused on covering her backside than acknowledging any problems, and then of course there is the team—the beneficiary of our client's policy. But the unknown question is, who benefits? From what I can tell, no one.

Given all that's happened there's only downside. The CEO looks incompetent, the facility manager has been fired, the county can't really afford the bad press, and the team gets no more insurance money than they actually lose."

"Curse or not, you're right," said Danielle. "People don't cut cooling pipes with a hacksaw for no reason."

"They used a hacksaw?" said Ron.

I shrugged. "I don't know exactly how they did it, but they did it."

"So who else is there?" asked Cassandra.

"The league, maybe?" said Ron. "Rival teams?"

"Maybe, but the thing is, I don't see rival teams benefiting either. Generally games get rescheduled rather than forfeited. There's usually too much TV money at stake to not play at all. And why would the league want to hurt one of its founding teams, in a brand-new marquee arena? Especially when the ownership seems to be shared across the venue, the team, and the league." I shook my head and took another sip. I had a brain full of information but no way to make sense of it all.

"I wonder if they got the basketball court laid in time," said Ron.

We had left with Monaro as he was escorted out, and his team had still been hard at work then. But they had just started the underlay, so they would cut it close either way.

Ron put his beer on the bar and then went inside to the main bar, a part of Longboard Kelly's we rarely frequented. The whole point of living in Florida was that you could spend time outside pretty much any day of the year. That wasn't to say you didn't get wet or cold, but being from New England, all things were relative.

We watched Ron walk over to a flat-screen television.

Mick walked out from the kitchen with a bowl of fish dip and crackers and stopped short when he saw Ron inside. He turned to me with a look of deep concern. "What the—?"

Not for the first time that evening, I shrugged.

The television was on some kind of talking-head news program that seemed rather pointless since the sound was muted and there were no closed captions. You couldn't tell from looking at it what they were talking about, or which side of the fence they sat, but whatever their position was they were awfully serious about it.

Ron flicked the channel over and over until he came to rest on one of those local stations that still broadcast in standard definition—the fuzziness of the picture made you feel like you'd forgotten to put your glasses on.

A basketball game was in full swing. I didn't know Mick had that channel or that Ron knew how to use the television. I didn't know who the teams were, and I hadn't realized that whatever competition they were part of got televised, but I knew where the game was being played. I recognized the arena logo on the floorboards. So it seemed that Monaro's team had gotten the floor laid in the nick of time, and for at least one more evening, life as we knew it would go on.

CHAPTER NINETEEN

DANIELLE AND I STAYED OVERNIGHT WITH RON AND CASSANDRA. They had a number of spare bedrooms in their apartment—I wasn't sure of the exact number—and always seemed excited by the notion of having guests. But I for one was starting to feel a little uneasy about the number of nights I was spending there. I still found my thoughts drifting around, like flotsam and jetsam, between the places where I was and the places where I wanted to be, between where I lived and where I should be living, and between waking up alone and waking up next to my wife.

Today was a good day. I woke up next to Danielle, and I didn't even groan when she suggested a quick run on the beach before breakfast.

She took it easy on me, and I got back to the apartment in minimum discomfort. We came out to the kitchen after showering and found that Cassandra had laid out a breakfast buffet on the counter. There were cold meats, slices of cheese, a variety of pickled vegetables, and two or three kinds of bread. She had yogurt and granola and hard-boiled eggs. No bacon and not an omelet or a pancake to be seen. I offered a raised eyebrow to Ron and he simply replied, "European."

We ate on the balcony overlooking the water.

"So how are you enjoying Miami?" Cassandra asked.

She could have been a psychologist, the way she eked information out of people. She knew full well that neither of us really considered Miami home, that we were there because for now, that was where Danielle's career had taken her. She knew that I had failed to put down roots there in the same kind of way that I had on the Palm Beaches.

"We have a great view," I said. It was true. A realtor friend had set us up with a phenomenal deal on an apartment on Grove Isle, with killer views over the marina in Coconut Grove.

"Views are nice," said Cassandra.

"Yeah."

"Not everything, but nice."

"Yeah." I shoved half a hard-boiled egg in my mouth before I said anything equally mundane.

"And how's your place on Singer Island doing?" she asked.

I finished my egg and took a sip of orange juice. "It's rented out right now, to some kind of healthcare executive, Penny tells me. Apparently he splits his time between West Palm Beach and Philadelphia. She says he prefers it to staying in hotels, and even a month's rent is less than a couple of weeks in a hotel, so his company is happy to pay. She says those are the best kinds of tenants: the ones who pay up but aren't around that much."

"That sounds just fine," said Cassandra.

"Yeah," I said again. "It's peachy."

I put some smoked ham on a piece of multigrain bread and folded it into a little sandwich. It was great ham, probably imported from Spain or somewhere else very far away. I chewed quietly, and Cassandra kept her eyes on me.

When I finished my mouthful I said, "Would you ever give it up?"

"Give up what?"

"This," I said with a nod toward South Ocean Boulevard and the Atlantic beyond. "The view, the island."

"The view, quite easily. The island, not so much."

"So if Ron had to go to Montana?"

"Why on earth would I have to go to Montana?" he said.

"I don't know. For the restorative waters, or the fresh air. To cure your lumbago."

"My what?"

"Just hypothetically," I said.

Cassandra put down her piece of toast and brushed her fingers with a napkin. "I'd go. No question. Just like you did. But that doesn't mean it would be an easy choice."

"So you'd miss Palm Beach?"

"Of course. But not the place. The place is just houses and hotels and stores, and a nice but rather unspectacular beach. It's the people that I'd miss. The ones I love, even the ones I don't care for so much. It's a rich tapestry. Some of it's fine art, and some of it's pulled threads, but it's my blanket, and, yes, I'd miss it." She looked me in the eye with the wisdom of a thousand ages. "And that would be okay."

I wasn't exactly sure what she meant by that, and I wasn't sure whether taking it further would be picking a scab or planting a seed, so I left it be.

She picked up her toast and took a bite then let her attention drift out onto the shining Atlantic Ocean. We followed her gaze and, for a brief moment, allowed the motion of the carpet of sea calm the chattering monkeys.

As is often the case, modern life butted its head in—my phone rang. I didn't recognize the number, and for a moment I considered not answering, but the noise had broken the spell. I stood from the breakfast table.

"Miami Jones," I said.

"Mr. Jones," said a woman. "This is Charita Jain."

I tried to place the name but failed. "Aha."

"We met the other day. Well, you met with my boss, Ms. Prior, at Palm Beach Events," she said, jogging my memory.

"Yes. I don't think we were properly introduced."

"Um, no." The way she said it implied she was often not properly introduced.

"How can I help you, Ms. Jain?"

"I was wondering if we could meet."

"Sure," I said. "I can come over to your office later this morning. You want to give me a time?"

"Um, well, I wonder if it's possible to meet somewhere else."

"You mean somewhere other than the government building?"

"Yes."

When a person wanted to meet at a place other than their office, they often had something interesting to say.

"No problem," I said.

She gave me a time that was an hour away, which was expected, and a location, which was not.

"Is that okay?" she asked.

"That will do just fine. I'll see you then."

CHAPTER TWENTY

I pulled into the nearly empty parking lot of the Manatee Lagoon in Riviera Beach and parked just inside the gate, at the far corner of the lot from the museum. I liked to park away from my destination, even when the lot was empty. It was those little spurts of effort, like walking an extra hundred yards, that kept the beer from settling on my belly.

I was a little early, so I wandered along the waterfront, around the large museum building that had been constructed to look like a plantation mansion, if plantation mansions were made of hurricane-proof concrete and were painted in pastel yellow.

It had been built by Florida Power & Light next to a natural-gas power plant, which had a warm water outflow into a small inlet on Lake Worth Lagoon, and the local manatees had taken to visiting it every winter.

Manatees were large aquatic mammals who didn't get up to much—they were known as sea cows for good reason, sort of floating around like waterborne rhinoceroses, munching on seagrass and doing their best to avoid the blades of speedboat propellers. The gentle beasts liked the warm waters of Florida, but like most people who lived in the Sunshine State for any period of time, they had grown soft, so when the water dropped below sixty-eight degrees, they went looking for any source of warmth and found it in Manatee Lagoon.

I leaned on the white barrier and watched a dozen or so manatees floating around in the outflow. They seemed content with their lot, as if they knew exactly where they belonged and didn't stray too far from their path.

The thought made me look across toward Singer Island on the other side of the intracoastal. I could see the tip of the island but not my house, the view of which was blocked by Peanut Island, sitting in the middle of the intracoastal. I didn't really need to see the house to picture it in my mind, and I wondered about the lone guy who was living there and whether he felt like his soul had been split apart, as if the two halves of his life—Singer Island and Philadelphia—didn't quite add up to a whole. I wondered if he saw my house as nothing more than a way station, a better alternative to a tiny hotel room, where he could leave a few fresh shirts and an unfinished six-pack for his next visit. I wondered if deep down he really wanted to be back in Pennsylvania, or if coming to Florida was an escape, a taste of something better.

I heard a voice behind me: "Mr. Jones?"

I turned and saw Charita Jain standing in the shadow of the Manatee Museum. She had forgone her gray uniform for an equally underplayed taupe.

"Folks call me Miami."

"Charita Jain—Charita," she said as we shook hands.

We both leaned on the guardrail and watched the manatees for a while. It was peaceful, the water lapping gently and the breeze a good deal cooler coming off the water. But I could feel the buzz coming off Charita, like she had a lot to say but was still working on the will to do it.

"The facility manager at the arena has been fired," she finally said, quietly as if she was concerned about disturbing the manatees.

"Francisco," I said. "Yeah, I know. I was there."

Charita nodded but didn't take her eyes off the manatees.

"Was it your boss who confirmed his firing?" I asked.

"Yes."

"Do you guys really think all this stuff going on is the result of his mismanagement?"

"It's really hard to know from our position."

"I've been down there," I said, "and I can tell you there's a lot of strange stuff going on, and a fair bit of it is above and beyond simply not maintaining the place."

"Ms. Prior gets her information from Mr. Gelphert."

"Has she spoken to Francisco?"

"No. She says it would be inappropriate. She says it's not her job to manage the staff there."

"She worried about losing her job too?" I asked.

"I think she's more worried about her next job."

"What's her next job?"

Charita glanced at me. "You don't know?"

"Ms. Prior's career hasn't been that high on my priority list until now."

"You know there's an election next Tuesday, right?"

"I guess. I saw something about it on the television."

"You are registered to vote?"

I nodded. I was, I just couldn't remember where. "Is she running for something?"

"Yes. She's running for an open county supervisor seat. She really has designs on the state legislature, one day."

"So she wants to distance herself from trouble."

Charita sort of shrugged, although it was hard to tell. She was petite, with shoulders like a bird. Her eyes drifted back to the manatees. They were grand animals—their gentle nature could teach us a thing or two—but I was fairly certain that wasn't the reason we were there.

"So, I saw most of this for myself, and the rest I could learn online," I said. "What can't I learn online?"

"I hear things."

"What sort of things?"

Charita shifted her feet and took a deep breath as if the air coming in off the intracoastal was better than the air-conditioned stuff she normally breathed. I was certain that was true.

"She thinks of me like a maid or a butler," she said. "Ms. Prior, that is. As if I should be not seen and not heard, melt into the background until she needs something. I'm sure sometimes she forgets I'm even there."

I recalled our previous meeting and how Jessica Prior, with her strong personality and bright attire, drew the eye, while Charita did the exact opposite. I had to admit there was a point during our meeting that I had almost forgotten she was there. The notion didn't sit well with me. "So what is it you hear?"

"She's having a lot of meetings that are not on her calendar."

"With who?"

"On the face of it, the arena management company."

"Isn't the county in partnership with the management company? Wouldn't she meet with them fairly often?"

"She would. So why keep those meetings off the calendar?"

"I don't know. I don't have a calendar."

"You don't answer to the people of Palm Beach County."

"Not if I can help it. So do you know who exactly she's meeting with?"

"John Trainor."

I vaguely recalled him from Lizzy's overview. "I know the name. Remind me."

"He's the one behind the management company, or at least he's the mouth behind the money behind it all: the arena, the league, even the team."

"So he raised the cash for the arena?"

"Goodness, no. That belongs to the people of Palm Beach County, by way of a bond."

"I didn't know that," I said.

"That's why you should pay more attention to county affairs. And vote. That's your money."

"Should I be worried about that?"

"I don't know. The thing is, the county offered the bond to finance the arena in the end, but we weren't going to."

"You weren't?"

"No. We have an investment committee whose job it is to look at when and where county funds should be used with or without private investment. The committee declined to invest in the arena. They recommended the board of supervisors stay out of it."

"But they didn't."

"No. Once the state got involved, suddenly everybody changed their minds."

"Why?"

"Because if the state thought it was a good thing, I guess the county supervisors didn't want to be left out."

"The state invested money too?"

"They did."

"So what did they see in it that your investment committee didn't?"

"That's the thing. The investment board in Tallahassee held the same opinion as our county committee. They said it wasn't a good deal for the people of Florida. But then a state senator took up the mantle, and he somehow got the governor on board. So suddenly everyone got interested, and they tacked a bunch of money for it onto an appropriations bill for the state budget and circumvented the investment board."

"Who was this senator?"

"Senator Vargas."

"Is he a hockey fan?"

"I have no idea, but I mean, really, is anyone? This is South Florida, not Detroit or Toronto. Whoever thought a second-tier hockey league was a good idea in eighty-degree heat?"

"There are plenty of northern transplants here," I said.

"They come here for a reason—and the reason isn't ice."

I couldn't argue with her logic. I had first come to Florida as a student-athlete, playing in a high school baseball tournament. I had instantly fallen in love with the place, its warm air and loads of sunshine and all the friendly people. Living near the water in New England, I was even used to the humidity. My dad had connections, having worked at Yale for most of his life. But as fine a school as that was, it was never really in the running for me. The moment I got my scholarship offer from the University of Miami, I mentally checked out of New England.

But I knew that pro sports sometimes transcended that line of thinking. There was an NHL team in Miami, and the one in Tampa Bay had even won the Stanley Cup. Sure, it looked ridiculous hoisting the massive trophy with a backdrop of swaying palm trees, but winning trophies was not really what professional sports was all about. At the core of pro sports, like most things in life, was money. And although I had no idea why the arena was being sabotaged, Charita had introduced a few new players to the stage, and a few new threads to pull on. Someone, somewhere was going to benefit.

We stayed and watched the manatees for a while. Then we walked back around toward the parking lot.

"Will you move upward and onward with Ms. Prior?" I asked. "Isn't that how these things work? The campaign manager becomes chief of staff and that sort of thing?"

"I think if she wins on Tuesday, she'll struggle to remember my name."

It sounded like a sad throwaway line, but I didn't hear disappointment in her voice, as if it was just a statement of how things were.

Perhaps this was when Lenny Cox would have given her a pep talk, delivering some ancient wisdom that set her off on her own path, and for a moment I rattled the old cage in my head for some wise parting words. But nothing came. And I wasn't sure it was appropriate anyway. She didn't seem upset that she was seen as part of the furniture, just disappointed that the furniture wasn't a little better appreciated.

I walked her to her car and thanked her a second time.

She looked up at me from behind the steering wheel. "It would be better for me if this didn't get back. I'm not even sure why I'm telling you. You just seemed like someone who might do something about it. I just feel like the people of Palm Beach County are going to be the losers here, and that just doesn't seem fair."

"It's never fair," I said. "So we do all we can to prevent it."

"What will you do?"

"In all honesty, Charita, I don't know. But don't worry, we never met." I gave her a wink. "You're invisible to me."

She gave me a little smile, then she backed out, and I watched her disappear out of the lot.

CHAPTER TWENTY-ONE

When I got back to the office, Ron and Lizzy were poring over some invoices and discussing billing and payment terms, so I motored right on through. When Ron finally came into my office, he asked me how the manatees were.

"Effusive," I said.

"Not what you usually get from manatees," he said, taking a seat on the sofa.

"They're enjoying the warm water. Didn't seem to want to get out."

"I've got some neighbors from Quebec like that."

I gave him the rundown of my meeting with Charita Jain and how she had mentioned the name of John Trainor.

"Lizzy said he was a Palm Beach boy," I said. "Do you know him?"

"No, but Cass might." Ron took out his phone and called Cassandra. When he hung up, he said, "She doesn't know him well. She's met his parents a few times, but the rest Lizzy already told us: local boy, boarding school, investment-banker type. Her impression was that he seems to do quite well, but at the same time he's not top shelf, if you know what I mean."

I knew what he meant. The top shelf in Palm Beach was a lofty perch. Even the people on the bottom rung in Palm Beach were doing just fine, thank you very much. The top shelf involved a lot of zeros on your bank balance and spoke of quiet money and generations of power. A guy could do pretty well—could do extremely well, in fact—and still not reach the top shelf, as defined by the Palm Beach set.

"Do you think—?" My phone vibrated on the desk, so I picked it up. "Miami Jones."

"Miami, this is Francisco Monaro."

"Francisco," I said, catching Ron's eye. "How are things?"

"I got fired, so, you know."

"Yeah. What can I do for you?"

"Can we meet?"

Some days go like that. You could be sitting in your office for weeks on end without saying boo to a soul, and then all of a sudden everybody wanted to meet.

"Sure," I said. "Where?"

"Can you come to my house? I have something I need to show you."

Francisco gave me the address, and I told him I'd be there directly. Ron and I headed over in my car. I was getting tired of having to borrow his keys all the time.

Francisco lived in an estate of old but neat little houses dotted around man-made lakes, just on the wrong side of the Turnpike off Okeechobee Boulevard. The streets were clean and the gardens were modest but impeccably maintained.

Francisco met us at the front door and ushered us into a very white house. Inside it was white tiles, white walls, white laminate countertops, white kitchen cupboards. The sofa could have been generously described as cream. It felt sterile to the nth degree, but whoever kept it clean did one hell of a job.

Francisco said he was just about to make coffee, so we waited while he put on a show involving a moka pot and a lot of gurgling noises. He poured three demitasse cups of Cuban coffee with crema then led us out into the enclosed patio. There was a round wooden table—not so much white as blond wood—surrounded by wicker chairs.

Once we were settled, Francisco got to the point: "I followed your advice."

"What advice was that?" I asked.

"I called a guy I know from the power company to go and take a look at the substation."

"Who's your guy?"

Francisco hesitated like he was a journalist protecting a source.

I hadn't really meant anything by asking the question, but all of a sudden, I really wanted to know. "I won't tell anyone."

"His name is Rico," he said, taking a sip of his coffee.

I did the same. It was rich and thick and bitter, the kind that started your heart better than a couple of electrified paddles.

"The point is, he found this." Francisco leaned toward a gas grill sitting against the mesh screen and picked up a large circuit board covered in transistors and capacitors and other components. Complex electronics were well outside my wheelhouse, but it looked too big and too industrial to be from inside a computer. It could have been from a rocket ship, for all I knew. The board was about three feet long and a good eighteen inches wide, and one side was blackened along the edge as if it had shorted out and caught fire.

"So your guy is saying the power outage was legit?"

"No," said Francisco. "He says this board was in the wrong place to get damaged like this. He says the system would have tripped breakers before this if there was a surge that could have done this kind of damage. But nothing was tripped."

"So what happened?"

"My guy says it looks like the power to the arena was purposefully turned off, at the substation. Then this part was exchanged in and the power switched back on, to make it look like a faulty part. But because the system didn't trip the breaker, when it was turned back on no power flowed through this faulty board, so nothing got through to the arena."

"So this is a fake?"

Francisco nodded and sipped his coffee. I got the impression it wasn't his first coffee of the day. His eyes were moving around like there was a touch too much caffeine pulsing through his body.

"Did your guy fix the problem?" I asked.

"A five-minute job."

"So if a qualified technician could spot the fake so easily, how would anyone expect to get away with it?"

"Maybe whoever put the bad part in was planning to be the one to fix it too. Maybe this part was just a temporary measure."

"Maybe," I said. "So why didn't they switch it back?"

"I don't know. Maybe they got caught on another job. Maybe they knew you were sniffing around the substation."

It was possible that whoever had inserted the faulty part had seen me checking out the gate. I didn't recall seeing an FPL truck in the area, but utility vehicles tended to zoom around the place unnoticed. What it did prove was that the sabotage was real, and the cutting of the dehumidification system's pipes was an escalation of the earlier power outage. But something about it didn't quite fit. Maybe it was the fact that one attack happened outside the arena and the others happened inside. Could the same person have access to both? Or was there a whole team of saboteurs on the loose?

We finished our coffee in relative silence. I was still trying to fit all these burned, broken, and cut pieces together. I suspected Francisco was thinking through his financial future. Ron looked noncommittal, like he might have been mulling over what to order for lunch.

When we were done with our coffee, Francisco showed us out and asked me if I could keep him abreast of any developments. I got the sense that he was still keen to clear his name, if not get his job back. I wasn't sure if that was possible, or even desirable. Sometimes once burned, bridges were difficult to rebuild.

We drove away, leaving Francisco standing on his front path, hands in his pockets.

CHAPTER TWENTY-TWO

BACK IN THE OFFICE, RON THREW A FEW LUNCH IDEAS AT ME, BUT AS IT was still only midmorning, I couldn't raise much enthusiasm for any of them. My limited brainpower was being directed elsewhere in a useless kind of way. I started to feel restless again. Sometimes I needed to stop and think—good hard conscious calculating—and sometimes I needed to just let things mull for a while. But it was impossible to do both at the same time.

I wanted to let my subconscious do its thing and connect some of the dots, but I couldn't help focusing on all the competing images in my head. The cut pipe and the burned circuit board. I wanted to know who it was that I had seen in the FPL truck in the gas station video. I wanted to know why what still appeared to be a zero-sum game was causing so much trouble. I wondered where exactly I was still registered to vote, a thought that caught me by surprise.

It made me think again of Charita Jain and the somewhat cynical yet pertinent question she had raised: who the hell thinks hockey in South Florida is a good idea? I knew someone who might have an answer to that. I made a call to the *Palm Beach Post*, not expecting my contact to be there. He wasn't in the Woodward and Bernstein business; his job usually saw him out and about a bit more. I left my number and asked the receptionist to pass on a message.

I placed the phone back on my desk and put my hands up behind my head and leaned back, kicking off my shoes to assume my thinking position. Then my phone rang.

"It's been a long time, kid," said the voice of a thousand smoked cigars.

"The carrier pigeon moves fast these days," I said in return.

"Damn cell phones," he croaked. "There's no hiding anymore. So what's up with you?"

"I just need to get some background on something. Thought maybe we could catch up for lunch. My treat."

The offices of the *Palm Beach Post* were on South Dixie Highway down near Southland Park, at the south end of town, so we met up in North Tamarind. I found myself outside a brick red barbecue joint just down from the rail yards. It was as charming as a bomb shelter and about the same size. I parked on the street and waited.

I heard two tons of Detroit steel coming up the street before I saw what it was: a low, wide, long convertible open to the elements like a cruise ship. It pulled into the tiny parking lot and stopped with a metallic *thwack-thwack-thwack* in front of the smoking barbecues. I wandered over and waited behind his car. As he got out, I noted that he may have added an inch or two to his girth but otherwise looked pretty much the same.

Punk Rowlands was the kind of local legend that nobody knew anymore because nobody read the local paper. Punk had been covering sports in South Florida for about as long as air-conditioning had been around. He had seemed old and wise and rather rundown when I first met him as a minor-league ballplayer during my stint with the St. Lucie Mets.

"Miami Jones," he said with a rumble as if coming from somewhere deep in his guts. It was a hell of a voice, one heard for many years on local radio from minor league ballparks and spring training. He had been with the *Palm Beach Post* when it was the only way people got their sports news, and I still saw his byline occasionally, wrapped around fish guts or lining the bottom of bird cages.

"Punk," I said, "you haven't changed a bit."

"Once tanned and leathered, always tanned and leathered." He slapped me on the back with a heavy paw that felt like an anvil, then pushed me in the direction of the small front door of the barbecue joint.

Journalists love a free meal. I had found this to be a universal truth dating back to my college days. If you ever needed to get some intel or local knowledge, there were few better sources than a local journalist, and few better ways to open them up than by feeding them.

The bomb shelter was Punk's choice. That was the other thing about most journalists: they were cheap. Not only because they were poorly paid—unless they cracked some massive story and ended up with a book deal and a lecture tour—but they tended to be no-nonsense folks, more interested in how things actually were than how they appeared to be. Substance over beauty.

The barbecue joint was all that. Inside it was as simple as could be: some plastic chairs for waiting customers but no tables or counters where you could eat. The smell set me drooling the moment the door was opened—there was something about that wood smoke smell that permeated the soul.

All the customers and staff were black, and a sign on the wall proclaimed the place to be a black-owned business. There were varsity pennants tacked up on the walls from historically black colleges and universities: Edward Waters, Spelman, Tuskegee. We may have been the only white folks in for lunch, but Punk didn't seem to notice, and I didn't care. Neither did the woman with the broad smile who met us at the counter.

"Well, Mr. Rowlands," she said, "so nice to see you again."

"Wanda, a pleasure as always," he replied. "This is my friend Miami Jones."

Wanda turned her bright smile on me. "Welcome."

She grabbed a notepad and began scribbling something down. Then she looked up at Punk. "The usual for Mr. Rowlands. And for you, sir?" she asked me.

It is my considered opinion, one that had been passed on to me by Lenny Cox, that when you are in an eatery—Lenny required there to be tablecloths to consider any place a restaurant—let your instinct guide you. If it smells good, it probably is good. And if it is good, then the people running the place know which food is best. It sounded like a risky strategy in a place like Palm Beach, where restaurant meals could easily drift into the high hundreds of dollars, and the cynical man might be concerned that a waiter would simply offer the most expensive dish. But in my experience, those kinds of restaurants smelled of bouquets and incense, not garlic and wood smoke. According to Lenny, if it didn't smell good, you didn't listen to the waiter; you just left.

"What would you recommend, Wanda?" I asked.

"If you ain't had our food before, you need to have the combo dinner. Ribs and chicken," she said with a definitive nod. "I make the corn bread myself."

"That's me, then," I said.

"And for your other side? Collard greens?"

I knew a lot of people in the South who claimed collard greens as some kind of national dish, but even they rarely ate it, and I wasn't a fan. But I heard Danielle in my mind telling me to eat some vegetables, so I went with it.

"And for dessert, we just made our famous pecan pound cake."

"Sounds fabulous," I said.

We each took a plastic chair to wait and caught up on old times. Punk had been a well-known face about town in the 1990s, but his celebrity waned as the news went online and even high school sports started appearing on cable television. He was a great writer and a decent enough radio commentator, but on camera he came across as grumpy and mean, although it didn't seem to faze him one way or the other.

When our food was ready, Wanda put everything in Styrofoam containers and bagged it up for us. She told me she hoped that I enjoyed my meal, and I told her that if the smell was anything to go by it was going to be fit for a king.

Punk led us back out into the parking lot. I thought we might sit in his convertible and chat, but he handed me the bag of food and proceeded to the trunk of his car. He opened it up and pulled out a couple of faded canvas director's chairs. Then he flipped open a small picnic table and set up a lunch spot right beside the smoking barbecues. I sat and doled out the food while Punk returned to the depths of his massive trunk and grabbed two ice-cold beers.

With the vacant lot across the street as our view, we ate one of the finest meals I've ever had in my life. The ribs were smoky and tender and had just enough bite to pull away from the bone without much effort. The corn bread was sweet and savory and delicious, and the greens had a smoky, bacon-y essence that made me reconsider vegetables entirely. We clinked beer cans and ate in silence for a while, until the threat of indigestion slowed us down.

Punk took a long sip from his beer. "So you're after some background?"

"Yeah," I said, licking tangy barbecue sauce off my lips. "I'm looking into some stuff going on with this new arena. You know, the one in Mangonia Park."

Punk nodded. "The hockey arena."

"What do you think of it?"

"Hey, I love the idea. I grew up in Buffalo, so I love hockey. But I wouldn't put my money in it." He bit into his pulled pork sandwich. Shredded meat squeezed out the back and dropped with a plop into his Styrofoam container.

"Why not?" I asked.

Punk chewed for a moment then washed his pork down with a slug of beer. "You know how many second-tier sports competitions folks have tried here? If they had bodies, they'd have filled the morgue. They've tried football—at least three times—and soccer. There's been basketball and lacrosse and even this World Team Tennis thing, out on Key Biscayne. Sports leagues down here are like property development: for every one that produces a shiny new building, there's a thousand lying in a grimy pile of broken dreams."

"But this one's not lying in a pile," I said. "They've got a shiny new arena, with tenants, and a new league."

"Look, I think the whole thing is folly. But I didn't think they'd even get that arena off the ground. They weren't the first ones to try. Since the old fronton closed back in the nineties, people have tried to do something good with that lot. I think they even wanted to put an Amazon warehouse there at one point. None of it came to squat."

"Until now."

"Yeah. I guess the guy behind it had some connections. I remember when they were pitching the whole idea. They started wheeling out all these old NHL stars—you know, the kinds of guys you'd only know if you were a hard-core Rangers fan, or from Canada. It felt like the same thing all over again. Until Lex Javits got on board."

"Lex Javits?"

"Yeah, you remember him? Hall of Fame defenseman for the Red Wings."

"Yeah, I kind of remember. He played when I was in college, didn't he?"

"Probably. But after he finished his hockey career—or maybe even before he finished—he got into coffee shops. You know, like them Seattle ones that you find everywhere now."

"Starbucks."

"Whatever. So he's got like a few hundred of them now, dotted around the Midwest and Northeast. He's worth a pretty penny, I hear. And he spends half his year in Miami."

"Is that right? So what happened when he got involved?"

"Like I say, up until then it was mostly a parade of B-grade stars and has-beens, but this guy behind it all brought in Javits and all of a sudden the thing seemed to get legs."

"Was the guy's name John Trainor?"

"Yeah, that's him. I heard he was a local kid but had gone to school in New York and had all sorts of connections up there. How he got Javits on board, I don't know. Maybe sweet-talked him by giving him a team."

"Javits has a team?"

"Yeah, the Miami team. And he's on the board of governors for the league."

"What do you know about the league? How's it going?"

"It's going the way you'd expect it to be going. It's hockey in South Florida, for crying out loud. Look, like I say, I love hockey. And like me, there's lots of folks down here who grew up in New York, Chicago, and Montréal. Folks who love their hockey. The thing is, most of those folks are old now. You may find this hard to believe, kid, but I'm no spring chicken."

"You weren't a spring chicken when I met you," I said.

"And you were just the same cheeky whippersnapper. What I'm saying is, these old folks, they don't go to the game. They're as happy as Larry to watch the NHL on their big-screen TV, chugging on a brewski while lying back in their Barcalounger. But to make it work, a league needs to attract a younger crowd. People who still need to go out to get their good times. Not people whose best days are all locked away inside their heads."

It was a good point. "So you're saying that the league is struggling?"

"Something new like this, it'll always take time to bed down. But the trouble is, the guys who sink the money into these things, they're usually not doing it out of a love for the game or civic pride. They're in it for the return. The cashola. They're usually not happy to lose money for ten years while a team grows roots in the community."

"But they're on television, too, aren't they?"

"Sure, if you want to call it that. The arena currently hosts development league basketball, which is on one of the secondary local networks, and hockey is on ESPN twenty-nine or some internet channel. I mean, you gotta be a diehard to put in the effort to find it."

"But minor league baseball teams are doing really well around the country, aren't they?"

"Some of them are, that's true. Some of these guys have found a smart business model: cheap ticket prices and low-cost concessions that bring in families just looking for a good time. But you gotta remember, baseball is ingrained in our psyche. It's part of who we are, our national pastime. I mean, don't get me wrong, I know most folks don't bleed it the way you and I do. And even you I'm worried about these days. But again, it's all still aimed at a younger market, a family market. If they're going to make this thing work, this South Sunshine Hockey League, that's who they're pitching at. But I've been to a few games. They're not hitting it just yet."

"Why not?"

"All of the above. It's not quite ready for primetime, so it's not so slick. Last game I was at, the scoreboard and the timer went out for half the game. I think they're not getting as much buzz as they hoped they would. It's a tough market. We got a lot of top-flight pro sports down here. NFL, MLB, NBA, even MLS. Most folks already have a team to root for, some way to spend their dough. So unless they start tapping into a cash-rich market pretty soon, I don't know how long this thing goes for."

"But they're not even through their first season."

"Exactly. Look, we had a hockey league here before, in the nineties. Only lasted a couple years. With soccer, one competition didn't even see out its maiden season. There's been arena and off-season football, which comes and goes bust and then disappears and maybe comes back again later but never sticks. Like I say, the money behind everything wants a return. They could go buy some of these internet stocks, you know what I mean? Double their money overnight and all that."

"So you think this John Trainor might be on shaky financial ground?"

"No, I think the guy's loaded. He lives in Palm Beach, for crying out loud. But my sources tell me the guy has tried to get action in the major leagues before. He's tried to buy into baseball, basketball, and even took a shot at the Carolina Panthers, I think. But he always comes up short. Word is he's rich and connected, but not major-league rich and connected. Those guys don't talk in millions or even hundreds of millions. Those guys are into billions."

Punk looked at his half-eaten sandwich and shook his head. "It's a hell of a thing to think you're poor because you can't buy into a major-league sports team." He ate a spoonful of baked beans that smelled like molasses. "It won't be this guy or his lack of trying that brings this thing down. You mark my words: it'll be the money. The money will run out of patience, sooner rather than later."

"But Trainor is the money," I said. "It's his company that owns the whole show, and half owns the arena."

"It's his company, but is it his money?" Punk shrugged his beefy shoulders. "I don't know. All I'm saying is, if you want to find a common thread in all these little leagues and teams and competitions that fail, it's that these guys never play with their own money."

This was also a good point. It made me think about what Charita Jain had told me. About the county issuing a bond to pay for their share of the arena. It made me wonder where the rest of the financing had really come from.

"You know, I didn't get that deep into this story. My beat is the games, not the politics behind them," he said.

"I know, Punk."

"But there was someone who came at this story from that angle —the business side, the political side." Before he even opened his mouth again, I knew exactly whose name he was going to say. "Maggie Nettles. She's a reporter at the *Post*."

"Yeah, I know Maggie."

Punk stuffed the final piece of sandwich into his mouth. "You should talk to Maggie," he said through sauce-covered teeth.

CHAPTER TWENTY-THREE

I returned to the office to find Ron hadn't had any lunch at all. Feeling sorry for him after my culinary feast, I drove him up to Longboard's to grab one of Mick's carved turkey and cranberry on sourdough sandwiches. Despite the early afternoon sun, the breeze coming through the courtyard had a cool tinge to it, the first hint that autumn was giving way to winter, such as it was in South Florida.

Ron and I were halfway through our beers and giving serious consideration to settling in for the afternoon when Ron's phone rang. He glanced at the screen. "The bride." He slipped from his stool and wandered to the back of the courtyard.

"No lunch for you?" asked Muriel.

"I ate already," I said.

"Don't let Mick find out you eat elsewhere," she said, offering me a wink.

"As long as I don't regularly drink elsewhere, I think Mick'll survive."

Ron returned to the bar but not to his seat. "So, Cass and Danielle were playing tennis at The Breakers."

"Okay," I replied.

"They've just gone out to the patio to have a late lunch."

"Do I need to know this?"

"You'll never guess who just walked past them into the Seafood Bar."

"Elvis?"

"Not Elvis. The guy you've been asking about, John Trainor."

"He's at The Breakers? Now?"

"Yes. But you didn't ask me who he was having lunch with."

"Who's he having lunch with, Ron? Tell me, tell me."

"Since you asked so nicely, I will tell you. He's having lunch with Senator Brian Vargas."

It was too good an opportunity to pass up. After Muriel put the rest of Ron's sandwich into a cardboard box, we dashed out into the parking lot and headed for Palm Beach. When we arrived, I stopped at the valet, and Ron and I strode up the steps into the lobby.

The Breakers was that kind of hotel that exuded quiet money. In a state that prided itself on glitz and sunshine, the lobby was dark and all kinds of New England clubby.

We walked down the wide corridor and around to the Seafood Bar. While the name engendered visions of fish and chips wrapped in newspaper and oysters by the dozen served in plastic trays, the Seafood Bar was the kind of place where you could run up a tab that some small Pacific Island nations would struggle to cover.

I didn't know John Trainor from a bag of malted barley, but when I scanned the room, I did recognize the face of Senator Vargas from television.

"Don't go too crazy," Ron whispered as I took off across the room. It looked like I was interrupting a cozy lunch, the two of them plotting world hockey domination, or some such thing.

"John Trainor," I said as I reached the table.

Trainor looked up at me. He was about fifty, with a decent head of blond but slowly graying hair. I suspected he had looked middle-aged in college. He had one of those faces. He seemed to be in pretty good shape, but he had the kind of jowls that meant he could have added or lost twenty pounds and either way it wouldn't have made any difference to the way his face looked. He offered me a confident if not quizzical smile.

"I'm sorry," he said. "Have we met?"

"No. My name is Miami Jones. I'm an investigator working on behalf of Stone Strong Insurance."

"I see."

He said nothing more, so I waited. People often don't like that uncomfortable silence and feel the need to fill it with the most interesting information. John Trainor was not one of those people. He had a glint in his eye as if he knew he was a golden child, and he had all the time in the world to wait for me to get to the point.

"I'm investigating sabotage at the new arena."

"Sabotage, you say? How mysterious."

"It's more than mysterious," I said. "It's criminal."

"Well, perhaps you should call the police. But I surely don't see what this has to do with me."

"Doesn't your company, Provents, run the arena on behalf of Palm Beach County?"

"Provents manages the arena on behalf of the stakeholders, both public and private, but I don't get involved in the day-to-day down there. Might I suggest you speak with Con Gelphert about it? He's the CEO, you know."

I knew. And I was pretty certain that he knew that I knew. And if there's one thing that gets my goat more than any other, it's people yanking my chain. It sometimes used to happen when I was pitching, back in college and in the minor leagues. I might throw one outside the box for a wide ball, or maybe into the dirt in front of home plate, and the batter would give some kind of lip like, "Nice pitch," or, "Cy Young material." My catcher could be fairly certain that the next pitch was either going to be a heater right over the plate for a strike, or a heater right at the batter's earhole.

"In the course of my investigation, I've uncovered a lot of things that make absolutely no sense. But top of the list has to be why anyone would be stupid enough to start an ice hockey league in South Florida."

I wouldn't want to play poker with this guy. I got the sense that if his hand was a dud, he could have bluffed his way to Babylon. He didn't flinch, he didn't frown, and the smug smile stayed plastered on his face.

"I can understand how these things would be beyond your intellect," he said.

I glanced at Senator Vargas. "And it seems like no one from the city, the county, or even the state wanted anything to do with this project until you got involved—right, Senator?"

Vargas wasn't quite so unflappable, but he wasn't a hothead either. He offered me a frown and shook his head. "I don't know who you are, and I don't particularly care for your tone of voice, but I can assure you that whatever you think you know, you're wrong. This was a great project for the people of Palm Beach County, and for the state of Florida. We've brought thousands of jobs here, and over the next ten years, hundreds of millions of tourist dollars will flow into the region because of the arena. I'm sorry you can't grasp that."

"Funny," I said, "the people who I spoke with that actually work at the arena all had jobs before, so I'm not sure you really created anything. And do you really think that tourists come to Florida to watch hockey?"

"You'd be surprised," he said.

"You got that right."

"Are you a resident of Palm Beach County?" asked Vargas.

"Yes, I live on Singer Island." The words came out of my mouth before I had time to check myself, to recall that I didn't live on the island anymore. Yet I didn't feel the need to correct myself. "Why do you ask? Drumming up votes?"

"As it happens, I'm not running for re-election this year. I'm retiring from the legislature."

"You don't look old enough to be retiring from anything," I said.

"Well, I've done my service for the people of Florida," he said. "Have you done yours?"

"Every day."

I felt the presence of someone at my shoulder and turned to find the bartender standing behind me.

"Can I offer you a drink at the bar, sir?"

It was as polite a way of saying *get out* as I'd ever heard, and I didn't want to make any more of a scene than I already had; I knew that Ron and Cassandra enjoyed the Seafood Bar on a regular basis.

"No, thank you," I said. "I think I'll check out the patio." I offered each of the two men seated at the table a nod. "Gentlemen," I said. Then I strode out of the bar.

I followed Ron out onto the patio overlooking the Atlantic Ocean. The days were getting shorter, and the sun was heading low behind us. Waiters were packing up the umbrellas and closing up the outdoor service. Danielle and Cassandra were sitting at a table looking out toward the water. They were each holding a Collins glass that could have been full of tonic water or vodka for all I knew.

"Did you see John Trainor?" asked Cassandra.

"We had a quick word," I said.

"And Senator Vargas?"

"Him, too, although he tells me he won't be a senator for much longer."

"Yes, that's right," she said. "He's retiring. But once a senator, always a senator. Isn't that how it goes?"

"Something like that. But if he looks after the Palm Beaches, I'm surprised I didn't hear about it."

"Maybe that's because we live in Miami now," said Danielle. "*For now*. I guess when we see anything about local politics, it's about Miami, not so much up here."

What she was saying made sense, but it still didn't sound right. It felt strange to be standing in Palm Beach talking about living in

Miami when I was only ten minutes away from my office but two hours away from my home.

"Did *you* know about Vargas?" I asked Danielle.

"About his retiring? Yes, yes I did."

"But you spend even more time in Miami than I do. I must really be out of the loop."

"Politics has never really been of great interest to you," said Danielle.

I shrugged. That was true enough.

"Besides, I happen to know the candidate who's running to replace him."

"You do?"

I saw Cassandra look at Ron and Ron look at Cassandra, and I got the distinct impression that not only was I out of the loop as far as local politics was concerned, but that I wasn't exactly going to enjoy being brought in.

"So who is running to replace Senator Vargas?" I had to ask.

"Eric," said Danielle.

She just left it at that, a single name. But I knew exactly who she meant: Eric Edwards. Her ex-husband. Currently state attorney for the 15th Judicial Circuit, aka Palm Beach County.

"Eric is running for the state Senate?"

"Yes."

"Why does that not surprise me?"

"Because it's not surprising," she said. "You know it's always been the direction he was going. Even as state attorney, he's an elected official. He was already a politician; now he'll just be a different kind."

"If he wins."

"The polls suggest he will."

"There are polls? I didn't even know the guy was running and there are polls?"

"Like I say, keeping up with politics is not something that lights you up."

"I didn't realize that you were such a politics buff either."

"I'm not. But he sent me an email."

"Why would he send you an email?"

"Why do politicians send anyone emails? To fundraise."

"Your ex-husband is asking you for money?"

"His campaign was fundraising. It's not exactly alimony."

"So," said Cassandra, cutting through the afternoon air like a front-end loader full of ice, "would anyone like a drink?"

I did want a drink. I wanted a couple—a couple of doubles. I didn't know why it was exactly that the news of Eric Edwards was getting under my skin. He and Danielle had been divorced for more than a decade, and the few times that he and I had crossed paths professionally, it had become plain for all to see that when it came to Danielle, I had won and he had lost. It was his mistake—his affair—that split the ground between them, and he regretted it, and he knew that his poor choices had ultimately been to my benefit. So why was he putting me on edge? For the same reason John Trainor—a guy I had never met and had no real knowledge of—had put me on edge. For the same reason that everything seemed to be putting me on edge. I just didn't know what that reason was.

"Actually," said Danielle, "I thought we might go for a bit of a run on the beach."

"Tennis wasn't enough for you?" I asked.

"I'm afraid at my age I'm not that much of a challenge," said Cassandra.

Danielle offered her a smile and shook her head. Then she looked back at me and gave me the face that I can never say no to.

"Okay," I said. "But not here."

Danielle and I headed back to the apartment in her car, leaving Ron and Cassandra on the patio with the claim check for my car. We got changed into our running gear. Then Danielle drove us off the island and went north up South Dixie Highway until we reached Blue Heron Boulevard.

We drove across onto Singer Island in silence, the birds flocking across the sky to perform their evening rituals. We parked opposite the shop that sold boogie boards and buckets and spades and towels then walked through the dunes and onto City Beach. We ran north in our regular formation, like the birds above us. Danielle in front, me bringing up the rear. She setting the pace, me comfortable with the view.

We had run this beach hundreds of times before. It felt completely familiar yet somehow unknown, like a favorite sweater that was pushed to the back of the closet only to be rediscovered years later. We reached the part of the island that thinned out into the state park, where Danielle turned, gave me a wink, and headed back for home. The sun was almost gone as we ran along the sand, the handful of condominium towers on Singer Island throwing patches of light across the beach like a chessboard. Many of the apartments were still shuttered, their snowbird owners yet to arrive for the winter.

We reached our starting point again and stretched on the beach. From the corner of my eye, I could see Danielle looking out toward the infinite darkness of the ocean. I was looking the other way. Beyond the scraggly grasses on the dunes, past the collection of shops and bars, and then down the street to the house where an executive from Philadelphia now lived. I thought for a moment about jogging past the old house, just to see it, but it wasn't really mine right now. Somebody else lived there, or at least they stayed there, like it was a transitory thing, a temporary state of affairs.

Danielle put her hand gently on my shoulder, and we walked back through the dunes toward her car. She drove us in silence off the island that was once ours but now wasn't and back to the other island that was never ours but somehow now seemed to be where we spent so much time. Back to Cassandra and Ron's apartment, itself starting to feel like a perpetual thing, a permanent state of affairs.

CHAPTER TWENTY-FOUR

THE NEXT MORNING I FOUND MYSELF PARKING ONCE AGAIN IN THE LOT next to my building but not going up to my office. After chatting with Punk Rowlands, I had called the *Palm Beach Post* to speak with Maggie Nettles. Unlike Punk, Maggie was the kind of reporter who spent a lot of time at her desk, typing copy and chasing leads. She was also the kind of reporter who didn't want to miss a tip, so when it turned out she wasn't at her desk, rather than leave a message with the receptionist, I was put through to her voicemail. She called back after my run on the beach and suggested we meet for breakfast.

Although my theory about buying food for journalists held true, I knew that Maggie Nettles would not be a cheap date like Punk Rowlands was.

I walked down South Dixie Highway in the general direction of Rosemary Square but stopped before I got to Okeechobee Boulevard. In a bland but newish office building, I found Loic Bakery Café Bar. The name covered a lot of territory, but the place was more or less a little French-style patisserie that did pastry-based calorie bombs and great coffee.

I knew Maggie Nettles from a previous case a good few years back. She had been on the trail of a corrupt senator who had wound up entwined in a case I was working, and we shared intel, which enabled me to solve the case and her to wrap up a series of investigative reports she had been writing. The strange part was we had never met. All our dealings had been on the phone. She was a prickly, no-nonsense person, but I hoped that our previous interactions and my willingness to share information might help her open up to me this time.

First I needed to figure out which person she was. The café was moderately busy both inside and out. People were ordering at the counter, and others were sitting at the tight seating inside. There were a few wooden tables and chairs, like fancy picnic sets, set up in the courtyard just outside the café.

I was surveying the crowd through the window when the voice behind me said, "Miami Jones."

I recognized it and turned to find a woman standing before me. In my mind's eye, I had created an amalgam of an angry librarian and my seventh grade English teacher, Mrs. Matthews. Maggie wasn't either of those things. She was blond and average height and weight, the kind of person who looks fit and healthy in real life but on television would look a touch pudgy. She had an attractive enough face that was set firm against the mild morning breeze.

"Maggie," I said, and we shook hands. "At last we meet."

"Yes, it's the highlight of my day too."

I shrugged off the barb, and we went inside and ordered breakfast. Maggie got avocado smashed up on toast with smoked salmon and a latte. I took a grilled cheese sandwich with a regular coffee. Then we wandered back outside to sit at one of the small wooden tables.

"So what have you been doing since we last spoke?" I asked.

"Living," she said. "And you?"

"I got married."

"How lovely for you."

As a server placed our coffees on the table. I said, "Didn't I see somewhere that you went to Washington?"

"I did a couple of years up there, *Washington Post*."

I had always imagined that working for a paper with the pedigree of *The Washington Post* was like getting a game in the major leagues, but she didn't seem boastful or even proud of the achievement.

"But you came back?"

I regretted the question the moment it left my lips without passing through my brain. Perhaps getting the big-time gig and then ending up right back where she started was the reason for her lack of pride.

"I wanted to write something important," she said, sipping the foam from her latte.

"And *The Washington Post* didn't do important stories?"

"Oh, they certainly thought so. What I realized was, those big national stories get all the headlines, but how much difference do they really make? I ask you, Woodward and Bernstein and the whole Watergate thing. It made them famous, but did it really change your life?"

"It ended a presidency."

"So it changed Nixon's life, but what about yours?" She gestured around the courtyard. "What about all these people?"

"Didn't change my life, but I wasn't even born."

"Don't get me wrong," she said. "It's important to keep all levels of government honest and on their toes. It's a government for the people more than by the people, so we can't just rely on them to do the right thing. Self-interest is a powerful motivator."

"But Palm Beach?" It came out sounding like the Palm Beaches was a terrible second option. I certainly didn't think so. I didn't want to live anywhere else, even though I did live somewhere else, at least for now. I wasn't so sure about Maggie Nettles. She didn't strike me as a beach kind of gal. She was blond, yes, but far from tan. And she wore none of the casual affectation that people who lived on the coast often had.

"It doesn't get more *for the people, by the people* than Florida. But it also doesn't get much murkier. Even now, there's still a good deal of the Wild West about this place, particularly with the folks in power. I just felt like my work had more impact here."

Our food arrived, and she cut a piece of her smashed avocado and ate it. I wouldn't have said it was the most unappetizing thing I'd ever seen, but it was on the list.

"Besides, I missed the beach," she said.

"You did?"

"Yes. You don't have to lie out on the sand baking like a Thanksgiving turkey to enjoy it. Truth is I don't go to the actual beach very often. But just being near it, it puts something in the air. It changes people. Gives a place a different feel. Something organic and real. There wasn't a lot of organic and real in DC."

I nodded and bit into my sandwich. The French didn't call their grilled cheese a *grilled cheese*, and there was good reason for that. It was a whole other beast. The bread had a tangy sourness to it that was offset by the creamy goopiness of the soft cheese inside and the crunch of the crusted cheese on top. It was seriously tasty.

We ate for a moment, enjoying our breakfast, until Maggie wiped her mouth with her napkin and put her elbows on the table.

"So, to what do I owe this magnificent breakfast?" she said. "I assume you want something?"

"I know we've been mutually beneficial to each other before," I said, sipping my coffee. "I thought maybe we could be again."

"What are you into?"

"The new arena."

Maggie leaned back in her seat and nodded. I saw her eyebrows furrow a bit.

"I hear you've been following the story," I said.

"Do you?"

"I do. So I'm wondering what you can tell me about how that deal was done."

Maggie shrugged. "Not much. Anything I know is in the paper."

"Hardly."

The server returned with a coffeepot. Maggie ordered another latte, and I got a refill. I offered the server a smile then found Maggie staring at me.

"What can you tell me?" she asked.

"Okay, you want to play it that way. But you know I'm good to my word."

"I know you were once. That's all I know."

"You're quite the cynic, you know that?"

"Takes one to know one. It comes with the territory."

"I have proof of ongoing sabotage. I'm trying to figure out who's behind it—I mean really behind it. And to do that, I need to know some of the high-level players."

"Can you get me quotes that aren't hearsay?"

"Not all I know is hearsay. I saw some of it myself."

"But I recall that you like to be *sources unnamed*."

"True. Yes, I can provide people in the know."

Maggie studied me for a moment longer then leaned forward, just as her drink arrived. We waited for the server to leave, then Maggie took a sip of her latte.

"So you know that the land has been a white elephant for decades."

"Yes. Lots of ideas, no traction. Until this new guy, Trainor."

Maggie nodded. "So you know Trainor."

"Not well enough. What can you tell me?"

"John Trainor, born into Palm Beach money. Lived on the island until he was shipped away to New England for boarding school. His daddy had gone to Princeton, and you know how those guys just love to keep the family lineage in schools. But old John didn't make it to the Ivy League, so they sent him to a private college—Clarkson University. Up in Potsdam, New York." She took a sip of her coffee and continued. "See, the defining trait of John Trainor is that he's always been *close but no cigar*. It's amazing how a privileged upbringing can make a guy look like a winner when actually he's been second-best his entire life."

"Doesn't sound as if you like him that much."

"It's the waste of opportunity that I don't like, and the whole façade of success that these kinds of guys put on. Even after college, he didn't quite hit the heights. Didn't get into a top-flight MBA school, so he went to Fordham."

"New York City?" I asked.

"Yes. And so the theme continues. Fordham's a good school, don't get me wrong. But to these guys, it ain't Harvard or Wharton. So he gets a job in a second- or third-tier investment bank on Wall Street. Once again, not a bad gig, making plenty of dough, at least for regular people, but when little Johnny came back to Palm Beach in the winters, he was considered somewhat of a disappointment. Seems like he spent his entire adult life trying to get accepted by the pride."

"I heard he tried to buy into the NFL, MLB, even the NBA. But no dice."

"Exactly. Those are the lofty heights to which he thinks he belongs, but in Palm Beach terms, he's just an ordinary Joe. I mean, it makes me sick. The guy probably earns a couple mil a year, he's got a brownstone in New York City and a bungalow in Palm Beach, but somehow he and everybody around him seem to believe he hasn't made it. Plenty of people would kill to be where he is."

"Plenty of people have," I said.

Maggie nodded. She probably knew more about that than I ever would.

"So what about this arena, this hockey thing?" I asked.

"Well, if you don't get accepted into all the best clubs, what do you do? As a mid-level mover and shaker? You start your own. Like Groucho Marx said, 'I wouldn't want to belong to a club that would have me as a member.'"

"But why hockey, and why here?"

"On the face of it, you gotta ask yourself, right? It seems crazy. What am I saying? It *is* crazy. But follow the logic. He went to Clarkson. Do you know Clarkson?"

"Not really."

"It's so far north in New York that it's practically in Canada. So what sport do you think they play?"

"Hockey," I said confidently.

"Right on the money."

"Did Trainor play?"

"No. But word is that he was tight with the team. Kind of like a booster, you know? He was the one who got the booze and drugs and that sort of thing fixed up for the players."

"You got evidence of that?"

"Nothing that I can write about. But you know the kind of guy I mean. Not a jock himself but likes to hang out with that popular crowd."

"I know that guy. So there is a hockey link there."

"Yeah, so we bring the two things together: he can't get into the top-tier leagues—his connections are all relatively small potatoes on Wall Street—but he has links to both hockey and Palm Beach," said Maggie. "Throw it all in the blender, what do you have?"

"The South Sunshine Hockey League."

"Exactly."

"Okay, so I hear that the county and the state weren't that interested in the deal, not initially."

"That's true. The county investment committee and the state board both rejected the proposals. But like all good Florida projects, all Trainor needed was his own booster, a champion to the cause."

"Senator Vargas," I said.

"You know more than you let on," she said. "Exactly, Senator Brian Vargas. He took the bit between his teeth and got the governor interested. Trainor arranged a parade of famous faces—former hockey players, old eighties TV stars—to sell the project. And if there's one thing Tallahassee politicians love, it's proximity to stardom. They might not get so fazed by it out in California, but Tallahassee can feel like a bit of a backwater that way."

"But what was Vargas's motivation? Why did he become the project champion?"

"The senator's wife acted as a consultant to the project to the tune of several hundred thousand dollars."

"He got his wife a job? Is that legal?"

"Did you arrive in Florida yesterday? Whether it's legal is not the question. It's whether it's ethical. And the answer is, no, it's not."

"Legal or ethical?"

"Ethical. It's all legal in Florida. You know he's retiring from the legislature, right?"

"I did hear that."

"And he's going to walk into the role of commissioner of the new league."

"It's hardly Roger Goodell," I said.

"Who?"

"Commissioner of the NFL. I mean, he earns a bundle. I can't imagine that's the case here."

"You're missing the point. This isn't about making money at that level. It's about giving the bird to the man. When you can't afford to buy into a team, you buy a whole league. It's about how many times you get in the newspaper or on social media and how many photos you can get with the rich and famous."

"That's for Trainor, not for Vargas."

"Don't make the mistake of thinking that just because the numbers aren't major-league big that they're not attractive."

"So is that how he got these old players and TV people involved? Appearance money?"

"Some, yes. He somehow found out that the governor's wife was a huge fan of that show about the kids at high school—you know, the one from the eighties with the bad laugh track?"

"I know it."

"You ever see any of those actors in anything in the last thirty years?"

"I don't watch a lot of television."

"That doesn't matter, because they're not on it. So when Trainor gets wind of this, he finds out that a couple of them live in Florida.

He throws a little money their way to come and meet the governor's wife and chat about this great new hockey project."

"And you're saying these people actually fall for this stuff?"

"You're a baseball guy," she said. "Imagine if Babe Ruth came and offered you the deal of a lifetime."

"At this point I'd be more impressed that Babe Ruth could talk. He's been dead for seventy years."

"All right, smart guy. But you know what I mean. If you hit the right buttons, people can be talked into almost anything."

"So he paid to have all these stars and hockey types talk up the project."

"No, he didn't have to pay the hockey types. Not directly, anyway. He just called up some favors."

"Favors from who?"

"From *whom*. Favors from his college freshman-year roommate."

"Who was his freshman-year roommate?"

"Lex Javits."

I sat back in my chair. "Lex Javits was freshman-year roommates with John Trainor?"

"Exactly. Javits played two years at Clarkson, then got picked up in the NHL. Apparently he was pretty good."

"He's in the Hall of Fame."

"Which I assume makes you pretty good."

I shrugged.

"So Javits becomes the front man for the league, the public face."

"Okay," I said. "I see how they played the game in Tallahassee. Is that where all the money came from?"

"Once the governor was on board and the state got involved, the county seemed to change its mind and go all in. They did a bond issue to raise three hundred million to fund the building."

"But that only paid for half, right?" I asked.

"No, that pretty much covered it."

"But I thought the arena was a public–private enterprise."

Maggie nodded. "Oh, it is. But that's the beauty of these things. The money comes from bonds, so the risk is shouldered by the people of Palm Beach County. Trainor's investors were all in the league and teams."

"So he doesn't own the arena?"

"That's where this deal gets seriously murky. The money for the building came from the bond issue. The county had already bought the land for cash and given a contract to lease it to the arena management company for one dollar a year, in perpetuity."

"Good deal, for some."

"Oh, it gets better. Even though the money for the building came from the county, the ownership of the arena is split. The argument was that without the league and the teams, and bringing in more top-flight entertainment—which is what Trainor claimed to be able to do—the arena wasn't worth a bean. So the county fronted the cash, the private side brought the tenants."

"I take it back. That sounds like a terrible deal," I said.

"Like you say, good for some. At this point, everyone was so starstruck and, frankly, in so deep that they would've offered the Taj Mahal to close the deal."

"Okay, that's all typical Tallahassee wheeling and dealing. What it doesn't do is answer my question: why would anyone sabotage the arena? Regardless of who paid for what, you would think the ownership is invested in its success."

"You would think that, wouldn't you?" said Maggie.

She finished her latte then sat back in her chair once more. I waited for her to follow up with a zinger and drop the mic. Instead she sort of drifted away, as if thinking deeply. Then just as suddenly, her eyes snapped back as if she had connected some dots.

"I need a list," she said. "Of all the people involved, the ones you know. I need details of the alleged sabotage, and I need to speak with someone—on the record—who knows exactly what's gone wrong and when."

"I can make that happen. But why? You know something. You

figured something out."

"It's the public–private enterprise. The holding company that owns the arena."

"Right. Half owned by the county and half by Trainor's company, Provents."

"No." A tiny grin slid across her face.

"No? What do you mean, no?"

"I mean it is co-owned but not fifty-fifty."

"It's not?"

"No. You're right, it was a pretty awful deal for the county, and a great deal for Trainor. But it wasn't a complete throwaway. Somebody somewhere included a clause. The county retains the controlling interest in the arena: they own fifty-one percent to Provents' forty-nine."

"How does that change anything? What's two percent between friends? Surely they all share in the arena's success, no matter the percent."

"At the arena level, perhaps. But the chain doesn't stop there. Trainor has that interest in the arena, but he's also into the league and team. That's where his private investors got involved. It costs a bundle to set something like this up—venues to procure, players to woo, relocating players and coaches and staff. Trainor even went to visit NFL and NHL headquarters and was at the drafts for both, and he visited a number of arenas and stadia. He went to the FA Cup final in England. And I can assure you, he didn't travel coach. With these appearance fees for celebrities and side deals for consulting, everything was done with glitz and glamour. That doesn't come cheap."

"What's your point?"

"My point is, if my math is correct, he's out of money. His New York investors are due a payment on their loan, and he doesn't have it. I know he's already tapped the team owners for more capital, and they've told him to take a hike. His New York investors might be next, and if they call in their loan, he's done."

"Okay, but what has this got to do with the two percent?"

"There's another clause in the contract that says if the arena fails to meet key performance indicators, the ownership flips."

"Flips?"

"Yes. Provents gets fifty-one percent, the county forty-nine. My contact says it was a clause added deep in the contract because the assumption on the private side was that a public entity wasn't capable of profitably running a venue."

"So what does that mean? It's still just two percent. Isn't it more incentive to make the place run well?"

"Not right now. See, once Trainor gets that two percent, he has the controlling interest of the asset. He can borrow against that asset. The county won't like that, but they won't be able to prevent it."

"So Trainor will be able to borrow money against an asset he didn't pay for."

"Exactly."

"Why would he do that?"

"Because of New York. The investors. He needs to make a payment, keep them on the hook but not snap the line. Like I say, if they call in their loan, he's done for. But if he can raise debt from the arena, he can keep juggling his plates for a bit longer. And that's how these guys roll. Just keep everything going for today, and worry about tomorrow tomorrow."

"Punk Rowlands tells me that most of these leagues collapse within the first year."

"He's right. It's dog eat dog, and most of the newborn pups don't survive."

"So you're saying that Trainor can raise this debt with the arena as collateral but that it probably won't help; it will just delay the inevitable."

"And the people of Florida will again be left holding the bag."

"So what do we do?"

"I can start working this on the financial side," said Maggie. "But we have to link the sabotage back to Trainor. It's the sabotage angle that gets this on the front page."

Then something hit me, something that had been staring me in the face for some time. Maggie's two percent game idea had crystallized in my mind.

"You say Trainor will get control of the arena if it doesn't perform. What would nonperformance look like? Would, for example, a canceled game cover it?"

"I'd have to check with my sources," she said. "I've seen parts of the contract, but it's not on public record. Work product and confidentiality and all that garbage. But, yeah, failing to host a scheduled game might do it. Why?"

"Because right now, underneath the basketball court, there is nothing but concrete. They had to take the ice out."

"Are you serious? When's the next hockey game?"

"Tomorrow night."

"Can they lay a hockey rink that fast?"

"I don't know. But the guy I told you about, the facility manager—"

"The one they fired?"

"Exactly. He's the ice master. He's the one who knows how to get it done."

"And they've got him out of the picture. It's a setup. Trainor's going to win, and once again the regular people lose."

"Not yet," I said.

"What can we do?" She leaned in toward me even farther than before. "You would say that the buzzer is sounding. Game over."

"No. What we're hearing is the two-minute warning. We're down, and we need a match-winning drive the length of the field, with no timeouts."

"You sporty guys really do have a language all your own."

"It means that we've got a chance. It means that they played a good game, but they've underestimated our offense."

I pushed my chair back and stood up. Maggie Nettles did likewise.

"It means it's time to go on the attack."

CHAPTER TWENTY-FIVE

I RAN BACK TO MY CAR. SUDDENLY IT FELT LIKE I NEEDED TO ACT FAST. I didn't go up to my office or even stop to call Ron. I just drove straight to the arena.

Devon, the security guard, was at his post at the front entrance. He had me sign in and went through the ceremony of writing out a name tag that we both knew I wouldn't wear.

"Pretty quiet today," he said.

Quiet wasn't the half of it. I wandered along the concourse, noticing the sound of my own footfalls. I took a quick look inside the arena. The basketball court, empty as a school gym in summertime, was shining under the lights.

I walked up to the suite level and stopped outside the door leading to the executive-floor stairwell. Amanda Swaggert had used her card to gain access through that door, so I tried knocking then banging but roused no one. I wondered for a moment if I could get a key card from Devon, but I suspected giving out security cards to visitors was not in his manual.

I dashed back down the steps then out through the concourse and into the arena proper. I found myself on the public walkway halfway up the stands, in the same position I had seen Gelphert when he had fired Monaro. I ran down between the seats until I got to the basketball court. It was then that I noticed that extra seating had come in from somewhere—probably the bowels of the arena—and now went right up to the edge of the court. I strode into the middle of the court. The polished floorboards glistened, with the arena logo on one side of me and a sponsor's brand on the other.

I took a deep breath—not one of my usual calming breaths, in through the nose, out through the mouth but deep into my belly, filling my lungs as much as I could. Then I yelled with all my might.

"Gelphert! Gel-phert!"

My voice rang out, traveling around the cavernous space. I figured I'd either get Gelphert's attention or that of someone from whom I might be able to grab a key card.

I took another breath and yelled out the CEO's name two more times.

Someone from Monaro's team appeared at the end of the court, looking at me like I was a lunatic, which was fair enough. I dropped my voice several decibels and asked him if Gelphert was in the building.

He nodded, seemingly unsure whether I was a danger to him or to his shiny basketball court.

"Get on the radio," I said. "Tell him to get down here." The guy didn't move. "Before I start smashing these chairs into your beautiful hardwood floor."

He pulled the radio off his hip and spoke into it. I couldn't hear what he was saying, but within thirty seconds Con Gelphert appeared in the walkway halfway up the stands.

"Oh, it's you," he said. "I'm calling the police."

"Don't bother," I said. "The insurance company will do it for you."

Gelphert strode down the steps and stopped on the edge of the court. "I've already told you: I don't have a policy with your insurance company. You mean nothing to me."

I took a moment to look around the empty arena. "It's like a ghost town in here."

"What do you want?"

"My client has concerns about why it's so quiet."

"You know why it's quiet," he said. "Because that maniac pulled all the ice out. If your insurance company has an issue, I suggest they take it up with the county. They hired that moron."

"Let me ask you a question," I said. "When the power went out the other day, who did you call at Florida Power & Light?"

"I wasn't on-site when that happened. Once again, our incompetent facility manager."

"That's funny, because everyone I spoke to that day claimed you were here at first, that you said you'd call FPL in, and then you left."

"That's not accurate."

"I have ten witnesses to your one saying that's how it went down."

Gelphert sighed and rubbed his chin. I was no expert on body language, but it looked like the sort of thing a guy might do when he was about to cheat while playing bridge with his grandmother.

"Oh, that's right. Now I remember. Yes, I called FPL before I was pulled away. I had a previous engagement. I had wrongly assumed that Monaro had everything under control."

"Who did you call?"

"I told you. FPL."

"Who exactly?"

"I'm not sure it's appropriate to disclose that."

"You're not an attorney, pal. And I'm not asking for the number of your favorite hooker. Look, this is how it goes. If the insurance company has to pay out to the team, they're going to want to know why proper procedure wasn't followed here. They're going to come looking for answers, and they're going to come to you. And then to the county, and after that, law enforcement will get involved."

"Why would law enforcement get involved?"

"Because it becomes very suspicious when strange things happen, like the power going out, but no one bothers to call the utility company to fix it."

"I did call."

"So you say, but you can't say who you called. It's almost like you wanted these bad things to happen, and that, my friend, will make the police very twitchy."

Gelphert rubbed his chin again, and I was becoming convinced it was a tell. He seemed to be looking for some way to squirrel out of a sticky situation, so instead of saying anything, I just took several steps toward him and waited for him to speak.

"Look, it's no secret. As CEO I have a contact at FPL. Of course I do. We don't just go through the switchboard, you know. The bottom line is, I called them, and we got the issue fixed, didn't we? Until Monaro ripped out all the ice."

"Who did you call?"

He hesitated again. "Our contact at FPL is Mr. Otto Barassi."

"And you're saying he's the one you called when the power went out?"

"Yes, that's what I'm saying. Now if you have nothing further, I think it would be best if you leave. I'm very busy. I have some press releases to write."

"Don't you have a PR person for that?"

"Of course I do. She's working on the initial drafts right now. But when we're talking about major announcements, like having to cancel hockey games, then I need to be involved."

"You're going to cancel the game?"

"We're going to cancel at least the next two." He turned as if to leave. "But who knows how much damage that man has done."

CHAPTER TWENTY-SIX

Gelphert left the floor, but I didn't. I sat on one of the seats alongside the court and called my client.

"I had a feeling you were going to call," said Peter Parker.

For a moment, I was going to say something about him getting that Spidey sense, but he didn't seem to have a lot of humor about the whole thing. Instead, I told him about the canceled games.

"That's going to mean a payout," he said. "And you say it's at least two games?"

"That's what the CEO is claiming."

"What do you mean 'claiming'? Is there anything we can do? The next game isn't until tomorrow night."

"Without a rink it's pretty hard to play hockey," I said.

"And they can't re-lay the ice?"

"If they could it would be some kind of speed record, I think. But that would depend on them having their ice master here. You know he was fired, right?"

"I heard."

"Isn't that risky?" I asked. "I mean, having all that knowledge in the head of just one guy? Don't you see that as a risk when you write a policy?"

"We don't insure the arena," said Parker. "We insure the team.

But in our risk assessment, the team certifies that these things are in place. That there are backups for such situations."

"Could that be reason to deny the claim? If they said someone else could do it but that wasn't true?"

"Maybe, but maybe not. Because the procedure is probably written down somewhere, it's enough to certify that the information is available. In practice there can be a fairly large gap between a manual and what actually happens."

I knew that for a fact. No one ever won a World Series by writing a book about baseball.

"The team here seems pretty capable, but I'm not sure how technical it all is," I said. "And even then, they're not going to be able to do anything without the CEO's okay, and he's writing the press release about the canceled games as we speak."

"There's an extra five grand in it if you can make that game happen."

I wanted to tell Parker that it wasn't about money. If I could do anything to fix it, I would, not just for him as my client but because it stuck in my craw that guys like Trainor got away with stuff like this. And he didn't even have to leave the island to do it. He could claim his hands were clean.

I told Parker I'd see what I could do, then I set off across the basketball court in the direction of the guy I had spoken to earlier.

I found him in the AC machine room. They had cleared out all the water. He was standing in the room watching another guy, who I didn't recognize, who was crouched down by the dehumidification unit.

Suddenly a burst of sparks came flying out past the guy on his haunches, and I realized he was welding the pipes.

I stood next to the arena guy and nodded. He gave me a sideward look suggesting he still wasn't convinced I wasn't a complete psycho, but he didn't run for the hills either.

"So, not an accident," I said, directing my chin toward the dehumidification unit.

"No," said the guy.

"Will it be fixed soon?"

"Maybe an hour."

"And you could start making ice again?"

The guy shrugged. "Not without Francisco."

"You guys don't know how to do it?"

"Sure we know. But it's not just science, it's an art. Just because I know how to kick a football, it doesn't make me Maradona."

I got what he was saying. Each team member knew how to play, but without the coach, the team couldn't function as a whole.

"So you can't just put down something temporary? Even if you had to pull it out again?"

The guy shrugged again. "The boss man don't want that. He says no ice until all the systems, including backups, are tested and working perfect. He says it's too expensive to remove the ice again. To me, it's more expensive to have no games."

"What would you need to get the ice ready for tomorrow night's game?"

"We'd need a miracle," he said. "And Francisco."

I left them to their work and made my way back out of the arena. I handed my unworn badge back to Devon and walked to my car.

After talking with Maggie, the beginnings of a plan started to formulate in my mind, but it all felt impossible without the one guy who knew how to build quality ice. And there seemed no way to get him back with the CEO watching from his lofty perch.

I got in my car and sat in the air-conditioning and thought about Gelphert. It made me wonder about this FPL guy, Otto Barassi. After punching the button on my steering wheel to make a call, Maggie Nettles's voice filled the inside of my car.

"Do you know the name Otto Barassi?"

"Oh yeah, I know Otto. He's a real peach."

"Tell me."

"He's with Florida Power & Light. One of those guys who never seems to have a job that you can quite pin down. He's the local union representative, but more than that, he's connected to all sorts of shady characters. He's been suspected of everything from racketeering to murder, but nothing has ever stuck. Even the union leadership doesn't trust him, but they can't get rid of him, because the rank-and-file members seem to love him."

"Or they're afraid of him."

"Right. How does he fit into all this?"

"According to the CEO, Otto's the arena contact should anything go wrong with the power."

"How convenient. It's more likely he's the reason that it went off, not the reason it came back on."

I nodded to myself and glanced across at the arena. It might have been the clouds overhead, but the building seemed to be losing some of its luster. Which led me to a completely unconnected thought. "Do you know anything about Senator Vargas's replacement?"

"In the legislature?" she said. "Yeah, he's the local state attorney for West Palm Beach."

"What are his chances?"

"From what I hear, pretty good. He's popular, and he has a good prosecutorial record. Plus, you know, he's photogenic. Why? Is he wrapped up in this?"

Half of me wished that he was, and the other half felt ashamed of that. "No, I was just wondering about Vargas and what comes next."

I hung up with Maggie, put the car in gear, and headed across the large empty lot. I tried to tell myself that I didn't know why Eric Edwards had suddenly floated into my mind, but the truth was I knew exactly why. But now that he was there, I suddenly saw a way Eric could serve the people of Palm Beach County before he even got into office.

CHAPTER TWENTY-SEVEN

I OFTEN HEARD PEOPLE AROUND TOWN COMPLAINING ABOUT HOW much they had to pay for a parking space. It seemed to be a perennial problem in big cities, like New York and Miami. I, on the other hand, was starting to question the value of paying for office space as I wandered from the parking lot where my car lived in the opposite direction of my office.

The Palm Beach County Courthouse was an edifice dedicated to the pursuit of justice, or the suppression of citizenry, depending on who you spoke to. An annex to the court also housed the office of the state attorney of Florida for the 15th Judicial Circuit. I found myself walking that way.

Eric Edwards sat on the corner of a desk, chatting to a young paralegal who seemed to be hanging on his every word. He smoothed down his tie as he spoke, his brilliant politician's smile turned up to about eight. The number dropped to a generous two when he saw me walk in.

"I'm very busy, Jones," he said, pushing his hips off the desk.

"It's important," I said.

"With you, it's always important."

"No, I mean, it's important to you. As in, your career might depend on it."

Eric was never really one to fall for my overly dramatic statements, but he turned and headed toward his office. "You've got five minutes."

He led me in then closed the door. Considering his position, the space was tight, packed full of leather-bound volumes of law books and Florida statutes. A pair of flags—US and Florida—hung from poles behind his desk. He swung around the desk like a reed on the breeze. He was marathon-runner thin, even after all these years, but I wasn't aware if he even owned a pair of jogging shoes.

"I really am busy, Jones. I've got a lot of cases to wrap up."

"Yeah, I heard you were running for the state Senate."

"Yes, I'm sure that will keep me very busy too."

"You haven't won the election yet."

"I wasn't talking about the legislature," said Eric. "I mean my move back into private practice."

"Private practice? I thought you were running for Senate?"

"I am."

"But you're saying you're moving to private practice? As a lawyer?"

"Yes, Jones. I'm not a carpenter."

"But how can you have a law practice and be a senator?"

If I didn't know better, I'd have said his expression was a look of disappointment. "You really pay no attention to the news, do you?"

"I get my box scores from the web."

"You are aware that in Florida we have a citizen legislature?"

"I surely have no idea what you're talking about, Eric."

"The legislature, Jones, in Tallahassee. It's part-time."

"Part-time? Seriously?"

"Yes. The legislature sits for sixty days each year. The rest of the time, elected officials return to their jobs. It's called a citizen legislature, whereby the members of the Senate and the house meet part-time and don't make their living as elected officials. They have other jobs. It's truly a government for the people, by the people."

I was reminded of Maggie Nettles suggesting the exact opposite. "It explains why it takes so long to get anything done in this state."

"You're very droll, Jones, but it is a system that's used in a similar way by many states. It ensures that all people not only have access to their elected officials but can also become one."

"You're saying if I were a street sweeper or a maid or a bartender, I could get elected to the Florida legislature?"

"Yes," said Eric. "That's the idea."

"And how many of our elected officials are maids or bartenders?"

"As far as I'm aware, currently none."

"And how many of them are lawyers?"

"During the last sitting session, I believe the number was twenty-seven percent."

"So not exactly a legislature for regular citizens then."

"Yes, I admit, there are structural impediments to some occupations enabling people to serve."

"You mean, some people have jobs where they can't just take off for two months of the year?" The idea of who *could* take off two months of the year sent me in a whole other direction. "So you're saying that people who run businesses get to vote on the legislation that affects those businesses."

"To some extent, yes. Obviously there are ethics rules to abide by. But in the end, wouldn't you want the representatives who intimately know an industry to be the ones making decisions about that industry?"

"And I'm sure those decisions never end up making them a ton of extra money."

Eric smoothed his tie aggressively. "What is it you want, Jones?"

So I told him. About the wheeling and dealing, about the bond issue—which, of course, he already knew—and about the funny business at the arena.

"It sounds like mismanagement," he said. "Not criminal activity."

"I want you to imagine something, if you will," I said. "Imagine a hypothetical guy. This guy happens to be running for a state Senate seat. Now imagine the county where this guy lives—and who he has worked for over the past decade—puts up several hundred million bucks on a bad deal that was sewn up by his predecessor in the Senate. Let's also imagine that the predecessor managed to get a very lucrative consulting gig for his wife from the company involved in this deal, all within your so-called ethics laws, of course. How do you think that would play in the media a few days out from an election?"

"I think it's you who lives in a fantasy world, Jones. The county isn't going to lose anything. I'd say from the outside looking in, it's a good thing for Palm Beach."

"Did you know that if the arena fails to meet certain KPIs, like canceling games, then the controlling interest of the arena switches from the county to the private management company owned by John Trainor and his investment group?"

"I did not know that."

"Furthermore, did you know that the management of this arena is also handled by a company owned by John Trainor?" I was starting to enjoy getting to talk like I was a character out of a John Grisham novel.

"He owns both the entity that manages the arena and the entity likely to benefit from the arena's mismanagement?"

"You got it. Word is, if they miss hosting a game, then Trainor could win big."

"Are they going to miss a game?"

"The next two. The CEO was writing the press release when I left. But the maintenance staff tell me they can be up and running in time to not miss anything."

"So why is the CEO saying otherwise?"

"Why indeed? He seems hell-bent on failure for someone who's charged with the arena's success. The facility manager has been sidelined, and he's the one with the expertise to get the ice in position fast. Of course, he's also the one the CEO is blaming for all the problems."

"Maybe he *is* to blame."

"I was there, Eric. Somebody cut the pipes on their dehumidification system. The ice was melting right before my eyes. If they didn't take it out, they couldn't lay the basketball court—they would've missed the basketball game last night, and Trainor would've already won. But getting the ice out quickly meant that the game went ahead. It bought them a couple extra days to sort things out, except they aren't trying to solve any problems. I'm telling you, the whole thing stinks."

"I still don't see a crime, Jones."

"That's because you're thinking like a state attorney, not a politician. And I'm not here to talk to the state attorney. I'm here to talk to the next Senate representative for Palm Beach County."

He stroked his tie again, and I saw the beginnings of a smile slide up the corners of his mouth. "Like you say, I'm not elected yet."

"No, but the county mayor is, and he'll listen to you. Because if Trainor gets control of the arena, he has the right to borrow against it to cover his other losses, and I have it on good authority that those losses are large and still mounting."

"You can prove this?"

"The clause to flip control is in the contract. I haven't seen it for myself, but my source is solid. I'm sure as a senator-elect you would be able to confirm exactly what it says."

"Don't get ahead of yourself, Jones."

"I'm not, Eric. But I'm telling you he's shifting deck chairs on the *Titanic*, and he's doing it right now. So if he leverages the arena and loses—and the numbers suggest he will—it's the county that will be out its three-hundred-million-dollar investment, and the mayor will be toast. Won't look too good for the local senator, either, whoever that might be."

He had stopped caressing his tie, and his hands were clasped together on his desk. "What are you suggesting?"

I proposed that Eric call Gelphert over to his office within the next hour. "An urgent meeting regarding some troubling malfeasance. I'll leave the legal babble to you. While Gelphert is off the property, the mayor makes a whistle-stop tour of the arena. He'll find the place more or less shut down. He'll ask for a reason and be given nothing in return, and he'll ask the guys who work there if they can get it up and running for the game tomorrow night, because he's got some important out-of-town guests he wants to impress with his brand-new, shiny arena. He'll ask if they can do that for him, and they'll tell him, yes, they can, and he'll tell them to get it done."

"And you're saying they can? Even without this facility manager?"

"I saw them remove an ice rink in an hour and replace it with a basketball court fit for the NBA within another two. But what I'm suggesting is, we get the facility manager back in. Just to make the ice. As it stands, he didn't really get due process anyway. He wasn't given a warning about his performance, and, as I said, much of the damage is from sabotage, not mismanagement. But there'll be time to sort that out later. If it turns out it was his fault, fine: fire the guy. But if it wasn't, not only does the county have a potential lawsuit on its hands, but you're gonna lose the mayor's new prize. Plus, I'm sure it can't hurt you, Eric, having the mayor owe you a favor?"

"That's not why we do these things, Jones."

The crazy thing was, I believed him. He really did buy all that mumbo jumbo about citizen legislatures and government for the people, by the people. He wasn't a complete fruitcake though; he knew there were problems with the system. There were always problems with the system. It didn't really matter what the system was. But some systems just stunk to high heaven from the get-go. Money and power and prestige would always curry favor, but as long as we the people had the power to apply pressure en masse in the voting booth, we could ensure that the checks and balances played their parts and together would keep our system on the rails. More or less anyway. This is Florida, after all.

Eric thought on it a moment. But he thought quickly. He was a litigator, used to thinking on his feet in a courtroom. He hit a button on his speakerphone and called the mayor and outlined the situation. The mayor said he had an opening in about an hour and could spare thirty minutes. He told the mayor that I would be there to meet him and show him around.

Then Eric called the arena and told Con Gelphert he heard some troubling rumors about insurance fraud and other malfeasance—I was impressed that he used the word that I had chosen, even though I wasn't a hundred percent sure it was the right one. Eric said they all needed to get their stories straight before the media got wind of it and told the CEO to get his carcass over to his office right away. I heard Gelphert say he was already out the door.

When he hung up, Eric looked at me. "You should be out the door too."

As I walked across the street toward the parking lot, I called Punk Rowlands. I told him there was a rumor going around the arena that the next two hockey games were going to be canceled. That he should call their VP of PR, Amanda Swaggert, and tell her he had to write a story about it but wanted to offer her the chance to give the arena's side of things. I suggested he meet her off-site and buy her a drink. I may have suggested that she was quite attractive.

"What's your angle?" asked Punk.

"I'll explain fully when I meet you at the game tomorrow night. Box tickets, all the beers and dogs you can eat, my treat."

"And who's gonna pay for this girl's drink?"

"Send me the bill."

CHAPTER TWENTY-EIGHT

I arrived at the arena before the mayor, but then I didn't have an entourage in tow. I found Devon at his post by the entrance. Clouds were drifting in, and while he hardly looked depressed, Devon's mood seemed as muted as the overcast sky.

"You need to get ready," I told him. "The mayor is on his way over."

"The mayor? Why?"

"An official visit. He wants to make sure everything's shipshape before he brings a party of dignitaries to the game tomorrow night."

"But the ice . . ."

"Where's Gelphert?"

"Um, he's not here."

"And Ms. Swaggert?"

"You just missed her. She said she had a meeting off-site."

I tried not to smile, but I was glad I had managed to get them both out of the building. It was always better to make your argument for something when the person arguing the opposite wasn't around.

"Should I call them?" asked Devon.

"No time. Just make sure you're ready to receive them."

The mayor of Palm Beach County isn't exactly the president of the United States, so he didn't travel with a police guard and a posse of fifteen vehicles. But he did have a big black Suburban, down from which climbed four people: the mayor, a driver, and two other aides of some variety. As they came up the steps toward Devon and me, one of the aides took the lead and moved out in front.

"You Jones?" he said.

"I am."

The guy shook my hand. "Arnie Parks, county administrator. Are you serious about this place being shut down?"

"Deadly serious. Let me show you."

Parks stood aside and introduced the mayor to me, and I introduced the mayor to Devon. I got the sense that both the mayor and Devon were a little perplexed by that—those in charge rarely get introduced to the doormen, and vice versa—but I figured Devon worked in Palm Beach and paid his taxes, so he was as much the mayor's employer as I was. Devon practically clicked his heels together and stood at attention.

As I directed the group into the arena, Devon whispered to me, "I'll take care of signing them in." I nodded and he left me with a wink.

I led the mayor and his people out into the stands and down onto the basketball floor. Only a few lights were on, but the floor still shone.

"Look at this floor, will you? It practically glows," he said, his face beaming like a teen with his first car.

Arnie Parks again asked where the problem was. I led everyone across the basketball court to the AC machine room.

The maintenance guy I had spoken to earlier was still there with the repairman, who was kneeling down, packing up his equipment at the dehumidification unit. I told the maintenance guy that I had the mayor of Palm Beach County with me, but he didn't appear to recognize anyone. That seemed fair enough—outside of hurricane season, the mayor didn't get a lot of TV time. I asked the guy to explain what happened to the AC system.

"They cut the pipes," he said.

"Who did?" asked the mayor.

The guy shrugged.

"We don't know yet," I said. "We're still investigating."

"But can you fix it?" asked Arnie Parks.

"It's fixed," the guy said, gesturing to the repairman, who didn't bother to look up. Perhaps he had bad hearing. Perhaps he didn't care for bureaucrats.

The mayor stepped forward and put his arm around the maintenance guy. I assumed it was a tactic he used to make his underlings think that he was one of them. The look on the guy's face suggested he was more concerned about the mayor making a pass at him.

"What's your name, friend?" asked the mayor.

"Javier," said the maintenance guy.

"Well, Javier, this facility that you're responsible for is important to our county, to the people of Palm Beach. And I have some very important guests coming from out of town tomorrow night to see the hockey game."

"No hockey game tomorrow," said Javier. "It's called off."

"Now, Javier, that's a problem. These are very important people. They could bring a lot of money into our county. You understand? Create a lot of jobs. But not if we don't have a game to see. If there is no game, these people will ask themselves whether they can trust us. Whether they want to do business with us. Maybe they will send those jobs to another town. You see what I'm saying?"

Javier frowned. I got the impression that he understood but that the weight of expectation was more than he could bear. "There is no ice."

"But can you make more ice? Can you do that for me, Javier?"

Javier shook his head. "Not me."

"Then who?"

"Pedro."

"And where is Pedro?"

"Cleaning the generator."

The mayor looked to me for guidance.

"The backup generator?" I asked Javier.

He gave me a definitive nod, and I told the mayor that this Pedro was on the other side of the arena.

The mayor dropped his arm from Javier's shoulder and shook his hand. "Thank you, Javier. You've been of great service to the people of Palm Beach County."

Javier looked relieved that the spotlight was being directed away from him.

I led the mayor and his posse back across the basketball court.

"Man, this thing really shines," said the mayor as we strode toward the machine room that held the backup generator.

As the five of us crammed inside with all the equipment and the three men already there, the machine room became tight quarters.

"We're looking for Pedro," I asked a tall guy with a thick black mustache.

"That's me."

"This is the mayor," I said, gesturing.

Pedro gave him a nod as if he didn't mind what the guy did for a living.

"The mayor has important dignitaries coming to the game tomorrow night."

"You haven't heard? The game's off."

"Because there's no ice," I said.

"That's right."

"Do you have everything back online to be able to make ice?"

"As soon as the AC system is working."

"We just came from there. It's up and running."

"Okay then, yeah, we can make ice."

I let the mayor step forward and give his spiel about important visitors and big business and creating jobs. I didn't get the impression that Pedro gave two coins either way.

"So I really need your help, Pedro," said the mayor. He hadn't gone for the big man hug this time, perhaps reading that his previous effort had made Javier uncomfortable, or perhaps it was because Pedro was a few inches taller than him and the whole thing would have looked weird.

"Mr. Mayor, we've been told not to put any ice down until all systems are go. I'm just doing my job."

"But didn't you just say that all systems are go?"

"Everything except the backup generator." Pedro nodded toward the large diesel tank. "We're still cleaning it out."

"But you don't need it to make the ice? It's just a backup?"

"Yeah, that's right."

"Then, Pedro, I need you to do me a favor. I need you to get this ice rink up and running. I need you to make sure this game goes ahead."

"But the boss said no."

"You mean Mr. Gelphert? He answers to me. You see what I'm saying? I will talk with Mr. Gelphert. What I need to know from you is, can you make me a new ice rink?"

"Yeah, we can make it."

"Then I need you to do it. I need you to get on that right now."

The mayor turned to the county administrator, and Arnie Parks handed him what looked like a business card. The mayor passed it on to Pedro. "If you have any problems, you call me. Okay? This is the number for my office. Let's get this done together."

Pedro didn't exactly jump at the mayor's call to arms, but he did nod, as if he was willing and prepared to do his job.

The mayor thanked him and directed his posse out of the machine room. I turned to follow, but Pedro grabbed my arm.

"Making new ice in less than two days is real tight," he said.

"But you can do it, right?"

"We need all our guys. The whole team. All the part-time guys too."

"Okay. The mayor's got you covered. Call them in."

"You don't get it. I don't call them in. I don't have their numbers. Francisco does."

"You want me to call Francisco? Get the numbers?"

"It would be better if Francisco was here. We can do it, but Francisco? He can talk to the ice. He knows how to make it sing, you know what I mean?"

"Can you get started on removing the court?"

"Right away."

"I'll talk to Francisco."

As I walked the mayor out, he asked me whether they could really do it. "We have a delegation of tourism operators from England here tomorrow. It would be great to bring them to the game. But I don't want to look stupid, you understand me?" The congenial tone he had given the workmen had turned serious.

"I understand you, sir. They can get this done if we can get the facility manager back in."

"Where the hell is he?"

"He was let go, by the CEO and one of your people at Palm Beach Events."

The mayor glanced at his county administrator. Parks shook his head. "Prior," was all he said.

"Isn't all this the fault of this facility guy?" asked the mayor.

"Like I told Eric, I don't think so. The pipes on that system were cut. That's not a maintenance issue. But even if it was, we just need this guy to make fresh ice. After that, you can run an investigation. Find out whether he really was negligent."

We stepped out past Devon, into the glow of the dull, humid day. The mayor stopped and turned to me.

"Do you think this facility guy was negligent?"

"From what I've seen? No. I think he's the hardest working person here."

The posse started down the steps toward the Suburban, and the mayor turned to follow them.

"Then get him back," he said. "And make this happen."

CHAPTER TWENTY-NINE

AFTER THE MAYOR LEFT, I STOOD ON THE CONCOURSE OUTSIDE THE arena and called Francisco Monaro.

"The mayor himself has ordered the facility to be opened," I said, trying to add some gravitas to the situation. "He has some dignitaries from England he's bringing to the game tomorrow night."

"What game?"

"The hockey game. He's personally requested that you come back, so call in your team and make your ice."

"It's not that easy to build a hockey rink," he said.

"That's why they need you."

"But I got fired, remember?"

"Listen, Francisco. If you get this done and the game can go on, the mayor will get to show off his brand-new arena to these people and he will owe you a favor. And trust me, being owed a favor by the mayor can be a very useful thing."

"So I get my job back?"

"You'll be making the best possible case for getting your job back permanently, and clearing your name."

"So you're saying I won't get paid?"

"You've got to look at the bigger picture here, Francisco."

"No, I don't. I've got work tomorrow on a construction site. I need to work. I need to earn money. My mortgage doesn't pay itself. My bills don't pay themselves."

"The mayor will make this right," I said.

"Did he tell you that? Or is he just using me because no one else can do this?"

"Okay, Francisco, let's put it this way. As of now, you work for me. My client is Stone Strong Insurance, and they need for this game to go ahead as much as the mayor. So if the mayor doesn't make it right, I will cover your salary, and it'll be my problem to recoup it from my client."

"Are you good for it?"

I rolled my eyes. I had to concede that the guy didn't really know me, so he didn't know whether he could trust me or not. But when you try to live your life being true to your word, the cynicism of those who've been burned can be tiresome.

"Okay. How about this? I will leave a down payment in cash in the control room. That should cover you for at least the next couple of days. Then you can show everybody whether you're worth keeping or not."

"You'll leave the money in the control room?"

"It'll be there, with your name on it, on two conditions: you need to call all your guys in right now, and you need to be here in the next fifteen minutes. We need to get this circus tent built."

"I'm on my way."

I killed the call and jogged down the steps to my car. I opened the rear hatch, leaned in, pulled away the felt-covered panel on the side wall of the cargo bay, and removed the first-aid kit tucked inside. I reached in farther, between the side wall and the exterior panel, and yanked out a small bag of wadded-up cash. I looked around the parking lot as if I were a drug mule.

But the cash was completely legitimate, just hidden because something lying in view in the cargo bay of a vehicle tended to get stolen. It was Lenny who had taught me the value of keeping cash at hand—he had kept his in a lockable gun compartment in the back tray of his pickup. He always said you could buy your way into almost anywhere if you could lay your hands on some cash, but the same could never be said of a credit card.

I took an envelope out of the bag and slipped some money inside. Lenny had always said keeping envelopes with your cash was a good idea, because you never knew when handing over a wad of cash might be frowned upon by authorities and bosses.

I dashed back up past Devon and down to the control room. The guy who seemed to be sitting in there twenty-four hours a day was there now, in the same seat, looking at the same laptop, whose screen appeared to be doing nothing at all.

I asked him if I could borrow a pen. Then I scribbled Francisco's name on the envelope and told him Monaro would be there in the next half hour. He offered a blank stare as if he hadn't realized that Francisco had ever left.

I strode back up to the public concourse and glanced in at the arena floor. The guys were already out there, pulling apart the floorboards and wheeling away the court-side seating.

Things were moving. But there was still one major issue outstanding. In theory we could get the ice in, make the game happen, and batten down the arena to prevent further attacks. But we couldn't batten down the entire county, which made me think of the sabotage that had occurred outside the arena. And who had done that, and whether they might do it again.

I jogged back to my car and drove to the other side of the tracks, where I found my spot and pulled over. Then I settled in to wait.

CHAPTER THIRTY

I PARKED ON THE SIDE OF THE ROAD ABOUT TWO BLOCKS FROM THE electrical substation where the sabotage had occurred. The facility I was watching—the FPL depot where the technicians left their service vehicles overnight—looked remarkably similar from the outside: cinderblock walls topped by razor wire, and another mesh gate. But that was where the similarities ended. This place was busy, and I saw no electrical equipment. I sat just down from the main gate and watched white truck after white truck coming in with single cabs and storage canopies built into the cargo beds.

I had been there about forty-five minutes when a truck drove by bearing the serial number I had retrieved from the gas station video. It slowed at the main gate and pulled into the large lot. I got out and jogged along the opposite side of the street to get a better view. There wasn't much in the way of hiding places, so I stood beside a queen palm that marked the entrance to a nondescript warehouse, and took out a small pair of binoculars.

I watched a guy get out of his truck—perhaps Asian, of average height and not flagpole-thin but not carrying much extra weight. Through the binoculars, I saw him go into a cinderblock building that I assumed was where they checked in and out of their shifts.

About five minutes later, he came back out, still wearing his uniform, and walked toward a sun-bleached Toyota Corolla.

I was back in my car when the Corolla came out of the depot and drove right past me. I did one of those moves you see in the movies all the time, where the PI does a not-so-subtle U-turn then follows their quarry as if no one noticed. It felt as obvious as hell, and I couldn't imagine the FPL guy hadn't seen me.

But he only drove a couple of blocks in the opposite direction of the substation before he pulled into the gravel lot of a bar. When he got out of his car he didn't look around as if he was being followed, and I started to wonder if the U-turn thing actually worked because drivers rarely bother to look in their rearview mirrors.

As he strolled into the bar, I pulled into the parking lot of a strip mall on the other side of the street. For a moment I tossed around whether I should just sit and wait, see where the guy went. But I wasn't learning anything more by staying outside, so I bit the bullet, crossed the street, and walked into the bar.

It was one of those workers' bars where you expect the jukebox to stop playing and every head to turn the moment you walk in. Except there was no jukebox, and no one appeared to pay me any attention.

I quickly surveyed the room for the guy. There were a couple of pool tables at the back, some tables and chairs scattered about, and a long bar that looked in dire need of a new coat of varnish. Everybody except the bartender seemed to be wearing a uniform of some description, most with a layer of dirt. Lots of Florida Power & Light logos, but those from other trades as well. They all seemed to be relaxed and in good spirits after finishing their day's work.

I saw the guy come out of the men's room, drying his hands. He headed for the bar, where there were two open seats. Rather than continue standing in the doorway waiting to be noticed, I headed in the same direction. We got to the bar one after the other, the guy first and then me, and we sat. He leaned his elbow on the back of his high-backed stool in such a way that he was half facing away from me, the way people at bars do when they don't know the person next to them.

The bartender nodded his head and said, "Hey, Neil," and slid the guy a bottle of Bud. Then he turned to me, and I pointed at the bottle.

After the bartender had passed me a beer, I glanced at Neil, who was watching a college football game on the muted screen behind the bar. I figured the one thing I didn't have on my side was time, so I put the chitchat in my back pocket and leaned toward him.

"Hey," I said.

Neil looked over and raised an eyebrow as if I were interrupting the game-winning play in the Super Bowl.

"So what happened at the substation?" I asked.

I sucked on my beer while I waited for him to answer, but all I got was a frown.

"Huh?"

"You know, the power to the arena. That fake burned-out circuit board. You didn't seriously think anyone was going to buy that, did you?"

"Who are you?"

"I'm the player to be named later. And you're Neil."

"Yeah, well, I don't know what you're talking about." He stuck his beer bottle into his mouth and tried to ignore me.

"Sure you do. You were at the substation the other morning when the power went out at the new arena. I've seen the video. I've seen the tampered circuit board. I watched you come in before the power went down and go out after. I'm not saying it was your fault, or at least your idea. I've got no doubt someone put you up to it. But you really need to come clean, because when the byproduct hits the fan, I don't think these guys are gonna stand up for you."

"You work for FPL?"

"No."

"But you have a circuit board from the substation?"

I didn't exactly have it in my possession, but I said, "Yeah."

"Well, that's stolen property, so you've committed a crime. Maybe *you* need to come clean."

Neil put his beer down and pulled a phone from the pocket of his shirt, then punched away at the screen the way people do, like they used to be part of the secretarial pool in a previous life.

"It's not stolen property," I said. "It's called evidence."

"Why don't you get lost?" he said, putting his phone down on the bar.

"You're missing the point here, Neil. I'm trying to help you. You think any of these guys are gonna visit you in the pen?"

He said nothing.

"Just tell me who's directing you. Who's telling you to do these things?"

Neil started peeling the label from his beer bottle, concentration etched across his face like he was performing surgery.

"Who is it? Is it Otto Barassi?"

I saw him flinch. His eyebrow went up again, before he returned his focus to his beer label. Then he stopped peeling and glanced my way. For a moment I thought he was going to open up, to tell me everything and blow the case wide open. But his gaze wasn't on my face. He was looking across my shoulder. Then, just as quickly, he turned his attention back to his beer bottle.

I felt a meaty paw on my shoulder and was suddenly yanked from my stool like a tarpon on a line. There were at least two of them, and although I only felt the one hand on my shoulder, the speed at which I was removed from my place at the bar and dragged across the room made it feel like I was being carried. I wasn't.

The second man—a big unit with a shaved head and a receding hairline—pushed the door open, and the other one, who had me by the scruff of the neck, launched me outside. I was about to stand and dust myself off and say it was all fine, whatever, I was leaving anyway, when I was picked up again and dragged around the side of the building.

Here, the first guy threw me against the cinderblock wall and gave me a second or two to consider my mortality. This guy looked like a carbon copy of the other one but slightly heavier, with maybe two days' worth of stubble on his head and a jagged scar on his left temple. I wasn't sure what it was about clean-shaven heads with these types of guys. It seemed like a uniform all its own. With a wicked snarl, he now looked at me like he was deciding where to hit me first.

He didn't ask me who I was, or what I wanted, or who sent me, or even my name, rank, and serial number. Instead he punched me in the face.

Hard.

My body fell back against the wall and my knees buckled some. There was no doubt my brain was bouncing around inside my head giving me some kind of concussion, and I wondered how boxers managed to stay upright for as long as they did.

Scar guy punched me again, a quick one-two-three in the gut, and I felt the sudden urge to vomit. I folded over. He seized the perfect opportunity for a feisty uppercut, which connected with the bottom of my chin and sent me back into the wall then onto my backside in the dirt.

After that, I just curled up into a tight ball, and the two took turns sticking their boots into me. I covered my head, but pretty much everything else was fair game. The kicks to the back stung the most, and I hoped like hell that my kidneys weren't gushing blood inside me.

It may have been thirty seconds or thirty days, but eventually they stopped and simply walked away, their message having been signed, sealed, and delivered in no uncertain terms.

CHAPTER THIRTY-ONE

I PROBABLY SHOULD HAVE GONE STRAIGHT TO THE HOSPITAL—I suspected Danielle was going to give me grief about it—but an urgent care waiting room was the last place I wanted to be. If I started coughing up blood, then I reserved the right to change my mind on that.

I set my sights on getting to the office instead. It took longer to get up, cross the parking lot and then the road, and ease myself into my car than it did to drive back to Banyan Street. I parked on the curb outside the bank branch that took up the ground floor of our building, then stumbled my way to the elevator. I got a few concerned looks from people on the sidewalk and those watching me through the window of the bank, but no one approached to see if I was okay.

I had read something about a scientific study that showed that groups of people were far less likely to offer assistance than a person on their own. Something about needing to conform to the tribe, or some such. I resolved to remember that if I ever really needed help, and if I ever saw someone else in need.

It didn't matter. I was in no position to help anyone, and I found the help I needed as soon as I opened the door to my office.

"Oh my Lord," said Lizzy, the closest she ever came to taking her Lord's name in vain. She practically vaulted over the desk and helped me into a chair in reception. "I'll call the paramedics."

"No, I'm okay."

"You're okay?" She got in tight to my face, as if she were inspecting my soul, or maybe just the whites of my eyes. "You must have a concussion if you think you're okay."

She turned toward my office and called for Ron. He appeared at the door, and his face dropped.

"What happened?" he asked. It was a fair question, and for a moment I considered the fact that Lizzy hadn't asked it—maybe she figured it was a question to be asked later.

She opened a metal case on the floor containing all manner of bandages and Band-Aids and ointments. It took me longer than necessary to realize she had procured a first-aid kit, but I had no idea from where.

She used a small towel to dab my face, and I was somewhat surprised to see the quantity of blood that came away on it. Once done, she touched up various parts of my head with antiseptic, then dressed my wounds.

"Take off your shirt," she said.

"Lizzy, I didn't think you cared," I said.

I didn't get the sharp rebuke that I expected. She and Ron simply pulled the shirt over the top of my head like I was a three-year-old boy, and I heard Ron gasp.

"Are you sure you shouldn't go to the hospital?" he asked.

I tried to inspect my wounds but given the fetal position I had assumed in the alley beside the bar, most of the damage was on the back side of my body.

"It's just a few bruises." Then I looked at Ron. "Isn't it?"

"It's more than a few," he said.

Lizzy had me take a series of deep breaths to see if it hurt. And it did, but not in a way that said major internal injuries. I allowed her to patch me up as best she could. Then I sat still for a long time in the reception area until I felt ready to move, thankful we didn't get many drop-in clients. My head was clearing, and I came to the conclusion that driving back to the office might not have been the smartest idea, for me and all the other drivers on the road.

Eventually I made my way into my office and lowered myself into the chair behind my desk. I didn't kick off my shoes or put my feet up on the desk. That felt like more activity than was warranted.

I wanted to understand how a bit of friendly sabotage could have taken such a dark turn for me. I used the speakerphone on my desk to call Sal, who had lived more lives than a cat and had more connections in dark corners of Florida than I could comprehend.

It took a number of rings for him to answer. I pictured Sally, in his little pawnshop on the wrong side of the turnpike on Okeechobee Boulevard, shuffling from one end of the counter to the other to answer the phone, cursing the entire way.

"Hey, Sal," I said. "It's me."

"You okay, kid?" he asked with a raspy voice, like his dry throat was about to hack a cough.

"I'm peachy."

"You don't sound so good. You been drinking?"

"Not nearly enough, Sal."

"What's on your mind?"

"Just wanted to throw a name at you, see what you knew."

"What's the name?"

"Otto Barassi."

There was silence down the line for a moment, and I figured Sal was entering his mind palace or whatever it was he did in order to rifle through the mental Rolodex he kept in his head. I presumed by the time I got to his age I'd be lucky to even remember what model of car I owned, let alone all the shady figures he seemed to be able to recall.

"Yeah, Barassi," he said. "He's old school. Union guy, in that Jimmy Hoffa kinda way. Only he's playing the part of the other guys, not Hoffa, if you understand my meaning. He's an old-fashioned racketeer, from back in the days when the unions had real power. Working guys like him loved to wield it in the face of all the white collars. You know, call snap walkouts and go-slows and all kinds of trouble, sometimes for better pay and conditions, and sometimes just because they could."

I heard Sal cough away from the phone—par for the course for him—then he continued.

"He's still connected, but these days the unions are trying to be more legit. So he's tolerated more than loved by union HQ. What's your involvement?"

"Not sure yet," I said. I closed my eyes for a second as a shudder of pain shot across my body like an electrical current.

"Well, whatever it is," said Sal, "be careful. Like I say, this guy's old school. He don't love publicity, and he knows how to shut things down in an old-fashioned way."

I considered how that might have been useful advice an hour or two earlier.

"Listen, Sal, I'm gonna be at the hockey game tomorrow night. You want to come?"

"You mean like ice?"

"Yes. At the new arena."

"I don't understand hockey in Florida," he said.

"It's the same as everywhere else, Sal."

"I can't follow the ball."

"They call it a puck."

"I can't follow that either. When I see it on TV, I'm not sure there's even a puck out there. It's just a bunch of guys skating around in circles."

"It's all the beer and hot dogs you can eat, Sal." This was always my checkmate move. Sal was a sucker for sports stadium hot dogs and beer in plastic cups. His preferred variety was minor-league ballparks. That was how we had met, years ago, when he came to St. Lucie to watch me pitch and sent me a note about something I was doing with my back during my windup.

"Aach, what else am I going to do?" he said.

"Good. I'll pick you up."

I ended the call and gingerly stood.

"Going somewhere?" asked Ron from my sofa. I had forgotten he was there.

"I need to go home."

"Where is that, exactly?"

It was good question, but despite his hospitality, I didn't mean his apartment. "Miami."

I took a step toward the door and was surprised at Ron's agility as he jumped up and blocked my exit.

"What are you doing?" I asked.

"You can't drive."

"I'll be okay," I said.

"MJ, it's not a polite inquiry. You can't drive, for your safety and that of everyone else, and I'm prepared to take you down to stop you."

"You're prepared to take me down?"

"I am."

I took a deep breath, in through my nose, out through my mouth, and it hurt like hell. Ron wasn't taking me down, and I wasn't going to give him cause to do so. But I didn't doubt he would try. Everyone should be so lucky to have a friend like that.

"I do need to get to Miami, Ron."

"I'll drive you."

"You're not driving me two hours just to turn around and drive back."

"You got a better idea?"

"I do," said Lizzy from behind Ron. We both looked at her. "Take the express bus."

"What express bus?" I asked. I wasn't, generally speaking, a bus kind of guy. I had done my fair share of sitting on buses during my baseball career. They don't call it the bus leagues for nothing.

"There's a new bus that runs from Palm Beach Gardens to Bayfront Park in Miami. Stops once in Fort Lauderdale."

So Ron drove me to Palm Beach Gardens. He didn't debate that

I needed to go, because he knew that it wasn't the *where* that I needed but the *who*.

We waited there in a parking lot of one of the large malls with an eclectic mix of folks. There were people who were clearly done with a day of shopping, as if Palm Beach had some tax-free status that didn't exist in Miami, and others who looked like office workers. I wondered why they traveled all the way from Miami. There were office jobs down there, I was sure of that. But then, there was plenty of investigative work in Miami, too, and here I was, spending my working days seventy miles from the apartment I called home.

As the coach pulled into the lot, Ron said, "Text me when you get home."

I embarked and found a seat by the window a couple rows back. Having come down off my adrenaline high, I fell asleep before the bus even left the parking lot.

CHAPTER THIRTY-TWO

I woke up just outside of Lauderdale with a pounding headache. Fortunately Lizzy had sent me on my way with a baggie of ibuprofen and a bottle of water. I took a handful of tablets, washed them down, then promptly fell asleep again until the bus driver roused me at Bayfront Park.

The city was dark by the time I disembarked the bus, so I stood on the sidewalk and sent Danielle a text message. Seconds later she replied: *Monty's? Remember?*

I forgot we had arranged to meet Lucas for a drink near the marina, so I flagged a cab. As we headed for the causeway, I returned Danielle's message, saying I'd be there in ten.

Monty's was a tourist favorite situated on the intracoastal side of South Beach, not far from the marina that Lucas managed. It was doing a roaring trade by the time I arrived, holidaymakers and snowbirds and locals intermingling with a buzz that set me on edge. My headache had gone, but a couple hours on the bus had stiffened every muscle in my body, so I was walking like a ninety-year-old man. From the glances people gave me, I may have looked like one.

I found Danielle and Lucas sitting at one of the tall tables overlooking the pool. It might have been heading into winter, but there were always visitors from Ohio or Indiana who thought it was still swimming weather.

I sidled up to the table and tried my best nonchalant face. Danielle wasn't buying it.

"What on earth happened to you?" She slipped from her chair and placed her hands on my cheeks.

"You should see the other guy," I said.

"Were you in a car accident?"

"Not so much."

When she moved a hand up the side of my head, I remembered the bandages. Danielle made me sit down, and she asked if a paramedic had applied the bandage.

"Lizzy," I said.

Danielle unwrapped it a little to take a look at the damage. I got the impression that the bandage had done its job and stemmed any blood flow, because she left it on the table. She told me to stay put and walked away.

"That's no car accident," said Lucas.

I shook my head very gently.

"How many were there?" he asked.

"Two. Big guys."

"When you get beaten, they're always big guys. You lay a hand on 'em?"

"Not a glove."

"I hate the sucker punches," he said. I knew he had some experience in this area even if I didn't understand the nature of it. He and Lenny had met during their military service—Lenny for the United States Marines and any number of three-letter-acronym organizations, and Lucas for the Australian SAS and whatever their sneaky, troublemaking organizations were called.

Danielle returned with a wet cloth and some more antiseptic and Band-Aids. She did a second patch-up job then checked over her handiwork before getting back in her chair. She was giving me that look that said there was going to be trouble if I didn't fess up soon.

"It's the case I'm working," I said. "The arena thing. I was following a suspect. I went into a bar that maybe I should have stayed out of."

"You need to call West Palm police," she said.

"I think technically it was Mangonia Park. But it doesn't really matter. There were two of them and one of me, and no proof."

"You said it was a bar? Was it empty?"

"No. It was full of workers who will back up the other guys' story. Just let it go. I'm chalking this one up to experience."

"I'm getting another round," said Lucas. He disappeared and Danielle resumed the frown. She was a law enforcement officer, and as such, she hated the idea that someone could get beat up and the perpetrators could get away with it—and she saw that happen all the time.

When Lucas returned, he passed a beer to Danielle, put another in front of his own chair, and handed me a glass of clear liquid.

"What's this?" I asked.

"H2O on the rocks," he said, slipping back into his chair. "I know a drink feels like a really solid idea right now, but trust me, it's not." He took a swig of beer.

"Are you sure?"

"He's sure," said Danielle. "Thank you, Lucas."

"Ma'am," he said with a nod.

We drank and chatted for a little while then ordered some appetizers to share. Fried calamari, and fish dip with crackers and chopped-up tomato and jalapeno. I could hear a low-level buzz in my ears, unsure if it was me or the ambience of the bar. It was a nice enough place, and people generally came to Monty's for a good time, not to cry in their pretzels. But it had a feeling of nothingness to it, as if good times were an illusion, the sort of thing you had on vacation, not in your day-to-day. It wasn't the kind of place I could relax and chat quietly with the bartender. That was to say, it wasn't Longboard Kelly's.

After another round, Danielle excused herself to the ladies' room.

When she was gone, I said to Lucas, "Do you come to this bar often?"

"Nah."

"It's pretty close to the marina."

"Yeah, it is."

"But it's not your local?"

"Depends what you mean by local."

"You know, the kind of place where everybody knows your name."

"*Cheers*, you mean."

"I guess."

"How many bars between your office and Longboard Kelly's?" he asked.

"I don't know, could be ten, could be fifty. Plenty, I guess."

"Right. So your local isn't just about distance."

"You have a local?"

"Sure."

"Why didn't we meet there?"

"Couple of reasons. One, they don't really like ladies in the front bar there, and two, it's in Brisbane."

"Back in Australia?"

"Yep."

"When was the last time you were there?"

"Decades."

"It might not even be there anymore."

"It'll always be there. In here." He pointed at his head.

"You don't miss having somewhere like that? Somewhere you know everyone and they know you?"

"Yeah, I do. But I came to grips with it a long time ago, that some people have roots that are shallow and some have roots that are deep, and mine were the former. I never really quite fit anywhere, not perfectly. Besides, there are good folks to drink with all over the world, and all it takes is one interesting mind to make a place worth your time."

I wasn't sure how much of what he was saying was about him

and how much was about me. Or maybe it was both, or neither. I wasn't in the greatest place to be thinking anything.

Danielle came back with two more beers and another ice water, and I told Lucas a little more about the funny business at the arena.

"Ice hockey, you say?"

"They just call it hockey," I said.

"Just hockey is played on AstroTurf, mate."

"Not in Canada."

"But hockey in South Florida? It's like cricket in Siberia."

"They have a team down here in Miami, too, you know."

Lucas chugged his beer then pointed it at me. "Yeah, you're right. Now that you mention it. One of the guys who has a vessel at the marina is involved in that caper."

"What's his name?" I asked.

"Lex."

"Lex Javits?"

"That's him. Nice fella."

"How well do you know him?"

"I'm not godfather to any of his kids, but we've shared a beer out on the docks once or twice. Why?"

"Do you think you could make an introduction?"

CHAPTER THIRTY-THREE

When I woke up the following morning, my mind was clearer than I expected, but my body was suggesting I stay in bed for a month or two. I stood under a hot shower until things loosened up enough to walk without grunting after each step. I could see the concern in Danielle's face, but she made no attempt to dissuade me from going out. Perhaps she felt consoled by the fact that where I planned to go, Lucas would be around if needed.

Lucas had called Lex Javits from Monty's the previous evening, and Javits had agreed to meet with me in the morning on his boat at South Beach Marina.

I took a cab from our apartment on Grove Isle, cutting across the causeway, and got out near the marina office. The parking lot was nearly full despite the early hour. Lots of deep-sea fishing charters ran out of the marina for the snowbirds who didn't own their own boats, and for reasons that I've never completely understood, fishermen always liked to get a super-early start to the day.

I stopped in at the office and found Lucas. He walked me out to the dock where Javits's boat was tied up.

The boat—more a fishing vessel than a yacht—wasn't quite as big as some, with a spotting tower high above and lots of brackets and braces to hold large fishing rods and various other pieces of equipment. The back deck was spacious: clearly Javits had not made plans to go fishing that morning. A table for six sat on the aft deck, where a game-fishing chair might normally have resided. Perhaps he had one that could be taken in and out, adding more functionality to the boat.

Lucas called out, then stepped aboard, and as I followed, I noticed the name of the boat on the transom.

Ice Queen.

The sliding door into the main cabin opened, and Lex Javits walked out. Lucas and Javits shook hands like old friends rather than client and marina manager. That didn't surprise me. Lucas had an easy way about him, the kind of personality that made you feel like you'd known him for decades after spending five minutes together.

Lucas introduced me, and I shook Javits's hand. He wasn't any taller than I was, but his fingers were a good inch longer than mine. It made me wonder whether those massive gloves hockey players wore were more about fit than extra padding. Despite not playing professional hockey in fifteen years, he hadn't gone to seed. He had thinning sandy hair that was graying at the sides, but otherwise I might have pegged him for a decade younger than I knew him to be.

"You look like you've just played a game of hockey," Javits said to me with an easy smile.

Lucas said he'd leave us to it and told me to drop in before I left.

Javits offered me a seat at the table and asked if I'd like some breakfast. The boat looked big enough to have a crew, maybe even a chef—there were lots of boats like that moored at South Beach marina. But when I said *sure,* Javits himself strode back inside and came out holding a tray with two mugs and a large carafe of coffee, no cream or sugar.

"You do the honors," he said.

He went back in, and I poured two mugs. The smell of the

coffee intermingled with the briny air in a way that suddenly made me hungry.

Javits returned and closed the sliding door with his foot, then carried another tray to the table. This one held a container of granola and a large bowl of yogurt, as well as a pitcher of orange juice with glasses and bowls and utensils. It wasn't the kind of breakfast I imagined a former hard-case hockey enforcer eating, but then it did feel very South Florida. It also told me a thing or two about Javits.

He had money, but clearly that money hadn't turned him into a snob. Plus it explained, in part anyway, how the guy stayed in such good shape. As with everything in life, he worked at it.

Javits sat and served up granola and yogurt, and I passed him a coffee.

"So, you live in Miami now?" I asked.

"Yes, part of the year. We winter in Miami but spend the summers in Detroit, Michigan." He shrugged his broad shoulders. "At least, that's how we've done it for the last decade or so."

I sipped my coffee. It wasn't Cuban, but it was extremely good. Not bitter, like I generally find black coffee to be.

"You played for the Red Wings, right?"

"Correct," he said, eating his granola. "Spent most of my career in Detroit. Then the last couple years here in Florida, with the Panthers."

"Did you enjoy it?"

"You play any sports?" he asked. "Even at college or high school?"

"Yes, college and minor-league baseball."

"And you're asking if I enjoyed it?"

"Detroit, I mean."

"I loved hockey, still do. And Detroit's a hockey town. I mean, they've got most every sport you could want, but folks there sure love their hockey. And I guess I fell in love with the town. And the people. People who live through that kind of weather, there's something real about them. You ever lived in a place like that?"

"I grew up in New England."

Javits nodded.

"So what brought you to Miami?" I asked.

"Honestly? Money." He took a sip of his coffee and looked at me. "By the time I came down here, I knew my best was behind me. But the Panthers were an expansion team, and they needed a few old-timers, some well-known faces, to try and get the snowbirds to come along to the games. But in the end, I fell in love with Miami. Or more specifically, I fell out of love with winter. More than a decade of crunching guys up against the boards makes it hard to get up in the morning."

This day of all days I knew exactly what he meant.

"Especially when it's below zero outside," he said. "I just found it easier to get going when the sun was out and there was no snow to shovel."

"Same reason a lot of folks come here, I guess."

"Still love Motor City though. That's where I raised my family, where my business is based—was based."

"Was?"

"Yeah, we just inked the deal to sell it."

"You were into coffee, is that right?"

"Correct. You ever heard of Tim Hortons?"

"Yeah, I've heard of it."

"It was started by a hockey guy, in Ontario in the sixties. These days, it's more Canadian than maple syrup. Did you know that eighty percent of all Canadians go for coffee or a donut at a Tim's at least once a week? That's some serious brand loyalty. They've tried to replicate the business in the US, but it never stuck. So when I was still in the league, an old college buddy of mine approached me with a plan to create a US version of Tim Hortons. He wanted me as the front man. About that time I was trying to figure out what life would look like after hockey, so I put in a bunch of the initial capital for the first restaurant—we started in Detroit—and then as we expanded, we got some private investment."

"So why did yours work when theirs didn't? Seems like there's so much competition in that space."

"There is. By the nineties, Tim Hortons had been sold off to a fast-food holding company, and they tried the whole Starbucks model—massive expansion. They thought Americans would love the brand simply because Canadians did. In the beginning, they focused on the border states, keeping close to home, so to speak. But they missed the mark. They discounted the part about Tim Hortons actually being Canadian. The brand might be in the DNA north of the border, but it's not here.

"So my feeling was, they got a little confused with their strategy. It didn't work anymore to pitch it as being purely Canadian when we're trying to attract an American consumer. And once you pitch it as being American, what makes you different from every other coffee and donut shop? They never answered that question, so a lot of those stores failed."

"But you answered the question," I said.

"I think we did. We focused on hockey regions first, but rather than it being another Tim's, we focused on what we had and they didn't, what all the other brands—Starbucks, McDonald's—didn't have either, as international chains. One, we were American and proud, and two, we were hockey and proud. We built from the local areas up, not corporate down. And yeah, it worked, to an extent. We had over fifteen hundred locations in eleven states when we sold."

"Why sell?"

"Somebody made me an offer I couldn't refuse." He put his coffee down and ate some granola, so I did likewise. I got the feeling it was homemade, that Javits may have made it himself.

"But you're not here to learn about coffee and donuts," he said.

"No, I was wondering about your interest in the new hockey league, and your position as a team owner. How did you get involved in that?"

"I get asked to be involved in a lot of things. I've learned it comes with the territory being a somewhat famous face. And honestly, most of these things just don't pass muster."

"But this one did?"

Javits leaned back in his seat. "Yes and no. Not as a business, not strictly speaking. If you're looking for a decent ROI, you'd probably do better in the stock market."

"But there were other factors," I said.

"Yes. It was hockey, and the idea of being involved with the game was attractive."

"You never thought about the NHL?"

"That's a billionaire's game now—I've done quite nicely, but not that nicely. Still, the idea that I might be able to give something back to the game that gave me so much? It had its appeal."

"I'm sure," I said. "But how much of a reason was John Trainor?"

Javits lifted his coffee mug and peered at me over the top of it. "You know John?"

"We are acquainted."

Javits nodded. "Yeah, John was part of it too. He was pretty convincing."

"I heard you two went to college together."

"He was my freshman-year roommate. You went to college, you know what that's like."

"Like a brother?"

"More like an invisible umbilical cord."

"You didn't room with a teammate?"

"No, not that first year. Initially I wasn't going to go to college. I was hoping to get picked up in the NHL, but all the teams that saw me in high school passed."

"I bet they regretted that when you made the Hall of Fame."

"I doubt they even remembered. Besides, you can't live like that. You gotta make your calls based on all available intelligence, and once you make them, you gotta own them. You win some, you lose some, and if you're smart and work hard, you'll win more than you lose. But you still won't win them all."

I agreed. "So you didn't get picked up?"

"No, but I got a scholarship to Clarkson, and I figured at least I'd be playing, so, yeah, I went kinda late and got paired with a nonathlete. But it was okay. He was a good guy, pretty popular, and always had enough cash and connections to get a few beers for the hockey team. And since most of us hockey players were pretty poor, a guy like John was always welcomed."

"And you kept in touch over the years?"

"In the way that you do, not often but always. Sophomore year I moved into a hall that housed most of our team, but John still hung out with us. And then before junior year, that's when I got picked up by Detroit. They sent me to a development league in Ontario for a year, and then it was Detroit for the next decade. But John and I stayed in touch. He went on to grad school and then Wall Street, I guess."

"And then he approached you about the league?"

"Yeah. He had a good pitch. And he was pretty focused on it. He had all kinds of people on board—or at least half on board—and he wanted a hockey name to front the whole thing. I'd used the same kind of tactic with the restaurants, and I was already spending half my year down here, so I figured, why not?" Javits put his coffee mug down and leaned on the table toward me. "Look, you know John, right?"

"Sure."

"So you know he's a solid guy, and he talks a good game. And he's got a great work ethic. You can't fault him about that. But . . ."

"But he's not quite top shelf?" I said, recalling the phrase I'd heard to describe Trainor more than once.

"Right, you know. You look at his record, it's good, but not great. And for a Palm Beach guy with his connections? You'd think he'd be right up there. But he's not. I mean, it's a rich man's problem he's got: he's worth millions but not tens of millions or hundreds or even billions, and that drives him, you know? He's annoyed by it. I think this league was his way of sticking it to the man. But the thing John doesn't realize is that to ninety-nine percent of people, *he* is the man. He's had all the advantages. Now I'm not saying he's not capable, and I'm certainly not saying he hasn't worked hard."

He poured some orange juice and handed me a glass.

"I've spent my working life since hockey in the business of coffee and donuts, and I took a trick that I heard they did at McDonald's HQ: I spent one day a week in one of our restaurants. Not just to see how things were running or spy on our employees. It was to meet the customers. Because I knew, at that point, that I really wasn't one of them anymore. I received a great gift—a career in the NHL—and that set me up in a way that would never have happened otherwise. If not for that, I'd still be a guy in the Twin Cities, maybe working in construction or something. And you might not believe this, but I think I would've been just as happy doing that."

He looked around at the other yachts in the marina.

"Well, almost as happy. My point is, but for that one stroke of luck, of being born with this body that could take so much punishment and dish out even more, *I'd* be the guy stopping in for a coffee and a donut on my way to work. But I didn't kid myself that I still remembered exactly what made them tick. Why they loved this game and why they even loved these dark, cold towns, the leafless trees, and the black snow by the side of the road. It's too easy to forget to look back down when you're busy climbing the ladder. But turning around and helping the next person up is exactly what we should do."

I watched Javits sip a little juice, and for a moment I said nothing in reply.

"So you got involved to help John up the ladder?"

"No, you're not getting it. I thought he was doing it to help others. You know, give these hockey players a second chance, or even a first chance. An opportunity to get seen by someone and maybe take the next step. But also to bring this game that I love back to the community. The NHL is such big business now. Sometimes it feels like it's left its roots behind. You must know what I mean. You said you played minor-league ball."

I nodded.

"That's what I'm talking about," he said. "Bringing it back down to the community. Don't get me wrong, I love my Red Wings, but there's something about local hockey, you know? The NHL is all glitz and glamour; it even smells different. Local hockey has a scent to it. The dry air and the ice and the sweat, and the, I don't know . . ."

"Rubber," I said.

"Yeah, there's that."

"So you got into the league to bring hockey back to the community."

"It wasn't all that, but that was part of it. All I'm saying is, it was never a blue-chip investment."

"What kind of an investment was it?"

"Not the monetary kind. Look, I've always run my business by the numbers. We didn't open ten thousand outlets because the numbers and our instincts told us it was a bad idea. But this, this is hockey. It's more about giving back. Sure, I'd like to make a return on it, but it was never the reason. Not then and not now. I just don't want to incur a loss."

"So are you incurring a loss?"

"I didn't say that. I'm just saying, if you're looking to make bank, minor sports leagues are probably not the way to go. But they can be profitable. The key is getting folks in the door. If you have an audience, you can find a way to make it pay."

He pushed his empty granola bowl to the side and took a long drink of coffee. "Like I said, the model is minor-league baseball. You keep the tickets and concession prices low so folks can afford to come and enjoy the game. That's not where you go looking for profit. If you're gonna make any, it's in sponsorships, TV rights, internet. Those are the places to look."

I recalled the minor-league teams that I had played for and against. Back around the turn of the century, teams flush with dot-com money were cleaning up their stadia to attract families. Most of the dot-com companies went bust, and the stadium names changed, but the product was a good one, and the people running everything seemed to understand it the way Javits did. At least that was the case in places like San Jose and Port St. Lucie.

"So do you have the audience?" I asked.

"Not yet. Not enough, anyway. It's the Tim Hortons dilemma. When they first launched restaurants down here in Florida, they were banking on the Canadians who already loved the brand to bring in the business then bring the locals with them. But the brand didn't have any kind of penetration, and often the Canadians didn't even know there was a Tim Hortons here, or if they did, it was too far away—for a coffee and a donut you're not driving across town, no matter how much you love a brand. Obviously people will travel a bit for a decent hockey game, but we have to reach them, show them the value, how good a product it is. And you gotta reach the moms. Sports isn't about shirtless men with team letters painted on their chests anymore. You've got to include the moms and kids. Our research shows fifty-five percent of new market business is women and families. But reaching those people costs money, and that's the rub. It costs to get them in the door, but if they don't know we exist, they won't come."

"And once they come," I said, "you gotta make sure they have a good time."

"Exactly. Moms are already a little skittish about hockey, you know, the contact and so on."

"So on? You mean the fighting?"

"Yeah, right. It's not like the old days. The old-timers loved a good punch-up, but not the moms. Now we need comfortable seating and decent food and entertainment during the breaks. We need to put on a good wholesome show."

"And it can't help with the Palm Beach arena having so many problems."

"What problems?"

"You haven't heard? That's why I'm involved. I've been

engaged by the insurer for the Palm Beach Chill. The new arena's been dealing with issues that extend well beyond the problems of a new facility."

"I don't know anything about that."

"So you don't know why someone might want to sabotage the arena? Hurt the team? Maybe hurt the league?"

"That makes no sense. You're nothing without the arena. As I said, you gotta have a good, reliable venue to attract the audience you want."

"You have such a place?"

"We do."

"You built an arena?"

"No. We already had one. The economics of building a new one didn't make sense. It's much easier to use what's there and put a fraction of the cash into refurbishment."

"But Trainor didn't do that."

"He didn't have an arena, so he had to do it differently. The way I understand it, he got a golden deal with the county. But still, there's gotta be a lot of financial juggling to make that work."

"Could part of the juggling involve getting financing on the back of the arena?"

"Nah, I don't think so. The county controls the place, as far as I know."

I finished my coffee and waited for him to say more, but he didn't.

"Did John Trainor come to you and the other owners for additional capital recently?" I asked.

"I'm not sure I can get into that with you. That's more proprietary information."

I took that as a yes. "Did you know that if the arena doesn't perform, if they have to cancel games because of these problems, control gets transferred to Trainor's management company?"

The look on Javits's face told me all I needed to know. "Is that right?"

"Yes. So let me ask you something. What's your downside if this thing doesn't work out?"

"Like I said, I didn't go into this as a blue-chip investment, so I didn't get in too deep. And I know most of the other owners can shift their positions to minimize their risk."

"Perhaps not everyone is quite in that position."

Javits frowned and it aged him. "Perhaps."

"You wanted to do this to give something back to the game of hockey," I said.

"Yes. What's your point?"

"You said you thought that's why John Trainor came up with the whole idea."

"I did."

"But he didn't play hockey. He didn't even grow up in a hockey town. So why would he be giving something back to a game that never gave him anything?"

"I hoped it was his connection to Clarkson, to us."

We sat on the back deck of Javits's boat listening to the gulls calling and the *tinking* of rigging on masts. I had no idea what Javits was thinking about, but I suspected it was in the same ballpark as me. If John Trainor wasn't creating the league to give something back, like Javits was, then his motivations were likely more self-serving. I wondered what that might mean if, in a financial sense, push came to shove.

I thanked Lex Javits for breakfast and told him that it was a pleasure to have spent time with him. It was. He seemed like a genuine guy, someone who realized just how lucky he had it and what the limits were when relying on nothing but hard work. Sometimes a person needed a break, a leg up, a helping hand. It made me think of Keisha, who had never gotten a break in her life, until I got the opportunity to look back down the ladder and offer her one. Now I had free haircuts for life, or at least until her debt was paid. But now she had an opportunity to be something. Not something newsworthy or extraordinary. But something better, something that might fulfill her potential.

Javits mentioned he had a meeting downtown so headed back together toward the office. As I walked I wondered if someone ever offered a helping hand to John Trainor, or whether his life of privilege had led everyone to assume that success was all but guaranteed. I'd seen guys playing Class-A baseball about to quit because they couldn't make rent, only to see it get covered by a local shopkeeper from whatever little Podunk town they were playing in, and that could be all the difference between a major-league career and oblivion. But I realized it went the other way too. Sometimes when you have all the opportunities in the world, you fail to grasp the value of them, and perhaps a quiet whisper in your ear, or even a life lesson or two, might be the thing that helps you realize that with great power comes great responsibility.

That line made me think of my client Peter Parker, the whole reason I was here. I needed to see him.

We stopped in on Lucas, and I said goodbye. Then I walked out onto the path overlooking the marina and shook hands with Javits.

"I hope it works out," I said.

"Do you think it will?"

"I'm no businessman. But I wouldn't want to be in it too deep."

Javits nodded. "There'll always be hockey. Even in South Florida. I'll make sure of that."

I left him standing by the water and returned to the office to find a taxi. I needed to get back to West Palm, for all sorts of reasons that were only now becoming clear to me.

CHAPTER THIRTY-FOUR

By the time the bus got back to Palm Beach Gardens it was nearly lunchtime, and I suddenly had a hankering for coffee and a donut. I got a ride-share downtown and jumped in my car without heading up to the office. Navigating like one of those cross-Atlantic birds that instinctively knows where it's going, I pulled into a small drive-through coffee hut, a little mom-and-pop place that looked like it had been there since the fifties. The coffee was bitter and unsatisfying, but the donut was fresh and delicious. I wasn't sure what message to take from that, but I found myself again heeding the earth's magnetism: I pulled off the freeway and cut down Australian Avenue to drop by the arena.

Devon, the ever-present security guard, gave me a nod as I came up the steps.

"What on earth happened to you?" he asked.

"Hubris," I said.

Devon frowned. "Mr. Gelphert is not happy with you."

"Mr. Gelphert can bite me."

"He doesn't want you on the premises," he said as I bent down to fill out the entry register. "It might be better if you don't sign in."

I was always in favor of any plan that involved less paperwork. "I don't want to get you in any kind of trouble."

"I suggest you stick to the lower levels, and keep your head down."

"I will. I appreciate it."

I headed straight for the maintenance level below the main concourse. I walked to the cutout that led to the playing surface, but stayed in the shadows. I could see that a layer of ice had already been laid overnight, and a team was out on the surface painting logos and putting down lines. I heard the soft electric whine of a golf cart behind me, but I didn't bother turning around.

Francisco Monaro got out and stood by me.

"Looks like you're getting this done," I said.

"It will be close," said Monaro. "And the ice might be a bit softer than the players would like, but it'll be good enough for one game. Our Zamboni driver will have his work cut out for him though."

I waited for him to thank me for leaving the cash for him, but he didn't.

"How's your CEO?" I asked.

"He is not happy. He doesn't seem very interested in keeping me here. But the mayor called and told him he's going to be at the game tonight, and from this point on, the boss's future is tied to mine. We both need to make sure this game goes ahead. He said we're all a team, and if one of us wins, we all win. But if one of us loses, we all lose."

I nodded. That was usually how teams work.

"I just hope something doesn't go wrong," said Monaro.

I looked at him sideways. "You're not going to mention that curse."

"No," he said. "You're right. A curse didn't cut the pipes on the dehumidification system."

"So what is it you're worried about?"

"I just hope the power doesn't go out again," he said.

"I doubt that lightning will strike in the same place."

I saw in Monaro's expression that he didn't share my optimism. It made me wonder if they could pull that trick again. A power outage from the substation would be pretty close to a fatal blow if it happened during the game. It felt like an unlikely play, but as I stood there watching the men work on the ice, I realized if anything funny was going to happen, Trainor would want to secure a decent alibi. And there's no better alibi than being seen by thousands of people at a game. Which made me recall that I was yet to secure entry for the game myself.

I quietly left the arena and drove back to the lot beside my building. Once again I didn't go up to my office. It was becoming a thing.

I walked down to Rosemary Square and dropped in on Stone Strong Insurance. I waited in the reception area for about ten minutes then joined Parker in his office.

"What on *earth* happened to you?" he asked with a little less concern in his voice than Devon.

"Disagreement with an ostrich."

"Pardon?" he said, confused.

"Looks like the game will go ahead," I said.

Parker pulled himself together. "That's good news."

"It's become an event to see and be seen at, if you know what I mean."

"A successful game is good for the team, so that is music to my ears. Thank you for all you've done. Feel free to send over your invoice."

"I'm not sure we're done," I said.

"But everything's fixed, isn't it? You said the game was going ahead."

"They've managed to re-lay the ice, or at least they will have before game time. But I've got to be honest, Mr. Parker, it feels like a temporary stop. Like a makeshift dam. I can't help but feel there's some kind of a tsunami out there we haven't spotted yet that just might break the dam apart."

"I don't like that word."

"Which word?"

"Tsunami. That's not a word we care to use in the insurance business."

"Understood. But let me ask you, do you guys have a presence at the arena?"

"What do you mean, a presence?"

"Like a corporate suite."

"We do."

"Are you planning on being at the game?"

"I wasn't. I'm not much of a hockey fan. But if the mayor is going to be there, perhaps I'll attend."

"If it's all the same to you, I'd like to have some eyes around the place tonight. Just in case. Is there any chance you can get me some tickets?"

Parker's regularly stern face grew even more serious. "Of course. I'll have some passes couriered to your office this afternoon."

CHAPTER THIRTY-FIVE

I walked back to my office, and although I didn't have the verve to take the stairs, as was my habit, I did feel slightly better. I got into the office and went through the expected interrogation with Lizzy and Ron. Yes, I was fine. No, I didn't have a headache or any pain, nothing beyond regular, old-fashioned bruising. When they were satisfied I was not at death's door, they let me take a seat behind my desk.

Ron sat on the sofa and threw me a bottle of water. I resolved that maybe we needed to get some kind of water-filtration system instead of powering through all the plastic. The label on my bottle said it was made from plants, so I could rest easy, but I further resolved to get Lizzy to look into that somewhat dubious claim.

I sipped my water as I told Ron about my meeting with Lex Javits. I mused aloud on my suspicion that something might happen tonight.

"It feels wrong," said Ron.

"How so?"

"This one feels like the battle you have to lose in order to win the war. Now that there's so much attention on it with the mayor being there, you can be sure all kinds of other hangers-on will get tickets too. Plus the story got out that the game was called off but suddenly it's back on, so folks got interested. Now it's an all-or-nothing proposition: either pulling something with the mayor and a big crowd there is the winning move—checkmate—or your play is to let it rest for a while, until people lose interest and look the other way again."

Ron was right. Pulling a stunt with the mayor there and all the extra eyes that would bring was a bold move. But he was also right when he said that it could be the winning move. The game might have been televised on some obscure cable channel, but I was sure the networks had reporters there now. It could be a record crowd. A blackout or some other kind of equipment failure would get a lot of attention. But it made me wonder whether attention was, in fact, what Trainor wanted. Ron must have been reading my mind.

"I think he'll want to cool his jets," Ron said. "There are too many eyes on this one. He doesn't need the publicity; he's not a terrorist. He gets control of the asset whether it's on the six o'clock news or not. And you gotta think less publicity is better, at least in this case."

It was sound logic, but I still wanted to be there.

Lizzy knocked on the door and stepped in.

"Courier package for you," she said, handing me a large, thin cardboard envelope.

I tore open the top and pulled out a smaller envelope bearing the logo for Stone Strong Insurance. Inside I found five laminated passes on lanyards for the corporate suite.

I held one up to Ron. "You want to go see a hockey game?"

"Do you need me there?"

"Only if you feel like using a free ticket."

"If it's all the same to you, I'll pass. I do enough hobnobbing in Palm Beach as it is."

"No sweat," I said. "I'm gonna take Sal anyway, and I promised a ticket to Punk Rowlands." I tossed three of the passes onto my desk and slipped the others back into the courier's envelope.

"Will those tickets get used?" asked Lizzy.

"I don't think so," I said. "Why?"

"Do you mind if I have them?"

The furrows in my brow deepened. I wasn't sure if Lizzy was asking to use tickets to a sports game, which seemed very unlike her, or if she planned to scalp them outside the arena.

"You like hockey?"

She pursed her vermilion lips. "Not particularly. But my boyfriend is from Pittsburgh, and he's a big fan."

I glanced at Ron and he at me. I could tell from the look on his face that he hadn't heard about this boyfriend either.

"You have a boyfriend?"

"Why is that so astonishing?" Lizzy frowned at me.

"Not astonishing, just news. I didn't know."

"There is life outside of Lenny Cox Investigations Inc., you know."

"So they tell me." I picked up the courier's envelope and handed it to Lizzy. "If your man's a fan, then go at it. Corporate suite, free food and drinks, the whole nine yards. He'll love it."

Lizzy took the envelope. "You're sure it's okay?"

"Absolutely. No reason for these tickets to go to waste. The game starts at seven, but hospitality usually opens about an hour before. If you want, I can probably get him a tour of the arena."

"I think these will suffice," she said, holding up the envelope. "Thank you."

Lizzy stepped out of my office, and I turned back to Ron.

"Did you know?"

Ron shook his head.

"You're regretting not coming now, aren't you?" I said.

"I want a full report tomorrow," he said.

"On the hockey?"

"I don't give two hoots about ice hockey."

CHAPTER THIRTY-SIX

I picked up Sal outside his pawnshop on Okeechobee Boulevard. I thought he might have gotten one of the kids around town to look after the store while he was gone, but Sal had locked everything up for the evening. If someone needed to pawn off a trumpet or Grandma's old rings, they'd need to come back tomorrow. Not that Grandma's old rings were Sal's main source of revenue. That, like religion and politics, was something that Sal and I chose not to talk about.

We got to the arena a good hour before the game. I wasn't much for pregame festivities, but I figured having given tickets to Lizzy I should make an effort to be there when she arrived, lest the insurance company folks look at her like she didn't belong.

We met Punk Rowlands at the gate, and I hung a lanyard around his neck like he was a gold medalist. Then we headed up to the expensive seats.

The suite looked like the others that I had seen on my previous tour, lots of polished wood and clean lines, punctuated by a wall print of the home team's logo. I said hi to Peter Parker and headed for the bar. Sally looked around the room like a choir boy at a mafia Christmas dinner or, perhaps, whatever the exact opposite of that might be. When I handed him a beer in a glass, he frowned, like he couldn't imagine such pointless finery.

"Lot of stuffed shirts here, kid," he said.

"Don't worry, Sal," I said. "We'll go out front."

I left Punk to hold the fort at the bar and led Sally over to a serving station, where a young woman with a brilliant smile prepared him a foot-long hot dog to his exact specifications. This aspect of the suite seemed to be much more to his liking. The woman was adding just the right amount of relish to his dog when I saw Lizzy and, presumably, her guy. They both looked a little out of place. In her Gothic style, she was dressed the way most folks would roll up to a funeral—especially their own—even if her makeup was relatively downplayed for the occasion. And he with his wide eyes communicated that the corporate suite was a thoroughly unfamiliar environment.

I left Sal at the hot dog stand and approached Lizzy. She seemed to relax some when she saw me, and I asked her if she had found the place okay, the way people ask those sorts of pointless questions.

"No problem," she said. Then she narrowed her eyes as if giving me a warning to be on my best behavior. "Miami, this is Christian."

I offered him a smile and shook his hand.

He looked young to me, but what his age was in comparison to Lizzy's I had no idea. The way she wore makeup gave her a sort of embalmed quality that made her timeless. But this guy looked like her polar opposite, like maybe an accountant, with his nice suit and tie.

"It's great to meet you, Christian," I said.

"You too," he said. "Lizzy's told me all about you, Mr. Jones."

"It's Miami. Mr. Jones was my dad."

"People call me Chris."

I led Lizzy and Chris over to the bar, where they each got themselves a Diet Coke, which felt a touch disappointing. I've got nothing against people who like to drink soda, but when it's an open bar on someone else's dime, top-shelf cocktails are always the way to go. I introduced them to Sal, and we grabbed some food.

People started pouring in. When everyone was plated up, I walked them through the crowd and out the door near the floor-to-ceiling windows.

There was a stand of about a dozen seats out front of the suite, designed for those hardy folks who preferred being out near the real action. I saw Sal nod, and I led him into the rear row. He slipped his glass of beer into the cup holder and sat down to begin working on his hot dog. I gestured for Lizzy and Chris to take the seats in front of us so we could chat.

I gave everyone a moment to eat and take in their surroundings, the new arena all lit up like a nightclub, with sweeping spotlights and a big screen over the ice showing slapshots and hot skating moves. None of the video shots were of an enforcer body checking someone up against the boards. Lex Javits would approve; it was the kind of video that would attract the moms and the families.

I looked around and saw no shirtless men with team letters on their bellies. He was right. It wasn't that kind of crowd. This was the sort of crowd that a league needed to base its future on. I looked back up above me, craning my neck to see if I could spot Con Gelphert's office, but I couldn't. As I turned back, someone caught my eye. In the corporate box next to ours, standing by the door in the floor-to-ceiling windows, was the FPL guy from the bar. I recalled the bartender calling him Neil.

It felt like too much of a coincidence that this guy was at the game at all, let alone in the box next door. The corporate suites themselves were separated by a cinderblock wall, but in the stands where we sat, they were only separated by a balustrade of blue steel pipe.

I told Sal I'd be back in a minute, then climbed over the railing and walked up the steps toward Neil.

It took him a minute to reconcile my bruised face with the one I had prior to him calling in my beating, but when he did, his jaw dropped.

"Neil," I said. "Of all the hockey arenas in all the world. You do remember me? Miami Jones."

He looked around as if searching for a fire exit.

"You know, I didn't get your name last time," I said.

"Yeow," he said.

"I gotta be honest, Neil, I didn't peg you as a corporate-box kind of guy."

"I was given some tickets. What are you doing here?"

"Me? I'm just here to keep the riffraff out." I stepped up to the doorway—nice and close so that Neil had to take a step back into the suite if he didn't want our lips to meet—and stayed there. It felt like a prudent move. Last time I'd come across this guy, I'd been taken unawares, and my sore body reminded me of that.

"You know, when we met we were rudely interrupted," I said. "And all I was trying to do was ask you about musical chairs. You know, the kids' game, where the music stops and the last one standing without a seat is out."

"Yeah, I know it."

"Well, the music's playing, Neil, and it's about to stop. Any second now. And whoever is behind you, working you like a string puppet, I bet they've got a chair all lined up. But I'm willing to bet you don't."

"Who are you, man? Why are you hounding me?"

I was about to get into it when somebody appeared beside him, short and stout like a fire hydrant with what looked like gorilla tape for eyebrows. I could see right over the top of his head, to the big unit behind him.

I recognized the big unit from the bar, the second of the two thugs who'd taken me into the alley. I hadn't really thought about it before, but now I figured that he was the leader of the two. He had sunk his boots into me, but not until the hard work had already been done.

"Can I help you?" said the fire hydrant.

"Yeah," I said. "I'll take a hot dog with mustard and ketchup. No relish."

He didn't smile. "I don't think you belong here."

"I was gonna say the same thing about you. I didn't think they let children into these corporate suites."

"You think you're very clever, don't you, Miami Jones?"

I figured while I was lying in the alleyway, his goons could have easily checked my ID.

"Yes, I know who you are," said the little guy.

"Well, I don't know you," I said. "Should I just call you Bubba?"

The better angel in my head was telling me to shut my smart mouth. Unfortunately, the better angel rarely won those arguments.

"I'm Otto Barassi," he said with a Don Corleone level of confidence.

I looked him up and down, which from my vantage point was mostly down. Though he could be one of those bouncing bombs the Brits smashed German dams with in the Second World War, I doubted he was as tough as he thought he was.

"How is it that an electrician gets into the corporate box?"

"Without us, this arena doesn't even get built," said Barassi.

"Is that so?"

"Of course. We power everything. The lights, the air-conditioning, the big scoreboard, even the cooling system that makes the ice."

I wondered what exactly this guy knew about the cooling system. I glanced at Neil Yeow, suspecting he knew plenty. Yeow didn't wear the same look of confidence as Barassi. It was clear who was the minion and who was the master, and the minion looked like he was about to lose his recently consumed hot dog all over his shirt.

"I can see how that might get your CEO an invitation," I said. "But they don't usually invite the grunt workers to these things."

"They do when the workers are part of a strong and vibrant

union," said Barassi, looking directly at me. "And that union doesn't take kindly to having its membership harassed."

"Harassment, you say? No, I'm just here to say hi."

"Is that so?"

"Sure. And to let you know that a beating doesn't change the fact that I know the power outages were sabotage. And I have proof."

Barassi's face contorted, as if he were attempting to smile but lacked the muscles to do it. The result was quite unpleasant.

"If you have proof, then show it or shut up. Just know that the union protects its own."

I wasn't sure if the little fireplug was referring to Neil Yeow or himself—or both. But this was the battle I needed to lose in order to win the war. I wondered when I might happen upon a battle that I would actually win.

"From what I hear, union leadership is just dying to cut you loose," I said as my parting shot.

I left with the vision of Otto Barassi smiling at me like a shark having a seizure.

CHAPTER THIRTY-SEVEN

I CLIMBED BACK INTO OUR SEATING AREA AND DROPPED DOWN BESIDE Sal, who was finishing his hot dog. Chris was looking at me like I was the class clown, but Lizzy seemed unsurprised by my behavior.

"Friends of yours?" Sal said.

"'Friends' might be stretching it a bit."

"That little guy you were talking to. That's Otto Barassi."

"Yeah, he introduced himself."

"Are those guys the reason you grunt every time you sit down?"

I saw Lizzy glance up at the door to the next suite.

"They might've had something to do with it."

"You remember what I said, right?"

"I do."

"Be careful," he said anyway.

The two teams made their way out onto the ice, skating around in random directions like atoms in an electrical current.

Chris leaned over and whispered something to Lizzy, then she turned back to me.

"Do you think it would be impolite if we had another hot dog?"

"Eat as much as you want. Your insurance premiums pay for this stuff."

She nodded to Chris, and I turned to Sal to see if he wanted something more. I didn't bother asking the question, because I knew the answer. Sal was an old guy now, and I got the feeling that when he was home he often ate a single piece of buttered toast for dinner, saving himself up for trips to the ballpark or visits to Cracker Barrel.

I was about to take orders when the woman with the beaming smile appeared in our aisle. "Can I get you folks anything more to eat or drink?" She made eye contact with each of us but reserved her extra wattage for Sal. Perhaps he reminded her of her grandfather, or maybe she knew a hot dog aficionado when she saw one.

We each gave her our order, and she took off with a promise to return very shortly.

"I could get used to this," said Sal.

"It's something, isn't it?" said Chris, turning around in his seat to look at me. "Thank you again, Mr. Jones, for inviting us."

"It's Miami, and you're welcome," I said. "Lizzy tells me you're a Penguins fan."

"That's right," he said. "I grew up in Pittsburgh. You know, it's really a football town, but my dad's a hockey guy, so he got me into the game when I was young."

"Did you play?"

"As a junior, yeah. Nothing serious. I was okay, but I was no Wayne Gretzky."

"The great one," I said.

Chris nodded. "What about you? You a fan?"

"Only in passing."

"Lizzy said you grew up in New England?"

"Connecticut."

"So does that mean you follow the Bruins?"

"Where I came from, it could go either way—Boston or New York—but if I followed anyone, it was the Bruins. My dad was a janitor at Yale University, and he cleaned up after the football games at Yale Bowl, so we were more into football. But he liked Terry O'Reilly. That guy used to end up in a lot of fights."

"Yeah, I've seen footage of him. He racked up over two thousand penalty minutes in his career, and if I remember correctly, most of them were full five-minute penalties for fighting."

"You like the rough stuff?" I said.

Chris glanced at Lizzy then back at me. "It's part of the game. But really I like watching good hockey, you know. Crisp passing and good team play."

"So you would be a Gretzky fan, then," I said.

"Probably more an Alex Ovechkin fan, myself."

"He's not from Pittsburgh, is he?"

Chris shook his head. "He's Russian, but he plays for the Washington Capitals."

"So who's your favorite Penguin?" I said, checking off another question I never expected to leave my lips.

"I've always been a Sid the Kid fan—Sidney Crosby. But my dad will tell you that Mario Lemieux was the best ever. My dad says he saved the franchise."

As the announcer called the players to line up for the national anthem, I wondered who would save the franchise in West Palm. If it turned out they needed saving at all.

We stood for the anthem. Then the vast majority of players skated to the bench, leaving five against five.

Our server returned with food and drinks just in time for the first buzzer. Players just skated around in crazy patterns without any obvious purpose. There was no movement directly up and down the ice, rather a series of random zigzags. I could see Chris gesturing in front of me, leaning into Lizzy and possibly explaining what was happening. The first period ended with no score, and I shared a look with Sal that said, *I have no idea what's going on either.*

Chris turned with a smile. "The standard's pretty good, don't you think?"

"My eyes are too old for this game," said Sal.

"What's your sport, Mr. Mondavi?" Chris asked.

"I prefer baseball."

"Well, you gotta retrain your brain, not your eyes. See, in baseball you think you're watching the ball from pitcher to catcher's mitt, or off the bat into the outfield. But actually, the only reason you're able to follow it is because all the cues are telling you where to look before anything even happens. I mean, there's only one place a pitcher is going to throw the ball to a batter, right? As close to home plate as he can. But imagine if there was a batter on each base, like the ultimate base-stealing team. Imagine if the pitcher could throw to any of the four bases on any given pitch. Then where would you look?"

"I'd look at the pitcher, I guess," said Sal.

"Right, but what would you be looking for?"

Sal shrugged.

"You're looking for cues," I said. "His body language. Whether he might pitch one down the middle, or pivot and throw it to first base, or even third. If there's a guy trying to steal third, the pitcher has to have eyes in the back of his head."

"Exactly. But what you're not focused on is the thing that you think you're focused on: the ball. You take hints from the players' positioning about whether it's going to be a proper pitch. It's easy if no one's on base and a little harder if the bases are loaded. But once he winds up, you know exactly where it's going to go, so your eyes are ready to follow it to the batter's box."

"I think that's the point," said Sal. "There is no batter's box on the ice."

"No, there's not. So don't try to follow the puck. It goes as fast as a baseball but in any direction, and from any player. What you're looking for are the cues, the movements. You take in the player, his body, his stick position, and then suddenly there are only three out of a possible thousand places it could go. Then you see him cock his wrist and turn his shoulders, and there's only one place for it to go, so that's where you're ready to look. You just need to learn the cues."

"I'm not sure I have that many years left in me," said Sal.

"It takes practice," said Chris with a smile.

"So, Lizzy," I said, "where did you two meet?"

I saw the crease form between her eyebrows as if it was some kind of leading question.

"We met at church," she said. "Why?"

"No reason."

"You think it's strange that people should meet and get together at church?"

"Not at all. I'm sure it happens all the time. At least you know you're going to share a common set of values. You know, because you're both . . ." I looked at Chris then back at Lizzy, and I saw her eyes narrow even more. "Your parents named you Christian?"

"Uh huh," said Chris.

"And you are a Christian," I said.

"Yeah, I know," he said. "A Christian called Christian."

"Now I know why you go by Chris."

He shrugged. "Could be worse. My parents could have been Buddhists. Then I'd have to go by Bud."

He smiled and offered me a wink. I realized he had heard what I was saying a thousand times.

"Or he could go by the city where he went to college," said Lizzy, her eyes on me.

"Touché," I said.

When all the players took the ice in preparation for the second period, Chris didn't turn around to watch them. Instead he pointed to the vacant seat next Sal. "Mr. Mondavi, you want to move over a spot?"

Sal, frowning as if he was unsure why he was moving, slid over to the next seat, and Chris clambered up from below and sat between Sal and me.

"Let me show you," he said.

The buzzer went off, and the players began their manic dance.

"You see number eight, for West Palm," said Chris, pointing.

Sal and I both nodded.

"Watch him, and only him."

I did as I was told. As the guy moved around the ice, Chris explained what the player was trying to do—how he was trying to position himself—like a sportscaster offering commentary.

"See, he's dropping back and center because they don't have the puck," said Chris. "Now they've got it, down back, so you see, he's skating out wide onto the wing. Keep looking at him. The guy bringing it up the middle is the center. He's kinda like the quarterback, unless you're Alex Ovechkin. Most of the great players are centers, but Ovechkin is a winger."

I kept my eyes on number eight, who, according to Chris, wouldn't move the lower half of his body, but the angle of his stick would turn toward the middle of the rink, where the puck was now.

"Watch," said Chris. "He's about to get the puck."

The puck hit his stick, and number eight took off along the side of the rink.

"Keep your eyes on the stick. If he closes the angle on it, he's gonna flick it back in for the center to take a slapshot. He opens the angle, he's taking it all the way to the red line."

I saw the head of number eight's stick turn so it was on the same angle as the length of the rink, closing the face, his hips slightly turned toward the center of the ice. Then, with a flick of the wrist, he shot the puck into the middle where the center swung his stick high in the air and drove it down like a golf swing, smashing the puck into the air, straight at the net. I couldn't see if the puck had landed inside, but the buzzer didn't go off, and I heard the slap as it hit the goalie's glove. I was amazed I had seen the puck at all.

"Hey," said Sal. "I saw that."

"And there you go," said Chris.

Next, number eight skated around behind the net, back along the other side, and zagged his way across to where he had previously been. He came off the ice with a quick step, like a ballet dancer covered in bubble wrap, and jumped up into the bench area. His replacement popped out as if from a dispenser.

"He's gone off, number eight," said Sal. "Is he hurt?"

"No," said Chris. "He's done his rotation."

"So he's taking a break?"

"Yeah," said Chris.

"But he was only on for maybe a minute."

"Actually it was more like forty seconds, and that's a pretty long rotation. You gotta remember, skating is hard work, especially when you're carrying all that protective equipment. Imagine running a full sprint on a football field in twice the equipment, on a surface that offers no traction. Football plays don't usually go for more than ten or fifteen seconds at a time, when you think about it. These guys go at pretty much full throttle whenever they're on the ice, so they have to rotate often or they'll burn out."

Chris continued his commentary for the rest of the period, telling us moments before where we needed to look, and, lo and behold, I kept seeing the puck in action. Then an offside penalty was called, and the official carried the puck to the face-off spot, so Chris took the opportunity to climb back down and sit with Lizzy.

Sal moved back next to me and whispered, "Kid knows his stuff."

I didn't realize how much he knew his stuff until I had to watch the rest of the period without his play-by-play. It must have been some kind of magic, because without Chris's words, my eyes didn't make contact with the moving puck again.

CHAPTER THIRTY-EIGHT

ONCE THE PLAYERS SKATED OFF FOR THEIR SECOND BREAK, LIZZY SAID she was going to use the little girls' room. Chris went with her and asked if he could bring back any food or drinks. Sally remarked that he wouldn't mind another beer and some of those nacho chips covered in cheese.

"No problem, Mr. Mondavi," Chris said, heading up into the suite.

Sal turned to me as they walked away. "Nice kid."

"Very," I replied, standing up.

It wasn't quite the seventh-inning stretch, but my muscles were more tender than usual. I didn't see any sign of Neil Yeow or Otto Barassi or the big bald unit in the suite next door, and no one I recognized in the stands. I wondered where John Trainor might be. Probably establishing his alibi in case something happened, though my instincts were telling me not tonight. But it *was* going to happen; I could feel it in my gut, and in the bruises across my body. People don't beat you senseless only to then give up on their plans. What I needed was to force Trainor's hand, to box him in, so I told Sal to keep my seat warm, and I went up into the suite.

I found Peter Parker chatting with an old guy who had a full head of hair the color of cocaine. I asked Parker over his shoulder where he thought John Trainor might be. Parker excused himself from the white-haired gentleman and started toward the door.

"He'll be in the owner's suite," Parker said. "With the mayor, I expect. I was just going to drop in. I'll show you where."

We walked out into the hallway and to the second suite along. Parker opened the door halfway, and an attendant on the other side opened it further. Parker showed the man the pass hanging from his lanyard. After a quick look and a nod, he stepped aside without a word and let Parker in. I just slinked in behind him before the attendant could get a good look at my bruised face.

Parker scanned the room and found the mayor of Palm Beach County standing by the bar, listening to a woman with hair so long it reached the backs of her knees. Parker headed that way, while I checked out the rest of the room.

I found John Trainor standing at a cocktail table by the window, in the company of Senator Brian Vargas and another guy, whose face I vaguely remembered but couldn't place. When he saw me approaching, Trainor winced. Senator Vargas's expression was much less committal.

"Have you been playing hockey?" asked the senator.

"Not lately."

"You look a mess."

"I know, and I'm sure you know nothing about it."

"I don't. But are you sure you shouldn't be in the hospital?"

"The jury's still out on that," I said, turning to Trainor. "But you must be very proud."

"Of?"

"Your maintenance team here at the arena. It's a credit to them that they were able to get the ice ready for tonight's game after so many problems."

"Quite," said Trainor.

I wasn't sure if he knew the role I had played in getting the facility manager back to put the ice in, and getting the mayor involved, but I didn't really care either way.

"You know what your problem is?" asked Vargas.

"I have a problem?"

"You do. It's called little brother syndrome."

"I don't have a brother."

"It's not about your family," he said, shaking his head. "It's about the little brother being jealous of what the big brother has. You guys in Singer Island are always so envious of everything that happens in West Palm Beach. It really makes you look sad and shallow."

I was surprised Vargas was so out of touch with his constituents. In Singer Island, there was less traffic—less hubbub in general—and most of the people there, even the new money that had flooded in, preferred the quieter lifestyle.

"If Saturday traffic on A1A is anything to go by, I'm usually pretty glad not to live in West Palm," I said. "Near, yes, but not in. And if anyone's got little brother syndrome, I expect that it's the politicians who run West Palm Beach. They all seem to be so jealous of the money over on the island. Isn't that right, John?"

"I can't speak to what the people of West Palm Beach are jealous of," Trainor said.

"No, I expect not," I said. "I'm sure it's hard to even see them from your lofty perch."

"If you're going to give me some speech about privilege, you needn't bother. I'm not buying your sob story."

"I don't have a sob story. My daddy didn't send me to a private college in upstate New York because I failed to get into Princeton. I'm not the one who had to do an MBA at Fordham because I couldn't get into Harvard. Or take a job at a third-tier Wall Street firm when all my friends and family expected me to be at Goldman Sachs. I heard you even tried to buy your way into the NHL, and that you tried to ingratiate yourself into the NFL, the NBA, and even major-league baseball, but you just weren't in that league, pardon the pun. The problem isn't that you've led a life of privilege; it's that you've been handed so much on a platter that all you can see now are the things you don't have."

"I never wanted to go to Princeton," he said.

"That's what you took from that whole story? Well, we know you crave the spotlight. You like being the big man on campus. Like at Clarkson, I heard you became the entertainment director for the hockey team because it was the popular sport on campus, but you weren't even athletic enough to play ping-pong."

"You jocks are all the same," he said. "You think being able to throw a ball or hit a puck makes you so special. But how do you think these kinds of sports happen? You think Clarkson hockey would've gotten their improved facilities without my fundraising?"

I gave him my cheesiest Tom Selleck grin, although it was closer to a blond surf bum who'd swallowed too much saltwater. "I know you used your old college roommate's fame and some of that third-tier New York money to create your own little competition."

"Little competition? I don't see your name on the letterhead of a significant sports league. You're a minor-league hack who never amounted to anything. You wouldn't understand the genius involved in creating something like this."

I took a moment to process the notion that he had just referred to himself as some kind of genius. "Yes, you certainly must have a big brain to come up with the idea of starting a hockey league. But the masterstroke was surely when you asked yourself, where on planet Earth would a hockey league succeed? And you came up with Florida. But now you've got a problem, don't you? The news that the ice was removed and the game would be canceled but then miraculously was pulled together has gotten you the biggest audience of the year, and it's still only two-thirds full. But is that enough to keep people coming back? From what I hear, you'd have to fill Yankee Stadium every night for a year to cover the checks you've been writing. Now your New York investors want their payday, don't they? So you're shifting cash from one hand to the other like you're Bernie Madoff."

A vein started pulsing in Trainor's temple. "If you ever suggest in public that this is any kind of Ponzi scheme, I will sue you into oblivion."

"Yeah, sorry to tell you that's not a long journey. But I didn't say it, you did. You're juggling more plates than a circus act, and you're running out of deck space on the Titanic for all those chairs you're shuffling." I took a breath. I needed to stop talking for a moment. I had gone for one too many metaphors.

"You're out of your depth, pal," said Trainor.

"As are you. I'm sure you think if you can get some more cash, you can pay off your New York investors—perhaps just a taste to keep them happy but on the hook—and you'll spend the rest trying to attract those middle-class moms who have the money to buy five-dollar tickets for hockey and five-thousand-dollar cruises from your sponsors. Until, that is, you run out of money, and word on the street is that will be any day now. You asked the other team owners for a capital injection, didn't you? They must be smart guys since they turned you down."

Trainor frowned and took in a quick breath that wasn't quite a gasp.

"And when you run out of money," I said, "who gets left holding the bag? Oh, that's right. The taxpayers of Palm Beach County."

"You think bringing this league down will save the taxpayers money? The bonds have been issued, the money has been spent. The only way they get a return is to make this team, this league, a success."

"That's it, isn't it? It's how you guys work. Too big to fail, am I right? Use the taxpayers' money to build your empire, and then when you've sucked all you can from it, you claim it will hurt the people more if they don't prop you up. Well, I'm onto you, pal."

Senator Vargas waved his hand to someone behind me. "I think you've said plenty," said the senator. "Now, can I ask who invited you into this suite?"

"The people of Palm Beach County," I said. "Remember them?"

A tall guy in a dark suit moved in between me and the senator.

I supposed when you passed enough legislation for rich people, favors like being provided with security came your way.

Regardless, the guy was a different class of heavy from the thugs I'd run into at the bar. He didn't lay a hand on me but stared as if the look alone might make me tremble. Obviously, the guy didn't know me at all. As a professional pitcher, I wasn't the one who got stared at. I did the staring. But I had rattled the tree sufficiently to dislodge a few nuts. So I wished them all a pleasant evening.

"Go Chill," I said, pumping my fist. Then I turned and walked out of the suite.

CHAPTER THIRTY-NINE

THE PALM BEACH CHILL LOST THE GAME TO THE TEAM FROM Daytona, one–zip. After the final buzzer we walked out with Lizzy and Chris, who shook my hand and thanked me again for the tickets. I thanked him for his hockey lesson and told Lizzy I'd see her tomorrow. Chris then shook hands with Sal and told him it was a pleasure.

"Good to meet you, kid," said Sal.

I realized Lizzy hadn't uttered a word to Sally all evening. She had a reasonable understanding of Sally's past and his connections to various Italian families in New York. Those connections likely didn't fit with her Christian values, despite the fact that all those families were Catholic.

I drove Sal home and said I hoped he had a good time.

"I like the baseball," he said. "I like being outside at night."

I couldn't argue with him on that count.

I left him at his door and drove away. I had every intention of returning to Miami. That late at night, it was usually an easy and fast drive, but all of a sudden I couldn't face it. I knew I could cut across to the island and crash with Ron and Cassandra, but once again I felt that sense of unease about overstaying my welcome there, even though I knew that wasn't possible.

I got on the turnpike and just drove north. Traffic was light—perfect conditions to think and drive while not thinking about driving.

I felt listless, like an anchor dragging along the sandy bottom, trying desperately to find something to grab hold of. I wondered if I was going about things all wrong. I had a responsibility to my client to find out what was happening at the arena, but that job didn't extend to stopping the actions from taking place. Technically that would fall to the police, but as I thought about it, I realized their job was typically after the fact. I might have suggested to Peter Parker that he hire some additional security, and then I could just walk away, but I knew in my gut that the likelihood of that was zero.

It had become more than a case when they decided to stick the boots into me. But I couldn't shake the feeling that I hadn't connected all the dots correctly. Or maybe I didn't understand my objective. What if Trainor's words were true: if he failed and the team folded, would that hurt the people of Palm Beach County even more than if his wheeling and dealing were allowed to succeed? Was I simply trying to take him down a peg or two out of jealousy? Did I really have little brother syndrome?

I tried to come up with a way out that didn't see Trainor's wealth enriched at the cost of the people who worked hard day in and day out. The folks who just wanted to escape for a few hours by enjoying a hot dog and a beer at a hockey game.

Driving into a tunnel of light along the turnpike, I felt fatigue kicking in, so I pulled off the exit ramp and cut across to I-95, this time heading south. As I drove, I called Danielle and told her that I was tired and I'd crash in the office. She suggested I head over to Ron and Cassandra's, but she didn't belabor the point when I simply said, "Nah."

I drove back toward West Palm Beach on autopilot. I was cruising down the off-ramp onto Blue Heron Boulevard before I realized what I was doing. My homing beacon had me heading for Singer Island again. I felt like some kind of creepy stalker, continually driving by the home of some celebrity or former girlfriend.

But Singer Island was closed down for the night. The stores and restaurants at City Beach were quiet. Across the lot, Seaside Bar and Grill was still burning a candle, but I could see a guy inside mopping the floor. I thought about turning down into the old subdivision and driving by my old house, but then the stalker sensation grew real. Somebody lived there. So at the last minute, I went the other way, into the street that led to the beach.

I parked illegally right in front of the beach supply store with its display still lit despite being closed, in case a late-night window shopper happened by to look at the visors or flip-flops or the naked mannequin. I figured parking enforcement officers had better places to ply their trade late at night than an empty beach near a closed-down village.

I wandered out through the dunes and onto the beach. The apartment towers were still throwing out their checkerboard light, but I stopped short of them, in the darkness, and sat down to watch the soft waves lapping against the sand. I took a long breath, in through my nose and out through my mouth.

The sea air made me feel better—I'd heard it had something to do with negative ions, but I had no earthly idea what that meant. My rationale would have been somewhat less scientific. Being at the beach beat sitting in traffic or watching the idiot box. The sound of the waves was repetitive and soothing. My phone was always telling me that I could get an app that would give me this very sound from the comfort of my bed, but I couldn't see how it could be any better than the real thing.

I lay back in the sand and stared up at the stars. There was plenty of light pollution in South Florida, but I could make out a bright celestial body with a tint of red to it. I wondered if it was Mars, and whether it was more logical to play hockey there than it was in the Florida heat.

My breathing fell into tempo with the soothing ebb and flow of the waves rippling onto the beach. For the first time in a long time, the weight of the world lifted from my shoulders.

Then my phone rang.

The trill was annoying, and I realized after a second that it had woken me from my nap.

I pulled the phone from my pocket and looked at the screen: Danielle.

"Please tell me you're not at home," she said.

I rubbed my face as I tried to understand what she was asking.

"No," I said. "I told you earlier, I wasn't coming back tonight." I wondered if I had dreamed that conversation.

"I know," she said. "I don't mean Miami. I mean Singer Island."

I sat up and looked along the beach. How could she know where I was sitting? "Why would I be on Singer Island?"

"Because it's your mooring, but that's not the point. The point is you're not there. That's all that matters."

"Why does it matter that I'm not there?"

"Because I just got a call from a friend in the fire department in Riviera Beach. It's the house. It's on fire."

CHAPTER FORTY

I was at the car in a flash. As soon as I pulled onto the road heading to the intracoastal, I could see the glow of flames. I had to park well before I reached the house—fire trucks and police cars with flashing lights blocked the way. A crowd had gathered behind a perimeter, people likely woken up by the piercing sirens that had failed to wake me on the beach.

I edged my way in between people to the front for a better look. Flames spewed from windows that appeared to have lost all their glass. The vehicle in the driveway had also caught on fire. A team of firefighters on the lawn pummeled the front rooms of the house with water, which seemed to be evaporating before it got the chance to do any good.

I slipped under the yellow tape and moved closer to the fire. A fireman stepped in my way and ordered me back. For a moment I didn't move, my eyes fixed on the flames leaping from every direction. It was both mesmerizing and terrifying, in a way that only fire can be.

"It's my house," I told the fireman.

"Sorry, but you need to stand back. Let them do their work." He gently placed his palm on my chest but applied no pressure. I took several steps back.

As I was about to duck back under the perimeter tape, I realized I wasn't watching my house burn at all. It wasn't my house, not really. I owned it, but that made me the landlord. Somebody else actually lived there, the thought of which made me rush back toward the fireman. He saw me coming and shook his head.

"The house is rented," I said. "Did they rescue someone?"

"No, they haven't gotten inside yet," he said. "But if someone is in there . . ." Then he shook his head again, this time conveying a very different message.

I retreated behind the perimeter and moved to the side and sat on the curb, watching my house burn, the way you stare at a campfire as logs turn from something tangible to nothing at all. I felt the warmth of the flames on my skin and saw the light bouncing off the windows of the neighbors' houses, but none of it seemed real. Despite the heat from the blaze, I was cold. The little energy I had left drained from my body. It was an effort just to sit upright. I leaned my elbows on my knees and looked at the faces of the people around me. There were no expressions of terror or sadness. If anything, the faces glowing in the firelight were blank, dispassionate. I knew the feeling.

Danielle had called this house my mooring. I had often conjured up an anchor when thinking about it. I now realized that her words rang true: an anchor weighed you down, but a mooring held you in place, right where you wanted to be. I'd given up this place, and suddenly I knew, with every fiber of my being, that I shouldn't have.

Now it burned.

Some of the original crowd drifted away, off to get some sleep, no doubt, so they could start workdays in only a few hours. Perhaps they figured they'd get a good look at the end result of the fire when they woke. Other people seemed to be arriving, like moths.

None of them came near me. Perhaps in the darkness no one recognized me, or those who were out were not the neighbors who I had connected with.

Surrounded by a growing throng of people felt strange and distant. Like most folks, I had been through my fair share of ups and downs. I'd lost people I deeply cared about—first my mother, then my father, then Lenny. I had found a new kind of family in Florida, yet until that moment, I had never felt completely alone in the universe.

Danielle was in Miami, and Ron and Cassandra were asleep, like every other person I knew—Sal and Lucas and Mick and Muriel and Lizzy. I wondered if having one of them beside me would change the way I felt. But it wasn't about proximity to another human. Watching my house burn was like seeing the tether break on my mooring, setting me adrift on a vast and empty ocean.

I didn't feel like crying; such emotion was far too much effort. Instead I laid my face in my hands, anything but to look at the burning structure across the street. I don't know how long I sat there.

Then a hand softly landed on my shoulder—not a tap or a jolt but a gently placed hand. I looked up to see the face of Detective Ronzoni of the Palm Beach Police Department.

CHAPTER FORTY-ONE

"If you've come to arrest me," I said, "that'll pretty much cap off the day."

"I'm not here to arrest you, Jones."

"What are you doing here? This isn't Palm Beach."

Ronzoni preferred not to leave the island of Palm Beach and venture onto the mainland, where West Palm Beach sat, and definitely not to the northern neighbor of Singer Island. His job, as far as I could tell, was to keep the likes of me away from the good people of Palm Beach and off the ritzy island altogether.

"I was working a case, and I heard the call. Heard the address."

Ronzoni sat on the curb beside me. He wore his standard-issue JC Penney wrinkle-free suit, its polyester fabric glistening in the firelight. His tie was loosened at the collar and hung so long it almost touched the concrete at our feet.

Ronzoni didn't say anything. He didn't ask me any questions or offer hollow condolences. He just sat beside me as we watched the firefighters gradually gain control of the blaze.

As the flames were beaten back, I could finally see the smashed-out windows and the large jagged hole in the roof. Even though I was sitting in relative darkness, the interior of the house looked black, like a missing tooth in an old man's smile.

I noticed another fireman chatting to the one who had kept me behind the perimeter. He pointed in my general direction, and the new guy headed over. He wasn't dirty or wet or soaked in sweat, so I pegged him as the fire chief. He stopped in front of us and dropped to his haunches.

"This your house?" he asked me.

I nodded.

The chief glanced at the detective beside me.

"What brings you here, Ronzoni?"

"I'm a frie—" Ronzoni glanced at me and then back at the chief. "Jones and I know each other. I heard the call on the radio. Just here in a personal capacity."

"You find anybody inside?" I asked.

"Not yet. There's a lot of debris, and although the flames are contained, it's still plenty hot. We won't go in now until the cops are done."

"What are the cops doing?"

"They help us out in situations like this."

"What kind of situation is it?" asked Ronzoni.

"The whole thing looks like arson."

The chief stood and asked if I could hang around in case the local PD needed a word. I didn't answer, but I got the sense that Ronzoni had nodded.

The chief walked away, and I felt Ronzoni looking at me.

"You got an alibi?" he asked.

For the first time in what felt like forever, something resembling an emotion fired in my belly. "Are you kidding me?"

"I'm not implying you did anything, Jones. But the Riviera Beach PD will have to ask the question. It would be better if you had an answer."

"I was at the beach."

Ronzoni frowned. "In the early hours of the morning?"

"I fell asleep." I looked him in the eye. "But I didn't burn down my own house." What I didn't say was that I had a decent list of candidates who might have.

We watched the crowd dissipate, the excitement of the flames giving way to the boredom of charred wood and smoke. The firefighters began rolling up hoses and packing away equipment.

Danielle called back, and I told her that the house was gone. For the longest time she said nothing, as if she was having trouble processing the notion, or maybe just finding it difficult to choose the right words.

"Are you okay?" she finally said.

I knew what she was asking. I wasn't in mortal danger, and I wasn't going to do myself harm. The urge I felt was to cause harm to someone else. I just had to figure out who that someone was.

A guy in a suit that looked like the tan version of Ronzoni's walked up to me.

"I have to go," I told Danielle. "The cops are here."

"Cops?"

"Yeah. They think it's arson."

I told Danielle that I'd speak to her soon, then Ronzoni and I both stood. I wasn't sure if it was the late hour or the lack of recent movement, but I felt dizzy for a moment.

"This is your house?" asked the cop.

"It was."

"And you are?"

"Miami Jones."

The cop looked at Ronzoni. "What's your connection, Detective?"

"Like I told the chief, I'm here in a personal capacity," said Ronzoni.

"I'm Detective Brookes, Riviera Beach PD. They tell me you don't live here?"

"No. The place was rented out. I'm in Miami."

"I'm gonna need an address down there."

"Fine."

"Jones is married to Danielle Castle," said Ronzoni.

"From the sheriff's office?"

"She's with the FDLE now," he said.

The detective made a note on a little pad then tapped his pen against the page. "So where were you this evening?"

"I was at the hockey game at the new arena," I said.

"I assume someone can vouch for that?"

"One or two," I said, thinking about all the people I had upset at the hockey game.

"That finished hours ago," said Brookes. "You didn't go home to Miami?"

"No. I was too tired to drive all that way."

"So where did you go?"

"I was at the beach."

"What were you doing at the beach in the middle of the night?"

"Getting some fresh air." I looked at the detective and could see he wasn't convinced. "I fell asleep."

Brookes turned to Ronzoni. "You saying that you can vouch for this guy?"

"I am," said Ronzoni. "I can."

Detective Brookes tapped his pad again and stood in silence for a moment. Cops like silence. It's not like they're not chatterboxes—get them in a cops' bar with a couple of beers under their belts and they can be impossible to shut up—but they liked silence when they were interrogating people. Perps had a tendency to blurt out the most interesting information in order to fill the silence. But I had nothing more to say.

"You should get your story in order," said Brookes. "And if I were you, I'd call an attorney."

"You think I burned down my own house?"

"In most arson cases, yeah, that's exactly how it goes down. I'm not saying you did anything. Not yet. But there's every chance we'll need to talk to you later this morning, once we find the body."

I nodded.

"You think there was just the one guy here?" he asked.

"That was my understanding," I said. "A business executive. Whether he had company, I can't say."

"Let's hope not," said Brookes. "So let me ask you, if it wasn't you, who would want to burn your house down?"

"I'm working a case right now, and I might've ruffled a few feathers."

"What do you mean, working a case?"

"I'm a private investigator."

The detective grunted.

"Maybe they thought I still lived on the island," I said.

"So who might these ruffled feathers belong to?"

I told him about Neil Yeow from the power company, and Otto Barassi, the union guy. I mentioned John Trainor, but the name didn't seem to ring any bells for the detective. "He's a rich dude from Palm Beach," I said.

"Aren't they all," he replied with a side glance at Ronzoni. "You haven't made many friends lately, have you?"

"No," I said. "And there's more. I forgot to mention the senator."

I saw the detective stiffen. "Senator? What senator?"

"Senator Vargas."

"You think a senator burned your house down?"

"No. You asked whose feathers I had ruffled, and Vargas is definitely on that list. Could he have gotten someone to commit arson? I can't put it past him."

"Well, I'm not going around digging up dirt on a senator," said the detective. "Or some rich guy from Palm Beach, for that matter. In the department, we call that career suicide."

"So what are you gonna do? Pin it on me?"

"If you didn't do it, then, no, I'm not going to pin anything on you. But you'll need more than a disagreement at a hockey game before I go accusing a senator of anything."

"He's right," said Ronzoni. "You need to be very careful about making public accusations against people like that."

It took me a moment to discern that it was anger welling inside not indigestion. I had shared a few run-ins with Detective Ronzoni through the years, but it was fair to say that we had seen each other's better sides and had given each other a little more grace. But the one thing I still couldn't stomach was Ronzoni the Palm Beach politician. Not in the literal sense—Ronzoni would never run for any kind of office; it would require buying a decent suit—but he had a tendency to bend over backward in order to ingratiate himself with the rich and not so fabulous of Palm Beach. However, at that moment, standing in the early morning darkness on Singer Island, I didn't see a lot of upside in saying so.

"I'll watch my mouth," I said.

Detective Brookes handed me a business card and told me to expect a call. As we watched him dip back under the yellow caution tape, I felt the weariness and loneliness pulling me back down. I wasn't sure that I wanted to be there anymore, but I didn't want to leave. I couldn't think of anywhere to go, so I was about to drop down onto the curb again when I heard my name.

"Miami."

I turned to see Lizzy striding toward me along the sidewalk. She looked like she'd seen a ghost, even paler than usual. Perhaps she had no time to apply all her makeup, having gone home to bed. She hit me with a hug that almost knocked me backward onto the street. I didn't wrap my arms around her in return. Not because I didn't want to, but because we didn't really operate that way. Physical contact was not something she ever seemed to enjoy. When she was done, she pulled back and held my arms.

"What are you doing here?" I asked.

"Ron called me," she said, turning her head.

Over her shoulder I saw Ron approaching. Lizzy stepped aside. Ron embraced me, then punched my back with his fist, the way men do, and pulled back with an expression that suggested he might have gone a step too far.

I didn't get the chance to speak. Ron moved to the other side, and Muriel appeared. Despite the coolness of early morning, she was, as always, wearing a tank top, the only noticeable feature of which was it didn't have a Longboard Kelly's logo. She launched into the biggest bear hug of them all and buried her face in my neck as if she might cry. After a while, I wondered if she'd ever let go. And I kind of hoped she wouldn't. When she finally released me, she ran her hands across my face, like my mother used to do when I had been crying. But neither of us had shed a tear.

Muriel turned slightly so I could see past her, to where Mick was standing with his hands in his pockets. Mick didn't come in for a hug. He just nodded.

"All right?" he said.

"Alive," I replied.

Mick nodded again. "Good start."

"What are you all doing here?" I asked no one in particular.

"Danielle called me," said Ron.

"And Ron called me," said Lizzy.

"Danielle called me too," said Muriel.

I glanced at Mick. He nodded at Muriel, as if that's where all his useful information came from.

I surveyed each of them: my business partner, my office manager, the guy who owned the local bar, and his bartender. Plus a detective who was up too late and out of his jurisdiction. It was a motley and eclectic crew.

I took in a long, slow, calming breath, the way I had a thousand times on the pitcher's mound, because all of a sudden every emotion I could possibly feel flooded into my body. I realized as I exhaled that when folks jumped on the phone tree and rushed to be with you in your time of need—especially at one in the morning—they weren't just people; they weren't even friends. This was family. Not the one I had been born into, but the one I had chosen, and had seemingly chosen me.

Ron stepped in and put his hand on my shoulder. "You'll come home with me," he said. "Then we'll all get into this in a few hours."

I nodded, and the six of us looked for a moment at the charred remains of my house. Then we each turned our backs and walked away.

CHAPTER FORTY-TWO

I woke with a start and the sense that I was still lying on City Beach. I pawed around myself, clawing at the sheets, and it took me longer than was necessary to realize I was in one of the spare bedrooms in Ron and Cassandra's apartment.

I lay back for a while and let my heart rate come down as the images from the previous evening replayed in my mind like a movie trailer from a show I saw years ago. I had no possessions in that house, so I had lost nothing personal. I still had joyful memories planted in my brain, but something made me feel as if they, too, had been burned to a crisp.

When we had gotten back to the apartment, Ron told me we would figure it all out, that he would contact the insurance company in the morning. But his tone suggested that he knew we were talking about something more than bricks and mortar.

I lay in the darkness of the bedroom thinking about two inconvenient truths: one, that I was likely suspect number one in the death of the tenant, and two, that the suspicions that it was arson told me somebody had deliberately set my house on fire. It wasn't drawing a longbow to conclude that I was the intended target, and that someone probably wanted me dead.

Cassandra had one of those apartments where the kitchen was tucked away in a separate room, typical for Palm Beach, where dinner was often prepared by a catering company, so kitchens were best closed off.

I stumbled out of the bedroom and into the dining room, where Ron and Cassandra sat at the table with coffee cups in their hands. They looked up at me, but my eyes were on Danielle. She stood, letting me come to her, and we embraced. I felt my breathing fall into sync with hers, and we stood there for a long time, until she stepped back and looked me up and down, the way law-enforcement types often do.

"What are you doing here?" I asked.

She shook her head. "You look a mess. I brought you some clothes."

Ron fixed me a cup of coffee while I washed up in the en suite bathroom. I stared in the mirror. I looked more than a mess, like someone in a war movie, the guy who lost. I was still bruised and puffy from the beating, but that was now complemented by ash and sweat that had run down my face like a topographical map.

I stood under the shower and watched the dirty water sliding down the drain, thinking about who it was that had taken a match to my house. The power company crew was one possibility, given their previous willingness to engage in physical violence. But this felt like a considerable escalation, and I had to ask myself if they had the resources to do it or to even find out the address.

I was fairly certain a state senator had such information at his fingertips. Clearly he already knew that I lived—or was supposed to be living—on Singer Island. Which left John Trainor. I had no idea what he knew, what his resources were, or what he was capable of.

When I came out, a cup of coffee was sitting on the table next to Danielle. I took a long drink. It was hot and acidic, nothing like the Cuban coffee Francisco Monaro had prepared for us, but the bitterness suited my mood.

"Would you like some breakfast?" asked Cassandra. "We have croissants."

"No, thank you. But the coffee is hitting the spot."

"Where were you when I called you last night?" Danielle asked.

"Just sitting on the beach," I said. "Clearing out the cobwebs, I guess."

She nodded and questioned me no further. She knew I had a tendency to contemplate the universe in the bleachers of empty baseball stadiums, and, short of a stadium, an empty beach was always an excellent substitute.

"Unfortunately that means I don't have much of an alibi for the time between leaving the hockey stadium and the fire starting."

"I spoke to the Riviera Beach PD this morning," said Danielle. "They've done a sweep of the street, canvassing all your neighbors, but they say they found nothing helpful. No useful witnesses."

"How did they know there was even a fire if there were no witnesses?" asked Ron.

"A neighbor called it in. An old guy out walking his dog. Apparently he doesn't sleep too well and takes to the streets in the wee hours. He saw the flames and ran home to call the fire department. But according to Riviera Beach PD, he didn't see anyone unfamiliar, no strange vehicles, just the dark-colored SUV burning in the driveway."

"Dark colored?" I asked.

"According to the witness," said Danielle. "The old guy who made the call told the police he didn't recognize the car, but he also said so many cars appeared in that driveway over the years that it wasn't so unusual not to recognize one."

I wasn't sure if that was a comment on how many vehicles I'd managed to work my way through or whether the tenant rented a great variety. But I also noted that I drove a dark-colored SUV.

"They get any kind of security video?" asked Ron.

"They didn't mention anything. They would have asked about it, especially where they saw cameras."

"Well, someone was there," I said, "and they didn't toss a Molotov cocktail from the intracoastal. They drove in."

"No doubt," said Danielle. "But they'll keep at it. Maybe somebody will come forward with something."

"I'm not sure how *at it* they will keep," I said. "The guy I spoke to last night seemed pretty gun shy about upsetting anyone important."

"They won't go off half-cocked, MJ," said Danielle. "But they'll get to the bottom of it. I won't give them any other choice."

I thought about old men wandering the streets at midnight, and quiet neighborhoods where people preferred the calm to the hubbub of West Palm. I wondered if anyone really had seen anything, or like me, they had all been asleep. Then I had an idea.

"Mrs. W.," I said.

"What?" said Danielle.

"Mrs. W.," I repeated. "She lives down the street, about halfway out to the main road. Anyone coming in from that direction to our place would have to drive right past her house."

"They have to drive past quite a few houses, MJ, but it was after midnight."

"I know. But last year her son asked me to install one of those video doorbells for her. He lives in New Jersey, remember? He ordered the thing off the internet and asked if I'd connect it for her."

"I remember," said Danielle. "But I'm not sure it'll be helpful; doesn't someone have to ring the doorbell for it to shoot video?"

"Yes and no. It has a motion sensor, so if someone walked up but they didn't ring the doorbell, it could alert her and start the video. It's supposed to be a deterrent to those morons who steal people's packages off front doorsteps—let's face it, robbers don't ring the doorbell. But there was a problem with it. I couldn't get the motion range to work properly, so it either picked up everything all the way out to the street, including passing cars, or it didn't work at all. And she didn't want to get an alert on her phone every time a car drove by, so we left the motion sensors on but turned off the alerts. Mrs. W. may well have video of the arsonist driving past and not even know it."

CHAPTER FORTY-THREE

After we finished breakfast, Danielle drove us back over to Singer Island. We headed north along Blue Heron Boulevard, past the stores and bars, and cut left onto one of the streets that headed west out to the intracoastal. Our house was on the bend where the street reached the waterfront houses and turned north. Our next-door neighbor got the glare of all the headlights coming down the street and had erected a large concrete wall as a remedy.

Mrs. W.'s house was one of the postwar originals halfway back toward the main road from the water. Danielle parked on the street in front of her house. For a moment we stood on the sidewalk to take in the neighborhood in a way we had never done before. Not so much home as crime scene. I didn't see anything out of order, except for the charred bones of the house at the end of the road.

I rang the doorbell and waited for Mrs. W. to answer. I was about to ring a second time when I heard the first of the locks turn on the front door. About thirty seconds later, she finished the entire process and opened up, peering through a screen door as if I was a mile away, or she had left her glasses on the kitchen table. Eventually she placed me, because a smile spread across her face.

"Oh, Mr. Jones," she said. "So nice to see you. Won't you come in?"

Danielle and I stepped into her small living room, and she immediately offered us coffee and Bundt cake. I glanced at Danielle, my look suggesting that we'd already had coffee and we didn't have time for any kind of cake, but the look I got in return said I should mind my manners and let a lonely old lady entertain us for a while.

Mrs. W. puttered around in the kitchen. Danielle went to go help, so I just looked out the window at the quiet street. I could hear them chattering away and the clinking of china.

Danielle reappeared with a tray of coffee and cake. Mrs. W. followed behind and waved us both to a sofa. Danielle served as Mrs. W. eased herself back into a recliner that looked like it might swallow her whole.

"Did you see any of the hubbub last night?" I asked her.

She picked up a pair of reading glasses off the table next to her and slipped them into a green case. "Oh, I heard all the ruckus, and I saw the flashing lights. But I didn't go out. I don't like to go out on the street in my nightgown. But I saw the debris this morning. I'm so sorry, Mr. Jones. But thank goodness you weren't hurt. And it's only a building, after all."

She was right and wrong. Not about the building just being a building. But wrong about someone getting hurt.

We sipped some coffee and I ate three pieces of delicious Bundt cake while Mrs. W. told us about the latest adventures her son was having in New Jersey. Apparently heating oil costs had gone through the roof, and the fall had been bitterly cold. It didn't sound like any kind of fun to me.

Once we had gotten the latest gossip out of the way, I asked Mrs. W. if she recalled the video doorbell that I had installed for her.

"Oh, yes. It's simply amazing. When the postman brings a package from my Henry, and he rings the doorbell, I can talk to him even when I'm at the bingo. He's a lovely man, Luis. He always hides my packages behind the chrysanthemums on the patio. You know, just in case."

"Good thinking," said Danielle.

"Mrs. W.," I began, "would you mind if I took a look to see if there was any video from last night?"

"I don't think the camera points toward your house, dear."

"No, you're right, it doesn't. But we thought it might show if anyone came in or out. You know, along the street."

"Oh, I see. Well, of course. You're the only one who knows how it works, anyway, so help yourself."

Mrs. W. went to pour another round of coffee, her hands shaking as she picked up the large carafe, but she didn't spill a drop. As she was working on it, I stepped over to a table with an ancient computer and a monitor the size of a small car. It took several minutes to boot up the clunky machine. Danielle brought me another coffee as I opened up the software to check the surveillance video.

"Do you know what time the call was made to the fire department?" I asked.

"No dear," said Mrs. W. "I'm afraid I don't."

Danielle smiled. "Twelve twenty-four a.m."

I checked the endless list of videos. The motion sensor seemed to pick up a leaf blowing as readily as it did a dump truck. Each activity was captured in thirty seconds of video, stored on the company's servers for thirty days, and then automatically deleted. I found the timestamp before 12:24. There were a number of videos between 11:30 p.m. and 1:00 a.m. The sensor would've gone ballistic with all the fire trucks and police vehicles, so I began checking in about an hour prior.

The first video I opened showed Mrs. W.'s porch, her front yard, and the street. There was no movement and nothing happening. A false positive. Probably the wind. The next video was a hit.

From Mrs. W.'s porch I saw a dark sedan drive through the picture at 11:55. The camera worked on some kind of infrared technology, so despite the dark street the picture was reasonably clear, although different colors were difficult to discern. I rewound the video and played it again, pausing the instant it started, with the car just leaving the frame. It was definitely a sedan, a large one. Maybe a Town Car or something similar. The kind of thing that had a trunk designed for a family of six carrying all their luggage on a ski vacation to Aspen. I let the video play through then checked the list and found another video, three minutes later. This was like the previous one but in reverse: the same car, driving in the opposite direction as if it had turned around at the end of the street and come back out. Typically a car would continue along the street and loop back out to the main road further to the north, so this was odd.

I sipped my coffee and emailed copies of the videos to myself. Mrs. W. and Danielle had dropped back into conversation about plans for the holidays or some such, so as I worked, I pondered the car. I wondered who it belonged to and how they had gotten onto the island. Coming down this street suggested they had come across on Blue Heron. And because they did a U-turn and drove out the same way, they probably wanted to leave via Blue Heron as well. That said they either intended to head south once they got back on the mainland, or they were unfamiliar with the area and were simply retracing their steps. Or both.

I looked at the time stamp on the first video. I hadn't been paying attention to the time while I was driving the previous evening, but it had to have been roughly the same time that I drove onto the island myself. Which took my thinking in another direction. Perhaps I had been followed. But I hadn't driven by my old house. As I recalled it, I had made the last-second decision to not be a creepy stalker, and I had pulled around the block of shops at the last moment to head over toward the beach. Was it possible that the sedan was following me and had simply lost me? Had they done a drive-by, knowing my address and, having seen the SUV in the driveway, just assumed I was home? Had they then set my house on fire?

There were a lot of questions without a lot of answers. But there was one thing I did know: if they followed me in off Blue Heron, then before they even got this far, they had passed a lot of eyes. Eyes that didn't sleep.

I swallowed the last of my coffee and shut down the computer, eager to get moving. I stepped around the coffee table and jinked my head at Danielle to say we needed to go. She simply lowered her eyelids and nodded toward the sofa, suggesting I sit the hell down—whatever I needed to find would be there in another five minutes, and while an old lady was holding court, the least I could do was relax and visit a little while.

CHAPTER FORTY-FOUR

After an hour that felt like a day and all the coffee and Bundt cake a man could consume, Danielle and I left. We drove back out to the shopping area at Singer Island, until I saw the building I was looking for. Right on the corner of Blue Heron Boulevard and the street that wound around the parking lot toward the beach. It was a prominent location, favored by fast-food hamburger chains, gas stations, and, in this case, a realtor's office.

Danielle parked the car in the large lot in back and we walked around to the realtor's. I stood for a second on the sidewalk as if interested in the property listings posted in the window. I looked back along Blue Heron Boulevard to the south—the way I had come onto the island the previous night—and then back the other way. Then I glanced up under the eaves of the building and saw what I knew was there.

A little bell rang as we stepped inside, and a woman smiled at me from the reception desk. She was seventy if she was a day, but to her credit she probably could have passed for fifty—thirty was pushing the envelope, as was the leopard print dress.

"Is Martin in?" I asked.

She doubled down on the smile. "Whom may I ask is calling?" she said, as if I was on the telephone.

"Miami Jones."

I turned and raised my eyebrows at Danielle, and she gave me a wink. We stood looking at the rental listings pinned up on a wall board. I knew the agent who ran this little operation. I'd never used him professionally, but we had shared a beer or two over a Patriots or Dolphins game at one of the bars along the beach. Like realtors everywhere, he was known around town. Realtors were a profession onto themselves, the only vocation I could think of other than actors who plastered their faces on every piece of marketing material they produced. Until I met them, I had no idea what my doctor, my butcher, the produce guy at Publix, or the local gas station attendant looked like. But I knew on sight every real estate agent for over a hundred miles in any direction.

Martin McConnell stepped out of his office and waved us back. We shook hands like old friends, and I introduced him to Danielle. When he offered us coffee, I felt bile rising in my throat and declined.

"So," said Martin, his cheeks glowing as red as the hair on his head, "how can I help you fine folks today?"

"I need a favor," I said.

Sometimes it was better to ease into a favor request, butter a person up with some casual chitchat or congratulations on their latest achievement. But not with realtors. It seemed to me that the real estate business was built on a foundation of favors. This was not something I cared to take advantage of except in the most dire of circumstances. Having my house burn down certainly fit the bill.

"Happy to help," said Martin. "What can I do for you?"

When I told him about the fire, he had already heard all about it. He knew how many fire trucks attended the call and which police jurisdiction was conducting the arson investigation.

"I was hoping to get a look at your security video," I said. "To see if we can spot any unusual vehicles coming or going."

He looked at me and then at Danielle. For a moment I was wondering if he was going to ask for a warrant or subpoena, but all he said was "No problem."

Martin moved us all to another office, where he tapped on a keyboard and brought a monitor to life. It took him all of about three seconds to retrieve the security video.

"Now, the fire was called in at twelve twenty-four a.m.," he said, as if he had been a reporter on the scene, not the local conduit for gossip. "How far back do you want to go?"

"We saw some video of a car going down my street at about eleven fifty-five. So maybe shortly before that?"

"Done." Martin maneuvered like a professional, and before I had a chance to even confer with Danielle, he had pulled up the footage.

Unlike Mrs. W.'s doorbell video, which was made up of thirty-second snapshots triggered by the motion sensor, this was a continuous feed.

When Martin clicked his mouse, nothing seemed to happen. Like Mrs. W's video, his camera used a kind of UV light system to capture night video, but the front of the realty office was lit twenty-four hours a day. The patches of bright and dark seemed to confuse the camera somewhat, and the picture shifted from bright to dim and back again.

But it was clear enough to see a car pull into view from the direction of where Blue Heron Boulevard bridged Lake Worth Lagoon. It was me, cruising around town, looking for something that couldn't be found.

We watched as I drove north on Blue Heron then pulled a hard right erratically onto the side street that ran to the beach.

"Were you drinking last night?" asked Danielle.

"No," I said. "Just a last-minute decision."

I drove out of the picture and, no more than ten seconds later, another car appeared: a dark sedan with similar lines to the one I'd seen in Mrs. W.'s video. It drove through the shot, but instead of turning right toward the beach as I had, it continued northward, where, off camera, A1A became North Ocean Drive, in the general direction of the side street to my house. Martin rewound the shot a little and froze it, with the car filling the frame.

"It's a Town Car," said Martin.

"Can you read the license plate?" I asked.

He leaned in close as if that would provide a better view. "Yep, I think so." He opened the drawer in the desk and pulled out a notepad with his picture on the page. Then he scribbled down the license plate number and handed the entire pad to Danielle.

"Keep it," he said.

"What state is that plate?" I asked. It didn't look like the standard Florida plate, with the oranges on it, but then half the plates around town didn't look like that anymore. Now you could drive around with birds and panthers and even manatees on your license plate. But this one was plain, with some kind of tagline written on it the way states like to proclaim themselves the *Sunshine State* or the *Garden State* or *North Dakota*.

Martin leaned into the picture again. "It's small," he said, stating the obvious. "But it definitely doesn't say Sunshine State."

Danielle leaned in next to him then stood back. "I know what it says."

"What?" I asked.

"*Official Senate*."

I looked to the screen and then back at Danielle. "Official Senate? As in a Florida senator? This is an official government car?"

"No," she said. "Senators don't get official government cars. That's not a perk of a part-time legislature. But they do get a vehicle allowance and special dispensation to have official legislative plates during their term."

"So whose car is it?"

Danielle shot me a look.

"I don't know," she said with a frown. "But I can find out."

I asked Martin if he could print me a copy of that shot, and with two taps of his mouse he did just that. I then asked him if he saved his video for a while.

"I can look up any second of any minute of any day going back six months." He seemed rather proud of that capability.

We thanked Martin and walked back into the reception area.

"If you need any help finding contractors or anything to fix up your house, just let me know," he said.

I thanked him again and felt bad that he wasn't going to get any business from me. But I recalled from my other realtor friend, Penny, that realtors play the long game. A good deed might not be returned directly, but people talk, and it might be a friend of a friend of an acquaintance who brings a realtor their next deal.

We stepped out onto the street. The clouds had built up over the Bahamas and were now drifting across South Florida. It wasn't a picture-postcard day, the ones the tourist boosters loved so much. It was the kind of neither-here-nor-there day that made South Florida locals pull out their slow cookers, in the hope they might be able to eat a stew in what passed for cold weather in this part of the world.

We walked back around into the parking lot and stood in front of Danielle's car.

"What are you thinking?" she asked.

"How many Town Cars with Senate badges on them would be driving right behind me on the night my house burned down?"

"Not many."

"It's Vargas, I know it. Maybe him and Trainor together, or maybe just him. He set our house on fire."

"Don't go saying that around town," said Danielle.

"Don't do a Ronzoni on me," I said. "You know it's him."

"I don't think that a state senator is driving around setting people's houses on fire, MJ."

"Well, if not him, then someone working for him. That's his car, for crying out loud. Think about it. His car, and the ability to mobilize fast. The ability to track me to my house."

"But you don't live there anymore."

"I know that, and you know that. But how would they look me up? DMV or utility records? I haven't bothered to change my driver's license, and the bills are still in my name, even though they're getting mailed to Penny. She advertised the place as an executive rental, utilities and gardener included. So if they looked up any of those records, they'd find me on Singer Island. And the senator made a remark at the hockey game about me being from Singer Island. It all adds up."

We slipped into the car and Danielle got on the phone. She called in the plate number from Martin's notepad and asked someone in her office for ownership details. She listened to a response, making notes on the pad, then thanked them and hung up.

"The car belongs to a law firm," she said.

"What law firm?"

"Doherty Banks Vargas LLC."

I didn't say anything. I just held out my hands as if to say, *See?*

Danielle said nothing. She just started the car, pulled out of the lot, and headed back across to the mainland.

"What now?" I asked.

"You need to pass this information on to Riviera Beach PD."

"What are you going to do?"

"I have to go to Miami. I need to get back to work."

"Are you going to look into this?"

"I'll raise it with my boss, yes. But this is Riviera Beach's case."

"Surely crimes perpetrated by a member of the legislature fall under the authority of the FDLE?"

"Surely they do," said Danielle. "But we don't have any confirmation of that yet. We need more."

"We've got them on video. What more do we need?"

"We've got a car driving along the road, in the general vicinity, but not committing a crime per se."

"*Per se?* We've got two videos, one placing the car on our damn street."

"I know you're frustrated," she said. "Believe me, so am I. But when you're dealing with people this connected, you have to tread gently."

"Why, because it's *career suicide*?"

"No. Because they have good lawyers. Hell, they *are* good lawyers. One little mistake taints the entire investigation. These people know how to pull strings to get out of trouble. So just promise me that you won't do anything stupid."

I made a motion with my head that might have been seen by some people as some kind of nod. Not Danielle.

"I'm serious, MJ. Promise me."

"Okay," I said. "I'm not going to do anything stupid."

Danielle headed back to Ron and Cassandra's apartment to drop me off before making her way back to Miami. The whole way I just looked out the window at the traffic, telling myself that I wasn't going to do anything stupid.

Burning down my house was stupid. What I was going to do was rectify stupid.

CHAPTER FORTY-FIVE

DANIELLE LEFT ME AT RON AND CASSANDRA'S APARTMENT WITH A stern look. I sat on the deck overlooking the glossy, silvery ocean and used my phone to look up the law firm of Doherty Banks Vargas LLC. Not surprisingly, their office was in Palm Beach. It wasn't my fault that it was a short walk from the apartment.

I wandered over to Worth Avenue, past all the shops I couldn't afford and restaurants I couldn't digest, until I got to a small, stout building—new construction made to look like old construction, with smooth stone designed to mimic the sandstone of a European university.

I checked the tenant listing, which consisted of two brass plaques. It seemed that Doherty Banks Vargas occupied the upper two of three floors. I took the stairs to the top floor, as it was a universal truth that reception areas were down low and partners' offices were up high.

I came out of the stairwell into a small elevator lobby and found plain wooden doors on either side of the building, beside which were magnetic pads, where a key card might unlock the doors. There were no phones or means of contacting anyone within. I supposed that was what reception areas were for. I further supposed that lawyers sometimes undertook actions that upset people, whether they be clients or the people they defeated in court, and it was prudent that any Tom, Dick, or Harry couldn't just walk in off the street with a sawed-off shotgun under his greatcoat.

So I waited. I could see the small security cameras in the ceiling of the lobby, and I expected that, at some point, a strange man mulling around would attract someone's attention. But I only had to wait about two minutes. I heard the heavy locking mechanism clunk as someone pushed at the door, and I took two quick steps to meet them.

I pulled the door open and gestured for the woman to step out before I went in. She did that with a frown. I pushed my backside up against the door to prop it open and held up my hands as if they were wet.

"Out of paper in the men's room," I said with a wry smile.

The woman nodded, and I slipped inside. The heavy door slammed closed between us, and I found myself in another small reception area, not unlike that which I'd seen in the offices of Palm Beach Events. There was neither a receptionist nor a desk. I assumed the tiny space was used just to shake hands and say final farewells to clients before sending them on their way.

I took the emptiness as an invitation to go wandering. I walked through an open office space that looked like it had been decorated by the interior designer for the Library of Congress. It was very clubby, all polished rosewood and hundreds of leather-bound legal volumes. The insurance bill covering the books alone must have been astronomical, and I couldn't help wonder if all that information wasn't kept online these days, making the books nothing more than affectation. People sat in cubicles, heads down, poring over documents or computer screens, paying me no mind. There were offices along the front side of the building that overlooked Worth Avenue, and as I strode by I checked each one for a familiar face. I didn't find one there.

I found one in the conference room. The interior wall was floor-to-ceiling windows, perhaps the kind that could be electronically darkened so as not to ruin the look with vertical blinds. Dark leather chairs surrounded the boardroom table, which gleamed like a wooden yacht. The space could have comfortably held twenty people, but only four were in the room. And I was only interested in one of them.

I pushed my way into the boardroom and stood at the end of the long table, my eyes firmly on Brian Vargas. I wondered if in the hallowed halls of his law firm he was referred to as Senator, or Mr. Vargas, or just good old Brian.

Vargas caught my eye and gave me a look that was more exasperation than surprise. "What the hell—?"

"I don't care who you are, or who you think you are," I said. "But you can't burn down a man's house and expect to get away with it."

Vargas stood. "What on earth are you talking about?"

"You know exactly what I'm talking about."

Vargas turned to the man seated beside him. "Call the police." He stepped around the man, who was reaching for a phone in the middle of the table, and took two steps toward me. We were still eight seats apart.

"How did you get in here?"

"I walked in."

"You're trespassing."

"I didn't see a sign, and no one told me I couldn't. Besides, you want to talk about trespassing? Let's talk about who was on my property last night when my house got burned down."

"Listen, Jones. I don't know what you're bleating on about, and I really don't care. But enough is enough. You cannot continue harassing me, or my staff, or private citizens who are doing nothing but trying to make this town a better place to live. Do you understand me? You've lost the plot, and it has to stop. I will take out a court order against you if I have to."

I didn't get a chance to fire a witty retort. Two security guards burst into the boardroom and grabbed me by the arms, pulling my wrists behind my back as if they were going to cuff me. They simply turned me and marched me out of the room, back through the bland handshaking area, and out into the lobby.

One of them used a key card to call the elevator, but neither of them let me go. Not that I was planning to run. The only place I would have run to was out of the building, and that seemed our general destination anyway.

We went down the elevator in silence, then the two guys led me across the building to the front door. We came out so quickly I thought for a moment they might be planning on throwing me through the plate glass and onto the sidewalk like in a movie. The one with the key card used it again to swipe the door open and pushed me out.

Detective Ronzoni stood by his car on Worth Avenue. I got the sense it wasn't a coincidence that he was there.

The two guys marched me up to his city-issued Crown Victoria. Ronzoni opened the back passenger door and let them shove me inside. He slammed the door closed, and I heard him say that he'd take it from here.

The security guards turned without speaking and headed back toward the building.

Ronzoni got in behind the wheel then swiveled to face me in the back seat. "Didn't I tell you last night not to go off half-cocked? These are serious people with serious power, Jones. You can't go accusing them of stuff without proof."

"I have proof."

"Tell me what you think you have."

"I have video, from two sources. Both showing the same car coming onto Singer Island and then down my street right before the fire was called in. The video shows a Town Car registered to this law firm with plates belonging to a state senator."

"Do you see them light the fire in this video?"

"No. But it places him at the scene. Circumstantial evidence is a thing, you know?"

"You don't need to explain the law to me, Jones. But I clearly need to explain it to you. Video of a car driving along a public road is no evidence of anything. It might work against some poor soul dealing with the public defender, but it won't work with the kind of legal firepower these people have. It's no kind of proof, and it's no excuse for the scene you just caused."

I could feel my blood pressure about to blow the top of my head off. I got the sense that Ronzoni could see it too.

He put his palms out to me. "Just cool it, will you? What you have isn't enough. It isn't even close to enough. But I'm not telling you it's nothing. You need to take your evidence to the investigating officer. He's the one who will build the case."

"You heard him last night. He's not going to build a case. He's gonna whitewash the whole thing. *Career suicide*, remember?"

"It's career suicide if you get it wrong." Ronzoni turned back to the wheel and shook his head. Then he glanced back at me: "Stay put." A rhetorical statement.

He exited the car and engaged the locks. As soon as he disappeared inside the building, I punched the back of the seat in front of me. It was softer than a brick wall, but only just. I must have connected with the framework under the vinyl because it hurt like hell.

I rubbed my knuckles, the one place on my body that had yet to be bruised. But the pain took the sting out of my rage. I started to think about what Danielle was going to say, and how she surely wouldn't agree about the level of stupidity of what I had done.

It was a good fifteen minutes before Ronzoni reappeared. He strode around the front of his car and got in. As before, he half turned to me in the rear.

"Okay, I've spoken with the senator. He says he's not going to press any charges, not right now. If I take you directly off the island and he never sees you again, he'll let the whole thing slide."

I went to say something about letting his act of arson slide, but Ronzoni didn't let me.

"Shut it," he said. "Do you know what a trespass charge and a court order against you would do for your little PI business? You need to cool your jets, Jones. Understand that you've gotten off lightly."

"So you gonna drive me to the county limits and kick me to the curb? What is this, a western?"

"This is how things are done. And the sooner you understand that, the better for you. These people can squash you like a bug. And you keep running out into the middle of the kitchen floor just looking for a shoe."

I was impressed by Ronzoni's turn of phrase. Glib repartee was not his strong suit.

"So you're gonna let him fob you off. Are you forgetting about the video? His car?"

"The senator has an alibi. He went home after the hockey game, and his wife can vouch for him."

"I'm sure she can. And you buy that?"

"Doesn't matter what I can buy or what I can't buy. It matters what I can prove. And so far, he has an alibi and you don't."

"How does he explain his car being on Singer Island?"

"He admits to sending a car to follow you from the arena last night."

"He admits it? Seriously?"

"Oh, he's very serious. He said that you accosted him in front of dozens of people and that he was fearful for not only his own safety, but for the safety of his constituents. The word he used was *deranged*. He had his driver tail you to make sure you didn't try to follow him home."

"I didn't go anywhere near his home."

"That's what he said. He said his driver followed you to Singer Island, and they lost sight of you as they crossed the bridge, but they did a drive-by and saw the vehicle at your house, so they returned home."

"And you believe that?"

"Like I told you, it only matters what I can prove. And so far, all the proof is on his side. It's his story that stacks up, not yours. So we need more."

"What do you mean *we*?"

"I need to remove you from the island, so that's what I'm going to do. I'm taking you to the Riviera PD. You're going to give them everything you've got."

CHAPTER FORTY-SIX

I told Ronzoni that my car was parked at Ron and Cassandra's apartment nearby, so he drove me around the corner and sat outside until I emerged from the underground parking lot. Like the marshal who rides the bad guy out of town, he followed me all the way off the island. I thought he might stop at the bridge and watch me drive off into the sunset, but instead he stayed right on my tail all the way to the Riviera Beach Police Department.

We stopped at the front desk of the station house. Ronzoni flashed his badge and said he was there to see Detective Brookes. I had no doubt this was going to expedite things. Cops didn't tend to make other cops wait unnecessarily. It was a fraternity kind of thing. I, on the other hand, might have wilted like a Twinkie in the sun waiting for Brookes to see me.

Brookes appeared, waved us through, and led us into a small meeting room with a round table and utilitarian plastic chairs.

I told Brookes about the two videos showing the senator's car in the vicinity of my house shortly before it burned to the ground. As soon as I uttered the word *senator*, Brookes groaned, and the further I got into my story, the further his eyes rolled back in his head. When I finished, I glanced at Ronzoni and waited for Brookes to follow up.

"Do you have homeowner's insurance?" he asked.

"Yes. Why?"

"Because I suggest you take the hint. A car doing a drive-by is not enough, as I'm sure detective Ronzoni here has told you. And the senator's explanation is not only completely plausible, it's totally understandable. You can't go around poking the bear, Jones. Eventually you'll get the horns."

I was going to question his mixed metaphors, but he didn't look in any kind of mood for an English lesson.

"So why don't you do everybody a favor and take your insurance money and go build your new McMansion, and I'll forget all about pursuing you for insurance fraud," said Brookes.

"Insurance fraud? Are you insane? Why would I burn down my own house only to use the insurance money to rebuild the same house? What's the upside?" It felt like the hockey arena all over again. People seemed awfully worried about claiming insurance on things that were a zero-sum game.

"Sure, Jones. You're going to build the same old dump you had before, not a brand-new two-story waterfront mansion. Why don't you go tell your tale to someone more gullible. You're gonna make out like a bandit in this deal. Look, do yourself a favor and read the writing on the wall. I can prove it was arson. This place burned from the outside in, using a gasoline accelerant. Right around the house, the car too. It was a thorough job, and it took more than the three minutes between your videos of the senator's car to set up. So don't make me follow this up, because none of it looks good for you."

I couldn't believe what I was hearing, and it wasn't just the clichés. Not only was I supposed to have burned down my own house just to rebuild it, but now I was supposed to live in one of the unsightly faux Tuscan monstrosities that dotted the Florida coastline. But I could see that Detective Brookes had already moved into covering-his-backside mode. He wasn't interested in the fact that I liked the house as it was. But there was one thing he couldn't skirt. One fact he couldn't conveniently dismiss.

"What about the guy in the house? You gonna sweep his body under the carpet too?"

"You're one lucky son of a gun," he said. "There was nobody in the house. If there was, right now I'd be charging you with homicide. But it looks like all your Christmases have come at once. We did the final sweep and found nobody in the rubble. So I made a few calls. I just spoke to the man an hour ago, at work, in Pittsburgh. Oh, by the way, your tenant says he's not paying rent this month. And you can consider your rental agreement terminated. He said he'd send you the bill for the clothes and the bottle of scotch he had there."

"What about the car in the driveway?"

"It's a lease. He gets a cab to the airport because it's cheaper than parking for a week or two at a time."

"So nobody died?"

"You got it, pal. You're all caught up. So listen to what I'm telling you. I don't need the aggravation of getting into the business of a state senator, and I don't have to work a case to prove insurance fraud against you if you don't make me. You know what they say: no autopsy, no foul."

After that I had nothing more to say, and Brookes had nothing more he wanted to hear, so I left without speaking another word. I assumed that Ronzoni took care of the pleasantries, because he took a good minute longer to appear out on the steps of the station house.

"All's well that ends well," he said.

I frowned at him, wondering if there was some kind of quote-a-day calendar that sat on the desk of every cop in the state.

Ronzoni told me to take the win and keep my head down for a while. Then he left.

I went and sat in my car but didn't start it. Something about what Detective Brookes had said was gnawing at me. No witnesses had come forward, beyond the one who called in the fire. And the fact was, in a sleepy part of town like where my house used to be, someone slowly cruising around in a Town Car would have been strange. The detective was right. It wasn't someone driving by with a Molotov cocktail. The Town Car had followed me, then, having lost me, continued into my neighborhood. But Mrs. W.'s video showed that the car had promptly left, in and out within minutes. Detective Brookes had suggested that the professional nature of the arson would have taken a little longer to set up. Certainly whoever did it wouldn't have brought out picnic tables and had a tailgate, but the more I thought about it, the less the time frame fit.

I started to wonder if there was some truth to Senator Vargas's statement that he had sent his driver out of an abundance of caution to simply follow me. I was sure that elected officials dealt with their fair share of angry constituents, but I wasn't sure if that hardened them or made them more cautious.

Either way, it was starting to feel less likely that they could have started such a comprehensive burn so quickly. But the fact remained that someone had. And they had taken long enough to make sure that the fire department would not be able to put it out fast. They knew what they were doing. And they were able to do it hiding in plain sight, without any witnesses, dog walkers, or other insomniacs noticing anything unusual.

I started my car, pulled out of the lot, and headed back to Blue Heron Boulevard. Because someone might be good enough to hide in plain sight, and they might be smart enough to set a fire to thoroughly burn a house, and they might have been lucky enough to operate in a quiet suburban town in the dead of night. Regardless, one fact remained inescapable: in order to do it all, they had to get there first.

CHAPTER FORTY-SEVEN

I parked in front of Mrs. W.'s once again and avoided looking down the street at the burned-out shell. I just didn't want to see it. It was already occupying way too much space in my brain.

I rang the doorbell and smiled at the video camera and waited an eternity for the old lady to unlock the front door.

Two visits in one day was almost too much for her—I thought she might go into cardiac arrest from all the excitement. But she was a hardy old bird, and she invited me in, explaining she was just about to prepare a late lunch. I had things to do elsewhere, but I took Danielle's words on board and allowed Mrs. W to enjoy the visit. Perhaps there would be a day in the future when I didn't have so many people around me, when I would crave human interaction instead of finding it so wearisome.

This time we stayed in the kitchen. I sat at her small Formica table as she made yet more coffee and prepared some sandwiches: pickle and ham on Wonder Bread, one side with mayonnaise and the other with Dijon mustard. I wouldn't have come up with that combination if I had only those five ingredients in front of me and a month of Sundays, but it was surprisingly tasty.

After we had enjoyed our sandwiches and had a bellyful of

caffeine, I asked Mrs. W. if I could take a second look at the videos on her computer.

"Help yourself, dear. I'll just take care of the washing up."

I waited for the old computer to start up again then found the list of videos triggered by the motion sensor. I could see a bunch more had been triggered since my last visit, probably cops and rubberneckers and someone from the local paper checking out what remained of my house. Videos I viewed earlier were now grayed out. I didn't look for anything earlier; I was fairly confident that if the senator's driver wasn't the bad guy, then he would have called in a fire had he seen one. Instead, I moved down the list looking for any videos closer to the time the fire was reported. I found one listed at 12:04 a.m., while I had been asleep on the beach. One that I hadn't bothered to open previously, once I had seen the senator's car in the neighborhood.

I clicked on it.

In the grainy black and white of the night vision, I saw a flash of white. Then nothing. I rewound the video and played it again, hitting Pause almost instantly.

What I saw was a truck. It was blurry, but I could make out that it was a worker's pickup, the kind a utility company technician might drive. I had no way of seeing who was inside, but a candidate came to mind.

It got me thinking. The cops had canvassed the area. No one saw anything. Not even the dog walker who had called 911. What kind of vehicle doesn't belong but is rarely paid any attention? A utility company vehicle—gas, phone, electric. They could park anywhere at any time and hide in plain sight.

I checked the list of videos to see if there was a shot of the repair truck leaving the scene. There wasn't. Clearly, the utility vehicle had left by driving the loop around past my house and to the north, then out to North Ocean Drive via one of the other streets that led in and out of my subdivision.

I leaned back and looked at the frozen image one more time. The white of the truck contrasted with the darkness around it, causing the picture to flare. While it was the kind of truck that Neil Yeow drove for a living, it was impossible to see the serial number on the side, or even the FPL logo. I had to believe that Detective Brookes and his team had been fairly thorough in their canvas of the area. He wasn't eager to investigate an elected official, and at that point he had to be thinking I was suspect number one and that I was blowing smoke at him about the senator. If his canvas had revealed no witnesses, then I was unlikely to find anyone who could tell me more about the truck.

Except that one of Danielle's lines was stuck in my head. When describing the police canvassing the area, she said that when the police had asked if anyone had seen anything, they would have asked about video footage, especially where they saw surveillance cameras.

But I knew there were two kinds of surveillance cameras. Those that were made obvious as a deterrent—like Mrs. W.'s—and those that you didn't know were there at all, and owners might not even admit having, like the one right next door to my house.

CHAPTER FORTY-EIGHT

I had the jitters from all the caffeine by the time I left Mrs. W's. I left the car parked where it was and walked down the street toward the intracoastal. Instead of dead-ending at the water, the road turned to the right and ran north with one block of houses on the waterfront side for those lucky few with million-dollar ocean views.

I had been one of those lucky few, although my view was worth more than my house. I had been fortunate to pick it up for a song as a fixer-upper during a downturn in the market thanks to Sal's connections and financial help. It was one of the many reasons I hadn't hesitated to help Keisha, my new hairdressing protégé. Most of the role models I had in my life had shared one common trait, something that they rarely discussed but always did.

Pay it forward.

Some of them had done it for me, some of them had done it for others in my presence, and some in my stead. I never really thought about it too hard, but it seemed like the tattoos that were imprinted boldest on our souls were the ones not inked with pressure but with consistency.

I was buzzing like an out-of-tune AM radio as I walked down the street. I couldn't have ingested more caffeine if I had mainlined it. As I reached the point where the street turned a hard right, I stopped and took my first look at the rubble in the cold light of day. Most of the basic framework was actually still standing, but great portions of the roof were gone, and the little I could see inside remained a black hole, devoid of life or memory.

I shifted my view from the burned ranch house to the double-story monstrosity next door. It was one of those new-build McMansions that people felt the need to erect with absolutely no consideration for the environment around them, in as ostentatious a style as was humanly possible. To me it just looked like a great big Greek wedding cake. I had nothing against Greek wedding cakes per se. I just didn't really want to live with one that overlooked my backyard.

I stopped outside the tall gray concrete wall that surrounded the mini compound. There was an intercom box built into a niche in the wall and a heavy steel gate painted to look like wood.

I had no doubt the cops had canvassed the houses on either side of the fire, and I was equally confident that both sides had seen nothing. That was the nature of mini compounds taking over what were once ranch-style single-family homes. People tended to lock themselves up and not engage with the outside world, except to collect their internet purchases from the UPS guy or the evening meal from a local restaurant delivery driver.

The police might have asked about video surveillance, but a decent study of the property beside mine would have shown no cameras anywhere, at least not the kind used as a deterrent.

I knew better. After a hurricane a few years before, my neighbor had attempted to buy my damaged property from me. The floodwaters had surged in from the intracoastal and settled in my sunken living room, destroying the flooring as well as the kitchen. My neighbor had offered me cash for the entire place with the intention of knocking the house down and building a luxurious pool for his trophy wife. When I had declined the offer—to my neighbor's considerable chagrin—he had gone and built a pool at the back of their own place, one that I suspected was much smaller than the wife had been hoping for. But she had used it plenty, or at least used the paved patio around the pool, for her regular sunbathing sessions.

It seemed the husband had grown concerned about his wife's safety, because under the guise of the pool construction, he had also brought in a company to install a state-of-the-art security system. It had looked like a pretty comprehensive job from the number of materials that went in and never made it out to the pool. Perhaps a panic room and motion sensors, the kind that didn't pick up every piece of passing traffic.

I didn't know for sure about what they had installed inside. But I did know about the cameras.

They were extremely discreet—invisible, really—having been integrated into the statuary of cherubs that guarded the front of the house. I had watched from the refurbishment of my own house as the team inserted tiny cameras inside the little concrete angels. Once I realized they were trying to hide the cameras, I just couldn't stop watching. It was an occupational hazard.

I had wondered at the time why they would bother to hide security cameras. Surely half the point of the cameras was for thieves to know that they were there, to act as a deterrent. I knew some gas stations and convenience stores didn't even hook the things up, not back in the old days, when video surveillance systems were expensive. Just having the dummy cameras did half the work. So why hide them?

The answer had been revealed to me months after all the construction workers had packed up and gone on their way. I started noticing people—sometimes individuals, sometimes groups of no more than three—arrive at the front gate and announce themselves using the intercom. But it seemed there was a design flaw: the angle of the cameras inside the cherubs under the eaves of the house were too low to see someone right up against the front fence, so all the visitors did the same robotic tango, taking three or four steps back and looking up to the sky, as if trying to spot Superman or Halley's comet. And the time it often took for the gate to open suggested their identification was being checked before they were granted entry.

The place was clearly not the beating heart of a Mexican drug cartel, or an international arms dealer's book club, but the owner sure as hell wasn't filling out all the appropriate paperwork with the IRS either. And that suggested if the cops had bothered to ask about the presence of video surveillance, they would have been given a resounding no.

With Danielle away in Miami, I had spent more time than necessary watching the strange comings and goings, the little robotic tango, and the brief visits at all hours of the day. Then I grew bored of it and forgot all about the invisible cameras in the all-seeing, all-knowing cherubs. Until I realized that a cherub that could see someone standing four paces back from the fence could also see anybody headed down the street in the general direction of my house.

I rang the intercom on the gate. From there I couldn't see any of the cherubs, but I knew the process was to wait until told to step back.

"Yes?" said a woman's voice.

"Hi," I said. "I'm Miami Jones, your next-door neighbor."

"My husband is not home," she said.

"Actually, it's you I need to talk to. Did you see my house? It burned down."

"My husband will be home tonight."

"Unfortunately, I won't be here since my house, you know, burned down. But the police want to interview all the neighbors again, and I thought it might be best if I had a quick chat with you myself. You know, leave the cops out of it."

I wasn't sure if I had overplayed my hand, if mentioning keeping the cops out was a little heavy-handed, given there was no implication that they had done anything wrong. At least not as far as my house was concerned. But in my experience, people with sneaky surveillance systems didn't like cops nosing around. My hunch was rewarded when the gate shuddered and slid partially open as if by magic.

The front yard was a thicket of palm trees and succulents, with a concrete path to the front door. I was about to knock when it suddenly opened, revealing my neighbor standing before me in a pink bikini. A discerning person would suggest that she wore it well, such as it was. I'd seen bigger napkins at a barbecue joint. She looked considerably younger than her husband, and though it seemed she'd been around the block a time or two, the distance had not done her skin any harm.

"What is it you wanted to ask?" she said, forgoing the neighborly niceties.

"The police said from their initial questioning that you didn't see anything, the night of the fire?"

She shook her head, and her brown hair fell across her shoulder. "No, I didn't see anything. I take sleeping pills."

"Of course," I said. "But I'm not so much interested in what you saw as what was seen by your surveillance system."

"We don't have a surveillance system," she said, flicking her hair again. "Just the usual alarms on the windows and doors."

I could see it was a well-practiced line, delivered with the kind of confidence you only derived from wearing a bikini so well.

"Look, I don't want to get into your business, or your husband's business, for that matter. But my house burned down, and someone did that. It was no accident. And I promise I won't tell a soul where I got the information, but I really need to see that video. And before you say anything, let me tell you that I know you have a surveillance system. I watched them install it."

She tilted her head and looked at me, not up and down the way people often do, but straight in the eyes. I didn't look her up and down, either, fighting every impulse to do so. I couldn't tell from her expression whether she was likely to invite me in or release the hounds, so I nudged her along by simply saying, "Cherubs."

She was obviously caught in her lie, but it didn't seem to faze her at all. She shrugged and held the door open. As I stepped across the threshold, it was then that I noticed she was wearing stilettos. It's always a little dent to the pride when a private investigator fails to notice something so obvious, but bikinis have a way of diverting the eye from someone's feet.

We walked into a large open-plan living area, leather sofas surrounding a flat-screen TV that took up the vast majority of the wall. There was a kitchen overlooking both the living room and the back patio. A lot of marble had died for that kitchen.

She offered me coffee, and, despite having a gallon of it pulsing through my veins, I accepted. I watched her use an espresso machine like a professional as she made me a double shot in a small glass that tasted like tar and heaven.

As she made herself an espresso, I glanced through the floor-to-ceiling glass across the paved patio and the sparkling pool toward the intracoastal beyond. The window had a tint to it that suggested it was one-way glass.

She noticed me looking at the pool. "It would've been bigger if you had sold your place to us."

"Sorry," I said. "I like the view."

"Me too. You want to sell now?"

"No," I said.

She shrugged her petite shoulders again and led me toward the sofas. I sat in one and she in the other. Mine seemed to grab hold of my buttocks and suck me down like it was quicksand, while she floated on hers like sunshine on a puffy cloud. She swung one long leg over the other, and I recoiled slightly as a stiletto went flashing past my face.

"Well, at least you can build something nice now, rather than that shack you used to live in."

I sipped my coffee.

Then she must have realized something because her face

dropped. "You won't build so tall that your windows will look into my yard? I like my privacy."

I wondered whether that meant she sunbathed naked, but I decided that the difference between naked and what she was wearing now was so immaterial as to be irrelevant.

"No," I said. "I won't intrude on your privacy."

Her mouth smiled but her eyes didn't look convinced. She watched me for longer than was necessary then uncrossed her legs in a fashion that reminded me of the Radio City Rockettes. Leaning forward, she picked up an iPad off the table and tapped the screen with a fingernail so long I feared for the structural integrity of the glass. She stood up, towering above me, all stilettos and long limbs and airline-sized napkins. Then she swiveled and dropped down on the sofa right next to me.

Right next to me. I had seen wrestling matches where the guys didn't get so close. I wasn't sure if she was trying to put me off my game, but I knew two things she didn't. One, I was a professional, whatever the hell that meant. It probably wasn't going to save me. But two, my wife carried a gun for a living.

She showed me her screen divided into sixteen squares, each displaying a different view of the property. I hadn't realized they had so many cherubs.

She tapped the screen again to open up a live view of the front gate and the street beyond. I could see the swaying trees in the yards of houses that lined the street out toward Blue Heron Boulevard.

She then tapped a few more times and brought up the same picture, but this time it was night, only discernible from a slight glow in the windows of the houses. Otherwise the picture was crystal clear. This was a whole other beast from Mrs. W.'s doorbell camera.

I gave her the time I was looking for, and she used some controls at the bottom of the screen to drag the picture back in time. Eventually she stopped, and we watched the empty street for a moment, until I saw a dark Town Car drive directly down the road toward the camera. The headlights flared in the shot for a moment, but the camera adjusted almost instantly. The Town Car slowed as it reached the turn, then it took the right-hand bend and drove out of frame on the left-hand side. About a minute later, the same car came back into view from stage left, turned away from the camera, and drove slowly back out toward Blue Heron Boulevard. This much I already knew.

We sat, crushed together, watching like teenagers engaged in a horror flick waiting for the guy with the chainsaw to leap out into the shot.

Another set of headlights approached from the dark end of the street and came to a stop about three or four houses short of the bend in the road. Again the headlights flared in the picture, making it difficult to see the vehicle. The headlights were turned off, and in the blink of an eye the picture cleared, and I saw the front of a large white pickup.

It eased to the curb and parked behind an old Saab. For a moment nothing happened. Then simultaneously the doors on either side of the truck opened, and two guys got out. They walked directly toward the cherub, one down the middle of the road, the other along the sidewalk. The one on the road was difficult to make out, but the large round-shouldered guy on the sidewalk was carrying something. A tool case or maybe a duffel bag.

The two guys walked across the picture, the one on the road disappearing off the left side of the screen, the one on the sidewalk dropping behind my neighbor's front fence. They were out of shot for about ten minutes or so, but we didn't fast-forward. I sat mesmerized by the view of the empty street and the scent of honey and lavender.

Then, eleven minutes after they had gone, they reappeared—as before, one on the road and the other on the sidewalk. I thought I recognized the lazy gait and rounded shoulders of the big guy, but I couldn't be sure. What I became sure of was what he was carrying: a gasoline tank, the kind of thing boaters used to power their outboard engines. They walked away from the camera, and the one on the road slipped back into the truck. The big guy walked past the truck to the rear, I assumed to put away the gas tank. Then he too got in.

But they didn't leave. For several minutes they just sat there. I wondered what the hell they were up to. I had never burned anyone's property down, but I imagined that if I did, I'd want to get out of Dodge as quickly as possible. But these guys wanted to see the fruits of their labor. Or maybe they were under orders to make sure the fire took hold. It seemed like a dangerous ploy, a great way to get caught.

After a couple of minutes, the video showed an old guy walking along the sidewalk toward the camera with a small dog on a lead. The man had a slightly stooped posture that gave away his age, and the dog was dragged along in a fashion that suggested it was no spring chicken either.

The man and his dog walked right by the white truck.

He walked the length of one house and stopped to either catch his breath or let the dog rest, then continued on, house by house. He was about to disappear behind the neighbor's large fence when he came to another stop. This time he didn't continue. He stood right below the cherub, exactly where the robotic tango people ended up, as if having his ID verified. But he wasn't looking up at the cherub. He was staring at something offscreen to his right.

Then I saw the dim glow in his face. The glow of my house burning.

He watched it for a while, obviously trying to process what he was seeing and what he should do about it. Fires can be mesmerizing, but eventually the old man turned and retraced his steps along the sidewalk, the rhythm in his shoulders suggesting he was trying to move faster. With no discernible change in speed, he reached the white truck and paused for a second. I wondered for a moment if he had indeed seen something, but he bent down the opposite way to pick up his little dog then shuffled back toward his house and out of shot.

Once the man was gone, the truck pulled away and headed

toward the camera. As they began the turn to head out, I made to tap the screen to pause it but landed instead on my neighbor's hand. Clearly she had the same idea. We sat with her hand on the glass screen, my hand on hers. She didn't make any move to pull her hand away, but after an uncomfortable second or two I did.

When she removed her hand, I saw a side-on shot of the white truck, clear as day. I could see the large guy in the passenger seat. I didn't just know the gait and the rounded shoulders; I knew the face. He was one of the thugs from the bar, the leader of the two, the one I had seen again at the hockey game in the company of Otto Barassi.

I couldn't tell who the driver was, but I could see a canopy on the back emblazoned with the Florida Power & Light logo along with *14646* on the side panel of the truck—the same serial number from the video of the power substation.

Neil Yeow's truck.

Now I had Neil at two crime scenes, and the balding thug at his own two. I wondered if pointing the finger at a couple of blue-collar types would be more palatable to Detective Brookes.

"Have you seen everything you want to see?" asked my neighbor.

I took a little longer to answer than I probably should have. "Yes, thank you."

I stood and brushed imaginary fluff off my shirt. "I should get going. Thanks for your help. I appreciate it."

She leaned back in her sofa and smiled. "Sure. You can show yourself out."

I edged sideways around the coffee table and strode to the front door. I stepped out into the junglelike yard and made my way to the front gate. I got right up to it before I realized that it was closed and I had no way through, so I turned back toward the house.

The woman was standing in the doorway, still in her bikini and stilettos, leaning up against the jamb. She didn't seem to move any, but the gate gave a little shudder and slid open enough for me to leave. I retreated backward, not taking my eyes off the woman until I reached the sidewalk, and the gate slid back into place.

Just as I lost her from view, I realized I didn't even know her name. Not introducing yourself to your neighbors is just bad manners. But the gate locked home with a jolt, and I decided the pleasantries would have to wait for another day.

CHAPTER FORTY-NINE

I didn't take the evidence to Detective Brookes. For reasons I couldn't quite understand, I felt the need to run it past Detective Ronzoni first. It occurred to me that I wanted his professional opinion, but that notion was so disturbing that I pushed it from my mind.

We met in the detectives' room at the Palm Beach PD building. Ronzoni had tall stacks of manila folders filled with paperwork on his desk, like a miniature forest. I had to peer around the columns of papers just to talk to him.

I told him about the new evidence and how I could place Neil Yeow and the union thug at my house at the time of the fire. I didn't tell him where I had seen it, and he didn't ask.

"So take it to Detective Brookes," he said.

"I don't want him to jump to a convenient conclusion," I said.

"What convenient conclusion would that be?"

"That these FPL guys were doing this off their own backs. I know they're getting their direction from higher up. And I know the senator's car might have had a salable explanation for being there, but that doesn't mean that Vargas or Trainor or both of them aren't the masterminds behind this whole thing."

"Did you just use the word 'masterminds?'" said Ronzoni.

"Whatever. You can't possibly believe that these guys committed arson without direction from above."

"You have annoyed a lot of people, Jones, but, no, I suspect their annoyance doesn't translate into arson. Obviously there's something bigger at play. And I can assure you that since the senator and Trainor both live and work on my patch, I'm the one who'll take the heat. But senator or no, they're not above the law. We have a duty. Because in this country, no one is above the law."

I waited for a moment for the swelling violins to kick in behind Ronzoni's speech, but he was too earnest a guy to not mean what he was saying.

"The problem is, if we're going to get anything on the guys at the top, we have to get the guys at the bottom to roll over. And in my experience, that's easier said than done."

"This is pretty compelling evidence. Enough for jail time, I would've thought," I said. "But is it enough to make these guys roll over? I don't know. Let's say Brookes goes after these two. They're pretty connected with the union, or at least the little faction controlled by Otto Barassi. So there's every chance they get a decent lawyer, and he'll argue it's circumstantial and that the video is unclear or whatever. And Brookes's motivation for charging these guys would only be to get at Vargas or Trainor, and he's made it pretty clear he doesn't want to do that."

"Of course not," said Ronzoni. "The fact still remains that you can't go after those kinds of people without rock-solid evidence."

"Like the minions rolling over on them."

"Possibly. But unless you can find something more, a good lawyer will get them off, or at least muddy the waters enough to get the state attorney to water down the charges. They might end up with community service, if that."

I thought for a moment about the state attorney. Not the one who would prosecute. The one who was half out the door.

"So how do you get guys this corrupt, this high up?" I asked.

"As a rule, you don't," said Ronzoni with a shrug that said he didn't love the idea but it was what it was. "But when you do, you basically gotta catch them with their hand in the cookie jar."

It was disturbing when Ronzoni made me think. "That's it," I said.

"What's it?"

"We need to catch them with their hands in the cookie jar."

"Meaning?"

"It's like Chris explained to me at hockey: you gotta watch the movements, the body language, in order to know where the puck's going. There are a thousand options, but the way the player moves in response to the defense cuts the thousand down to ten, then three, then one."

"What the hell you talking about, Jones?"

"We need to corral Vargas and Trainor into a corner so they have only one play. And we need to be ready when they call it."

"One play? Like what? Cutting the power?"

"That's the obvious play, given everything, but it's not so much about what as when. There's a Hail Mary out there they haven't used. I thought it might be in play last night at the game, but I upset the apple cart by involving the mayor, so with him and half the city there, it became too high profile, too high risk. But there's another game in a couple of nights, I think. And the Hail Mary is still in play."

"What Hail Mary?"

"Shutting down an actual game," I said. "As in midgame, midplay. Crowd and all. Kill the whole damn thing. A little bit of panic would be great press. I mean, terrible press, but that's what Trainor wants. It gets a very obvious strike against arena management. It might be enough to enact the ownership clause. And it would be easier to pull off without all the added security and eyeballs that the mayor's entourage brought yesterday."

"They could call in a bomb threat," said Ronzoni.

"Possibly, but they can't control the reaction to that. Maybe whoever gets the call overreacts, but maybe they underreact. And there's a legal gray area as to whether that would be considered the arena's fault, as far as meeting KPIs is concerned. Maybe that's kind of like an act-of-God type of thing. Not the arena's fault. Whatever happens, it has to be the arena's fault. Trying something like this is a big risk, a onetime play. Trainor would have to be sure he was going to get the controlling interest. So it has to be something they can definitively blame on the arena, but something that they can manage."

"What can they manage?"

"They can manage the power systems. They've got all kinds of people in place for that already. Neil Yeow, Otto Barassi. Who knows who else?"

"That still leaves a thousand opportunities. They could disrupt that system almost anywhere. How do you whittle that down from a thousand to ten to three to one?"

"We cover all the bases except one. We offer them one last opportunity and no second chance."

I left Ronzoni after the standard warning about not going near or even whispering the names of important Palm Beach residents.

It was time to set up the play. As I drove back across the bridge into West Palm, I called Peter Parker and asked if he knew who the investor was behind Trainor's league financing.

"Yes, I do," said Parker. "He winters in Palm Beach. I think that's how John met him."

"The guy's in Palm Beach?"

"No, not right now. I think he's still in New York. He usually comes down in the new year, if I recall correctly."

"Can you get me five minutes with him?"

"On the phone?"

"No, it needs to be in person. I've really got to sell him on this."

"Sell him on what?"

"On something that will save your insurance policy and may well earn you some new business. Can you get me time tomorrow?"

"I'm not going to regret this, am I?"

"No, you're gonna stop this guy from losing sixty million dollars."

CHAPTER FIFTY

THE NEXT DAY I CAUGHT THE MIDMORNING FLIGHT FROM PALM BEACH International to Westchester, New York. Both airports were secondary commuter facilities, each conveniently close to the Palm Beach winter nests and the tri-state manor houses of the super-wealthy. They were both nicer to use than any of the big airports in those regions, and I wondered how much the local money at both ends was responsible for that.

I strode out of the airport into a gorgeous New York fall morning. There was a light frost on the ground and a chill in the air, which was only accentuated by the fact that I'd forgotten to bring any kind of jacket. I got more than my fair share of sideways glances from people wrapped up in coats and scarves as I made my way to the taxi line in a pair of chinos and a palm-tree print shirt. It wasn't the first time I had landed at Westchester in need of a jacket, and I resolved once more to remember to bring one with me should I ever land there again.

The ride out to where John Trainor's investor was based took us through the winding back roads of Greenwich, Connecticut. We drove through a tunnel of red and yellow leaves falling from the trees like glittering rain. Many of the estates north of Greenwich were so large that the houses weren't visible from the road, but the rolling green hills and the fall foliage made me miss the Northeast, for a moment at least.

The taxi dropped me at an uninspiring office complex called the Greenwich American Center. I stood in the lobby and checked the tenants' board. There was a feature film animation studio and a lot of companies with names that included words like *management* and *capital* and *partners*.

Trainor's investor was in a beige office on a beige floor, but his view looked out over a blanket of burnt gold and amber trees. I was offered coffee and a danish, and despite still coming down from my caffeine high of the previous day, I gleefully accepted both.

I was done with the danish and sipping my coffee when the receptionist led me to the investor's office. He wasn't quite what I had expected. This was no Gordon Gecko. He was tall and thin yet chubby in the face and bald with a ring of hair, as if somebody had stuck Danny DeVito's head on John Cleese's body. He wore round glasses on the end of a long nose and looked over the top of them as the receptionist quietly knocked on the open door and announced my presence.

He came to the door, and we shook hands.

"Miami Jones," I said.

"Goldblum," he replied as if he was one of those Brazilian soccer players who only had one name.

He pointed to a comfortable-looking chair beside his desk, and I sat.

"You have five minutes," he said. He didn't say it in a nasty kind of way; he just seemed like someone who blocked out his calendar with ruthless efficiency.

I told him about the concerns of the insurance company, and the sabotage of the arena, and how John Trainor was attempting to shift money around like he was playing three-card monte.

Goldblum listened then leaned back in his chair. "What do you have against John Trainor?"

"Personally, nothing," I said, despite questioning whether that was true. "He's going to call on a payout from my client, plus he's gonna take down a lot of county money if he fails, which he will if you look at the house-of-cards financing he's built."

"What does this have to do with me?" asked Goldblum.

"I hear that he's late on a loan payment to you."

Goldblum shrugged. "It happens. Look, I can tell by your sense of style here that you're not a money guy. That's cool. But let me tell you, creative financing is all part of the game. Moving money here and there, there's nothing unusual in any of this, not in private capital."

"Except that the league is broke, the team is trying to defraud the insurance company to stay alive, and the other owners are shifting all their assets out of their teams so they don't lose their shirts." I knew this last part wasn't completely true, but Javits had said he and the other owners could take steps to mitigate their losses. "And if the arena fails—and I believe it's part of John Trainor's plan to make sure it does—he'll gain majority control of the asset so he can borrow against it to pay you back."

"Okay. So what exactly is my problem here? If he gains the asset and pays me back, why do I care about any of this?"

"You care because it's not going to happen. He's not going to get control of the arena. He has to take down the county's finances to do it, and I'm not going to let that happen. So I'm here as a courtesy to you, to give you a chance to call in your debt before every other creditor in town gets in line and you end up with a dime on the dollar. I assume you can do that?"

Goldblum steepled his fingers against his chin. "I can call in the loan within forty-eight hours. He is well past due. But why are you helping me? What's in it for you?"

"Look, I can tell by your sense of style that you're not a people guy. So you won't get it, but I love where I live—the locals and the tourists and the fact that people from all four corners of the globe come to our part of the world to get away from it all. I love the beaches and the bars and the traffic snarls. It's my home. These are my people. And I and every other taxpayer in the Palm Beaches have sunk over three hundred million bucks into this thing, and if we lose it, we lose a lot more than money. We lose jobs, houses, neighbors. We lose faith, in our institutions and our leaders and each other. Plus, as it happens, I'm getting paid by the insurance company, so in a way, all I'm doing is my job."

Goldblum tapped his steepled fingers against his chin as he looked at me over the top of his little round glasses. For a long time he said nothing. I hoped this wasn't counting against my five minutes.

"So what do you think?" I said.

"What did Reagan say? Trust, but verify. I'll check out what you're saying."

"It'll stack up. And when it does?"

He dropped his hands and sat up. "I don't like losing money. And despite what you might think of me—and trust me when I say I really don't care what you think—I also spend part of the year in Palm Beach. I spend a lot of it in West Palm, or Delray, or Boynton, or Singer Island. I like it there. I also like the people. I like the fact that when I'm there I spend time with the kinds of people that I don't know here. I go deep-sea fishing with tradesmen and storeowners. If I have the choice, I'll take my money from John Trainor rather than the people of West Palm Beach. But in the end, I will take my money, from whoever has it."

"So when will all this verification happen?" I asked.

"You're flying back to PBI today?"

"I'm headed straight back there now. I'm not equipped for a long stay."

"I will know what I need to know, or not, before you're even in the air. If what you're saying is true, John Trainor's hourglass will run dry at midnight tomorrow night."

I called Peter Parker from the cab on my way back to Westchester County Airport to ask him if Con Gelphert had put any extra security in place at the arena. As far as he knew, and despite everything that had gone on, security hadn't been beefed up at all.

"Can you give him a call?" I said. "Tell him that I've solved the problem and everything looks good."

"Have you? Does it?"

"No. But John Trainor is going to lose his league financing sometime today, and when he does, the last option he'll have is to pull something at tomorrow night's game."

"I don't want him pulling anything," said Parker.

"No, what you don't want is him getting away with anything. Do you have it in you to pay for a few hours of extra security for the game?"

"How can I tell Gelphert it's all fine but he also needs extra security?"

"You're not. I'm going to supply the extra bodies."

"These are registered security people?"

"Better."

I got to the airport, checked in, and breezed through security in a way that people getting through La Guardia or JFK could only dream of. I had some time to kill, so I settled in at an airside bar and called Danielle. I asked her if she had any contacts at the Palm Beach County Sheriff's Office who might be interested in organizing a little after-hours work at double-time rates. She said she couldn't think of one who wouldn't and gave me a name.

"How is it up there?" she asked.

"It's autumn in the Northeast. It's beautiful."

"Does it make you want to move back?"

"Let me put it this way: the happiest people I've seen all day are sitting here at the airport, knowing they're about to hop a flight to South Florida."

I told her I'd see her soon, and she said she hoped so.

By the time I got on the plane, I'd had my fair share of winter, before any snow had even arrived. People squeezing into the tin can that was about to fly south were wearing boots, heavy coats, and gloves, and scarves and muffs and beanies. For once, I had all the right clothes on.

For the first time in days, I felt some semblance of relaxation. I hadn't really achieved that much, not yet, and there was every likelihood that my plans would go awry, so I didn't know if it was the couple of beers or the thin air at thirty thousand feet, or a combination of the two, but I kicked back in my seat and took a well-earned and well-needed nap.

By the time we landed in West Palm, the sun was all but gone. As we walked through the concourse, people around me started pulling off their heavy winter gear, shedding it like reptiles discarding their old skins. The sight of them doing that made me smile, and my smile seemed contagious. Or maybe it was the sixty-eight-degree temperature.

I drove straight from the airport to the sheriff's office on Gun Club Road and requested Sergeant Castañada. I asked him if he and five of his best might like to do a few hours of lazy work at the new arena the following night.

"Trouble?" he asked.

"More a deterrent," I said.

He told me he'd put a crew together, and we arranged to meet an hour before the game.

"Who do we bill?" he asked.

"Cash money," I said.

The sergeant gave me a big smile. Even law enforcement loved cash in hand.

I left the office and joined the slog south on I-95. My plans had been laid, my traps set. I figured if there weren't any more than the usual number of accidents on the freeway, I might make it home to Grove Isle for a nice dinner with my wife.

CHAPTER FIFTY-ONE

It seemed that the people of West Palm Beach weren't as enthusiastic about the next game at the arena as I was. I had spent a pleasant evening with Danielle, sitting on the patio overlooking the small marina at Grove Isle, tucked underneath a blanket as the cooler breeze gave us our only sense of the change in seasons.

Danielle had asked me about my plan but not with any enthusiasm. I suspected that she was worried about me, after getting beaten up and having our house burn down. But she also knew those events were more likely to drive me on than stop me, so she expressed her concern in a simple but perplexing statement.

"You're not as young as you used to be."

I returned to West Palm the following morning and spent the day in the office, making sure all my pieces were in place. That took maybe five minutes, so I spent the rest of the day like a bruised cat on a hot tin roof. I paced the office until I drove Ron to distraction, then I walked down to Flagler Drive for a walk near the marina.

By the time I arrived at the arena for that night's game, I might have been a nervous wreck except for one thing—I was now moving, doing things, making it happen. Action was always preferable to inaction; playing was preferable to sitting on the pine.

Peter Parker had provided me with staff entry passes, so I didn't need to check in with Devon, who wasn't on door duty anyway. I stood outside with a security guard called Remus, who wasn't interested in talking, smiling, or doing anything than scrolling on his phone.

When the team from the sheriff's office arrived, I decided I was in good hands. There were six—five men and one woman—wearing matching plain blue polos, khaki trousers, and khaki bomber jackets, under which I suspect they were each carrying some kind of firearm. They looked like the advance team for a private army.

I explained the nature of the issues at hand and how I needed protection for some of the more vulnerable areas. I then took them around the maintenance concourse and showed them the various machine rooms to which I wanted to restrict access. Next, the sergeant assigned posts to his team and positioned himself outside the room that housed the incoming electrical systems.

Devon came around the concourse from the opposite direction and headed over to him.

"Can I help you?" asked Devon.

"No," said the sergeant.

Devon paused. "Are you here for the game?" It was still a good hour until the first face-off, so there weren't too many reasons to be milling around in a nonpublic area.

"No," said the sergeant.

Devon frowned. He clearly wasn't sure where to go with his questions at that point, so I wandered over.

"Devon," I said.

"Mr. Jones."

"I was just on my way to see you. We've beefed up security."

"I wasn't informed," said Devon.

"No," I said. "We can't be sure who is responsible for the sabotage, so the county has provided this backup. This is still your show. We still need you in your public role, keeping the crowd safe. This is just to ensure you don't have to waste your time down here."

Devon eyed the sergeant. "Is he licensed? We can't have civilians running around down here."

The sergeant reached into his jacket and pulled out his sheriff's ID, which he held in front of Devon, so he couldn't see the officer's look of contempt.

"This is Sergeant Castañada, of the Palm Beach County Sheriff's Office," I said.

Devon looked at the ID, snapped to attention, and saluted him.

"At ease, kid," said Castañada.

"We need you to take care of things as per normal," I said to Devon. "And it might be best if you kept all this to yourself."

"Yes, sir, Mr. Jones."

"Good man."

"Do you think something might go down tonight?"

"I think we're on top of it, Devon. But keep your eyes open."

Devon marched away, and I offered the sergeant a nod.

As I walked toward the playing surface, my phone rang. "What's happening, Ron?"

"You've got me doing something I thought I'd never, ever do."

"What's that?"

"I'm sitting outside a bar watching some other guy drink a beer while I'm in my car with a Coke and a cuban sandwich."

"That's not the worst dinner."

"Not the best either. Your man, Neil Yeow, he's inside. He dropped his truck off at the depot about thirty minutes ago and went straight to the bar. Been here ever since."

"He sounds like a creature of habit, Ron, so keep a lookout. We've covered all the bases here. The substation is the only obvious target we've left open. He'll hit it soon enough, and you need to be watching when he does."

CHAPTER FIFTY-TWO

THE WEST PALM BEACH CHILL PLAYERS CAME OUT OF THEIR NEW locker room and followed the rubber trail out toward the ice. I stood aside and let them pass. It was the prudent thing to do. They were all big guys carrying hockey sticks and wearing more protective equipment than the knights of yore.

As the last of the players launched himself onto the ice, I walked out between the temporary stands where the front-end loader had entered only days before. The gap was now just wide enough for the Zamboni to come and go. It was parked to the side, ready to smooth the ice after the first period. Right behind the Zamboni was a golf cart, which I assumed belonged to Monaro, although I didn't see him anywhere.

I stepped out into the arena and looked around. I didn't care to toot my own horn, but it was clear that my conniving to get the mayor and his entourage to the last game, perhaps combined with the news of the game being canceled, had drawn a bigger crowd then. Tonight's crowd, however, was around half the size, with more open seats than occupied. If this was more representative of the audiences the team was getting, it helped to explain Trainor's financial predicament.

As the announcer shouted the names of the players, I strolled to the walkway halfway up the stands then out to the main entry gate.

Maggie Nettles stood outside, waiting for me. I gave her a pass on a lanyard and ushered her inside.

"Do you know anything about Trainor's league investor calling in his loan?" she asked.

"No," I said.

"Word is he's called in the full sixty million."

"High finance really isn't my area."

Maggie frowned. "If that's true, Trainor's toast."

"Unless he gets control of the arena."

"I'm not sure even that will save him now. He'd basically have to get control, like, tonight."

I shrugged, and Maggie gave me a look.

"Something's going to happen, isn't it?" she said.

"Not if I can help it."

"Jones, why do I feel like I'm being played?"

"We're all being played, in one way or another. But you should take comfort in the fact that if you are being played, you're not the pawn, you're the queen."

I walked Maggie to the elevator that accessed the corporate suites. I told her the pass around her neck would get her into any room she wanted and that all sorts of interesting people awaited. She gave me one last frown as if she didn't trust me, but she knew a gift horse when she saw one. Even a series of *no comments* was going to tell her something.

Maggie showed her pass to the attendant at the elevator, and I walked back out into the arena. The game had started, and ten men were zooming around the ice with the finesse of figure skaters and the power of rugby players. I strode up the steps to the very back, the nosebleed bleachers. Only a handful of hardy souls were up there, most having moved down the half-empty stands to get closer to the action.

I didn't watch the game. Without Chris, I couldn't follow the puck. I tried studying number eight's posture, but it changed like the wind, and I started to realize why fans loved seeing players get crashed against the boards and the fights that often ensued: they could see them happen. Otherwise it was like watching golf, admiring a good swing and just trusting the commentator to tell you that, yes, it had landed on the green.

My mind turned to John Trainor. If what Maggie said was true, then Goldblum had called in his loan, and I was confident that Maggie would get in Trainor's face about it, making sure he knew he was left with no options. No options but one.

I called Ron.

"Yeow left the bar," he said.

"I knew it."

"But he didn't go back to the depot to get his truck."

"He didn't? He went straight to the substation?"

"No. He went home. I'm sitting outside his house now."

"Home?"

"Yeah. So if he's going to pull something, he's a pretty cool customer about it."

I told Ron to keep on it, and I killed the call. It didn't make a lot of sense. Yeow was good for the substation job, so why wasn't he there? The game was nearing the end of the first period, so if he was going to shut things down, he was cutting it close.

I worried that I had it all wrong. Was Trainor not planning on pulling anything? Or were they just worried about doing the same trick twice? A good magician knows the secret to performing the same trick is to get you looking in a different direction. Perhaps I was looking at the wrong person or in the wrong place.

But I was reasonably sure that I had covered the other bases and left the substation option open, and I could place Yeow at the substation during the previous outage. I had seen the evidence of that sabotage in the form of a burned-out circuit board—Francisco Monaro had shown it to me.

I could link Yeow to the bar and to the thugs who beat me up, and I could connect one of those thugs to the arena suites and the union guy, Otto Barassi. I could then place that thug at my house when it was set on fire, along with Neil Yeow, which brought me full circle.

Except it didn't. Suddenly the pieces didn't all fit. There were gaps in the story. Some of the facts I had admitted into evidence in my head were nothing more than smoke and mirrors. I had made assumptions that were faulty at best and outright wrong at worst.

There was another player in the game. Someone I hadn't accounted for.

I called Danielle.

"You okay?" she asked.

"Fine. Stupid but fine."

"What have you done now?"

"I've fallen for the three-card monte. Listen, do you guys have a database of known associates of Otto Barassi?"

"The union guy? I'm sure we do."

"I need to find someone. Someone close to him, someone I haven't accounted for yet. All I have is a name. Maybe first name, maybe last, I don't know."

"MJ, I don't think it's appropriate to use law enforcement data for your private work."

"Then do it for the County of Palm Beach. Do it for all the people who are going to lose out when Trainor wins. And do it for me, so I nail the guys who burned down our house and beat me senseless."

There was silence for a long moment, then: "What's the name?"

I gave it to her, and she told me she would get back to me. I called Ron again and told him to go knock on Neil Yeow's house.

"You think he jumped the back fence or something?" asked Ron.

"Or something."

I told Ron what I needed to know then called Sergeant Castañada and asked him to meet me at the security office.

"You want to get some cover for this room first?" he asked.

"No, I'll meet you at the office in two."

I made my way down the steps all the way to the floor. The

buzzer sounded to end the first period, and I had to swim against the tide of people heading up toward the concession stands on the main concourse. I got to the boards around the ice and edged over to the space in the stands that led down to the maintenance concourse, where I flashed my badge at an usher and vaulted over the barrier.

The Zamboni was gone, but the golf cart was still there. I turned and saw the Zamboni chugging around the rink. As I strode into the bowels of the arena, my phone rang.

"You'll never believe what I heard," said Ron.

"Let me guess," I said. "Yeow says he never went to the substation. He says he was told by the union some story about guys hassling FPL workers and was given a number to call or text if he had any trouble. Then he was given tickets to the suite by the union for being such a team player."

"Well, that's pretty much it. He said on the day of the power outage, he wasn't even on the roster to work. So how did you know all that?"

"My brain started working again, just way too late. What about the truck?"

"Yeah, he said it was his regular ride, but there was nothing really stopping someone else from using it. And there's a log of who takes what truck and when, but there's no guarantee it gets filled out."

The mention of a log gave me a thought. I thanked Ron and called Devon.

"Meet me in the security room."

When I reached the security room, Sergeant Castañada was waiting outside.

"Trouble?" he asked.

"Maybe. I might have missed someone."

"What can we do?"

I thought for a moment. "You have arrest power even off-duty, right?"

"Even off-duty we're still sworn deputies. Why?"

"Trouble might be closer to home than I thought."

Devon arrived and made to salute Castañada, but I waved him off. He opened the door and let us in. The room wasn't like security rooms in the movies. There were just plain tables and cheap chairs and a couple of small displays offering views around the arena.

"What's up?" asked Devon.

"When you have visitors sign in, what happens to those logs?"

"We file them in here." He pointed to a row of gray steel filing cabinets against the wall.

"For how long?"

"Don't know. Forever, maybe."

"You got the logs for the day of the last power outage?"

"I guess." Devon opened one of the cabinets and started flicking through the files.

"Why isn't this digital?" asked Castañada. "I thought this place was supposed to be state of the art?"

"It is," said Devon. "Well, it's supposed to be. But the software to log people in and out was left off the initial spec, so it was ordered later and just hasn't happened yet."

I looked at Castañada, and he rolled his eyes like he'd seen it all before. Then Devon pulled out a file and opened it.

"This is it. Everyone who came in and out that day."

I dropped the file onto the table and ran my finger slowly down the list of names. The signatures were varied and largely illegible, but the handwritten names were clear enough. Then my phone rang.

"MJ," said Danielle.

"Hit me," I said as my finger continued down the list.

"You said the guy who provided the proof of the substation sabotage was called Rico, right? Well, I found a Rico on Otto Barassi's list of known associates."

I continued scanning the list of unfamiliar names. A lot of people came in and out of a sports arena. There were food and beverage deliveries, toilet paper and cleaning supplies, and cooking-oil exchanges. It was run like a small town.

"I'm sure Otto Barassi's list of associates is long and distinguished."

"Very. But this Rico works for the power company. He's an FPL repair guy. And here's the kicker."

"What?"

"He's Otto Barassi's brother-in-law."

"That figures." Then my finger came to a stop.

"His name is—"

"Rico Martin," I said, tapping the entry log.

CHAPTER FIFTY-THREE

I TURNED FROM THE ENTRY LOGS TO LOOK AT THE SIX MONITORS IN front of me. I now had a better option for who and needed to open up one of our covered bases to create a better where and how.

"Can you control these cameras?" I asked Devon.

"We can turn them from side to side, if that's what you mean."

"That's what I mean. I need you to turn the cameras in the concourse outside electrical room one so they're all pointing north."

"But then we won't be able to see anyone coming from the south side of the arena."

"Exactly."

Devon used the keyboard and a small joystick that looked like something from a kid's computer game to adjust the view of the cameras in the maintenance concourse. When he was done, I told him and Sergeant Castañada what I needed them to do.

"And there's one more thing," I said to Devon. "I need to borrow your keys."

We left the security office and went in three separate directions. I headed directly for the machine room that held the electrical panels. It was a bold play, but I realized as I heard the crowd cheering on the second period of play that Trainor was out of time and the fastest and best bet he had was in that room.

When I got to the door, I noted that the security cameras were all pointed in one direction, such that I wouldn't be seen on any screen in the security room. I used Devon's keys to unlock the door, and I stepped inside, flicking the switch on the wall.

The room burst into light. I'd seen it before, when Rico Martin had arrived to check the fuse boxes to confirm everything was in order. I had stood with Francisco and watched Rico at work, not realizing he was simply resetting switches that he himself had probably tampered with. How he got access I didn't know, but I felt like I was about to find out.

I gave the room a quick scan. When I'd visited previously, I was concerned with other things, other places. Now I looked at the panels on the back wall, and the five-foot-tall electrical boxes that looked like something you might see controlling the traffic lights at busy intersections. I focused on one of the boxes closest to the side wall and marked that as my spot.

I turned off the light, plunging the room into utter darkness, then edged my way with an outstretched hand toward the spot behind the electrical box, and I slipped in between it and the wall to wait.

My other senses kicked up a notch. I could feel the pebbly texture of what had appeared to be a smooth, painted cinderblock wall. The room that had seemed quiet grew loud with the hum of motors and circuits, and the dull sound of the cheering crowd was like distant freeway noise. I put my hand in my pocket and wrapped it around my phone like a gunslinger at the ready.

I didn't dare check the time on my phone or my watch for fear of becoming night blind, but I got the sense that the second period had ended. We were somewhere into the final break between periods when I heard a new sound.

The metal on metal of a key sliding into a lock, then a loud snap. I saw a spear of light shoot across the room as the door opened, then disappear just as quickly as it gently closed with a metallic click.

For a second nothing happened, and I held my breath, straining for any sound. Then I heard the flick of a switch, and the room exploded into bright light once again.

I had underestimated how blinding it would be, and for a moment I could see nothing beyond the metal box before me. I pulled out my phone and hit the button to begin recording, holding it out.

From my hiding spot behind the boxes, I couldn't see the room, but I could see the screen of my phone as I slowly edged it around the corner of the box.

There was a man standing with his back three quarters to me so that I could see his left shoulder but not his right, and not his face. I couldn't see the logo on the front of his shirt, but I knew from the color and design that it belonged to the electric company. I watched the screen as the man moved over to one of the electrical panels on the wall and, using a set of keys, opened up the panel.

He punched a series of buttons then pulled a couple of levers, and I got the sense that some of the background hum of the arena had disappeared. I couldn't really hear anything outside the room, and I wondered if the arena had gone dark.

The machine room certainly hadn't. I saw the guy move to the next electrical panel and unlock it as well. This one was different. Fewer buttons and switches and more large fuse breakers. I saw him flip all the breakers across to what I assumed was the off position. Then he pulled a couple of the larger breakers completely out of the box and put them in his pocket.

The room fell back into darkness for a second. Then the emergency lighting system must have kicked in, as one small lamp in the far corner sent long spear-like shadows across the space.

The man quickly moved to the third panel and opened it up. In the semidarkness I saw him pull out a large breaker, and with that, the emergency lighting died.

I couldn't see him anymore. The room was pitch black once

again, and I heard the man step across to the door of the room and yank it open. There were no shards of light shining in from the maintenance concourse. The entire arena was in darkness. It was dead in the water. I could hear the pensive hum of the crowd outside the door, that quiet uncertainty when a large crowd is trying to comprehend what is happening, in the seconds before panic sets in.

I was moving before I heard the thunk of the door closing. I dashed across to the electrical panels and hit the icon on my phone for the flashlight. I wasn't going to be able to do anything about the backup system if the man had taken the breaker fuse with him, so I went straight to the first of the boxes, the one with all the buttons and switches.

I hit every button that was green and yanked every switch and lever that was pointing down into an up position.

The lights came back on in the room, but I wasn't sure about the arena.

I strode to the door and pulled it open. My efforts hadn't been as fruitful as I had hoped. There were patches of dim light coming from the arena, possibly the glow of a large scoreboard rebooting. But the majority of the lights were still out. I held up my phone flashlight and saw Sergeant Castañada. He had a man against a wall, his hands already behind his back in cuffs, with Castañada's hand at the base of his neck, pushing his face into the cold concrete.

"Rico Martin, I presume?" I said, shining my flashlight into his face. He grunted and snarled but said nothing.

"What about the lights?" asked Castañada.

"Yeah, good call." I reached into Rico Martin's pockets and pulled out the breakers he had taken and shined my flashlight on them for the sergeant to see.

I moved back inside the room and, like a kid doing a puzzle, tried to match the right breaker with the right hole. I managed to replace the breaker for the emergency lighting first, and under the dim light of the backup halogen lamp, I shoved all the other breakers back home.

When I stepped out of the room, I could hear the sound of people clamoring for the exits. I didn't hear yelling or screaming, so it didn't sound like mass panic, more like a collective agreement that the game was over.

"Are we good?" asked the sergeant.

"Better," I said.

I looked at Rico Martin. I recognized him. I'd seen him at the arena once before, talking with Francisco Monaro, doing the so-called repairs after the previous sabotage. And I recalled one other thing: he had gained access to the electrical room using a set of keys I had seen him hand back to Monaro.

I put my hands back in Rico Martin's pockets.

"Hey man," he said. "You some kind of pervert?"

I simply yanked out the set of keys and held them up. They were nothing special—just an ordinary set of keys—but what drew the eye was the pink flamingo hanging off a chain on the ring.

CHAPTER FIFTY-FOUR

As Sergeant Castañada dragged Rico Martin along the maintenance concourse, we heard the arena announcer telling everyone to be cool. I thought *calm* might have been the word such a person would use at such a time, but then I thought of Amanda Swaggert and the too-clever-for-words nickname of the hockey team, so telling people to be cool was on-brand for a team named Chill. The announcer said there had been a temporary electrical problem but that it was all fixed now, and he would make another announcement shortly about the restart of the game. As we passed the gap near the playing surface, I saw a sliver of the crowd. They didn't seem to be getting the message. Most folks looked to be making for the exits.

Castañada called his crew in, and we deposited Rico Martin with Devon in the security office. When the first two of Castañada's men arrived, he turned to me.

"Your show, Jones. Clock's ticking, folks are getting away."

I tried to think what the next move would be. I couldn't stop the crowd from leaving, and I wasn't sure if that would be enough to trigger Trainor's control clause, unless we managed to nail him. We had Rico Martin with his hand in the cookie jar, but there was still a lot of air between Martin and Trainor. Then I thought of the keys.

"This guy got into the room using keys that belong to the facility manager. He's the next link in the chain."

"What about your senator or this Trainor guy?"

I shook my head. "Trainor's not going anywhere. He's up in his cushy suite, watching the kind of panic he thinks will get him control of the arena. We'll get to him, but when we do, it's got to be a slam dunk."

"You use a lot of sports analogies, you know that?"

"Doesn't everyone?"

Castañada shrugged. "So what about the senator?"

"I think he's a crook, and I think this whole *govern while you run a business that profits from your legislation* is as corrupt as all hell, but, no, I don't think he's involved. This was a gravy train for him, nothing more. All about lining his pockets in an ethically bankrupt but technically legal way. I think he sent his crew to follow me as a caution."

"Riviera Beach PD might have been a bit more helpful if you hadn't gone down that rabbit hole."

I shrugged.

"So where's this facility manager?" asked Castañada.

"I know exactly where."

As we walked, I explained my thinking to Castañada and his team.

"It was all a fake-out, from the minute I got here. It was the facility manager, Monaro, who suggested the substation as a possible weak point, and that got me looking at it. That's when I found evidence of Neil Yeow's involvement—I have video of his truck there. And then Monaro got fired, but I figure that was a fake-out too. It put me right off his scent. But it was after his so-called firing that he presented me with the evidence of the sabotage: the burned-out circuit from the substation. So now I had Yeow at the scene, and the evidence of the damage caused."

"So where's this Yeow?"

"He's at home. Because he didn't do it. He was never at the substation. That was a setup, and Yeow was the fall guy. His truck was there, but he wasn't driving it. And the burned board that Monaro showed me? He didn't want to tell me who found it, but when I pressed him he gave me a name: Rico. I'm willing to bet dollars to donuts the whole circuit board thing was done after the fact, to make it look like the substation was the hub of all wrongdoing, when it wasn't."

"What was?"

"It was all here. Right where they could control it. Rico Martin's name is all over the entry logs, apparently here to fix things, but I'm willing to bet he was actually here to break them. We'll need to check all the video feeds, in due course."

"So you're trying to say you were wrong, without saying you were wrong," said Castañada. "That's a tough act to pull off."

"I'm saying they got me looking the wrong way for a while. Looking at the wrong henchman. But the guys behind it all are still the same: Barassi and Trainor. See, they doubled down on framing Yeow by using his truck when they set fire to my house. But we can place one of Barassi's goons there, and I'm willing to bet the other was Rico Martin, not Yeow."

"If we get a solid on the arson, we might be able to apply pressure, get them to roll over."

"I'm not sure how far we'll get with that," I said. "The thug is Barassi's personal enforcer, and Martin is his brother-in-law, and from what I hear, they're a pretty tight crew."

"So who then?"

"Yeow already told my partner that Barassi put him up to calling me out, which led to me being assaulted. I think you'll get something from him."

Castañada got on his phone and called in a unit to pick up Neil Yeow from his home.

"But he didn't do anything," I said. "Not really. He was the patsy. We need to roll the facility manager."

"Who is he again?"

We reached the door of the facility control room, and I pushed it open.

"Francisco Monaro," I said.

The sergeant and his deputies stepped into the room as Monaro looked up from his laptop.

"What's going on?" Monaro asked me.

"Maybe it's a voodoo curse?" I said.

"Francisco Monaro?" asked Sergeant Castañada.

"Yes? Who are you?"

"Palm Beach Sheriff."

Monaro frowned, and his look only grew more intense as Castañada read him his Miranda rights.

"You're arresting me?"

"I'm reading you your rights, so you understand that anything you say can be used in a court of law."

Monaro looked at me. "Is this serious?"

"I think being arrested is generally pretty serious, yeah. But, look, Francisco, we have Rico Martin in custody. You know him, right? He's the guy who just turned off all the lights and tried to kill the game. And you know how he got into the electrical room?"

I dangled the keys with the pink flamingo. Monaro's face dropped.

"Now, unless you want to go down with him, you best start talking."

Monaro set his jaw and looked at Castañada then back at me. I thought he was going to clam up, which was going to be a problem.

But he caved. He sung like a canary.

"Look, I didn't want any of this, you know? Rico came to me during an inspection visit and told me to turn a blind eye to a few things. He offered me cash."

"Everybody likes cash," I said.

"Well, I turned him down, said no. I reported it to Mr. Gelphert. I told him everything. Next day Rico returns and says that running to the boss man was not what friends do to each other. Then he showed me a photo of my wife and kids in our driveway, and he said friends also don't hurt each other's families. So I said okay. I wasn't going to do anything; I'd just look the other way."

"But you didn't just look the other way," I said. "You fed me the story about the crazy voodoo curse."

"Oh, that was real."

I shook my head. "You showed me the fake damaged circuit board."

"Rico gave it to me. He said I should show it to you."

"So the firing was a fake-out?"

"No. The boss fired me. That was real. But Rico said I could get my job back."

"How?"

"He didn't say, but then right after, you called and said I needed to come back, so I figured you were all in on it."

"Do these bruises look like I'm in on it?" I gave him a moment to take in my battered appearance. "Did Con Gelphert ever say anything more to you, after you told him about Rico approaching you?" I asked.

"Yes. When I saw him later, he said I should just keep my head down, do what they wanted. I asked him why he wanted to damage his own arena, and he said it was above his pay grade, that it was just big business. He said just take the money and be happy."

I looked at Castañada and we raised our eyebrows at each other.

"It's not enough," he said.

"What is it with you guys and not enough?"

"We have to present a case in court, not in a bar. And it's just he said–he said. One guy's word against another."

"Not really," said Monaro.

"What do you mean, not really?"

Monaro pulled out his phone. "After Rico first approached me, I got scared. I recorded everything after that."

CHAPTER FIFTY-FIVE

Castañada had one of his deputies take Monaro back to the sheriff's office and called another from the security room to do the same with Rico Martin. Then we headed for the corporate suites.

"You sure they'll still be here?" he asked.

"They'll be loving this crowd leaving, more than any hockey game."

Castañada flashed his ID, and we took the elevator up. There was an usher on the suite level who pointed us to the box where we would find Con Gelphert.

He was standing in the suite overlooking the arena, still a quarter full of folks who had paid good money for hospitality and weren't leaving until the final buzzer.

Gelphert frowned at me and opened his mouth to tell me to get out, or some such bravado, but was shut up by Castañada reading him his rights.

"You're arresting me? For what?"

"The list is long and growing," I said. "Let's start with willful damage and fraud."

"You can't arrest me. I haven't done anything."

"All evidence to the contrary," said Castañada. "But if you want to deal, you can tell us who ordered what."

"I will say nothing without a lawyer."

"I'm sure there's one in the building," I said.

"That is your constitutional right," said Castañada. "You can call one when you get to jail."

Gelphert's jaw dropped so far I thought it might smash against the floor.

"Jail? I can't go to jail."

"That's where arrested people go," said Castañada. "But don't worry, no one will speak to you until a lawyer arrives, and that won't take any longer than forty-eight hours."

"Forty-eight hours? In jail?"

"We don't hold people in hotel suites, Mr. Gelphert."

"No, you can't do that. I haven't done anything. Do you know what my neighbors will say if they hear I've been in jail?"

"I've got a fair idea," I said.

"Look, I didn't do anything, I tell you."

"That's funny," I said, "because right now, you're the one holding the bag for everything. We have recorded evidence of you orchestrating the sabotage, the fraud, the whole enchilada."

"No, no, it wasn't me. It was John Trainor."

"We can't talk about this," said Castañada. "You've requested a lawyer."

"I changed my mind. I revoke my request."

"You hear that, Jones?" said Castañada. "He revokes his request."

"I hear it."

"Yes, I do. I'll tell you what you want to know. John Trainor said we needed to show that the county wasn't capable of running a facility like this, which, let's face it, they're not."

"Why did he need to do that?" asked Castañada.

"Because he needed control of the arena. It's better that way. What do politicians know about running an arena?"

"What do *you* know?" I asked.

"I know plenty."

"But all these problems, the missed games and lost revenue, that all looks bad for you."

"John said it might look bad for a bit, but . . ."

"But what?" asked Castañada.

"He said that if I took one for the team, then soon the league would need a new commissioner."

"That's funny, he offered the same thing to Senator Vargas," I said.

"He did? Why that—!"

"Did Mr. Trainor order you to sabotage the arena?" asked Castañada.

"No. He said someone would take care of it."

"Who?"

Gelphert inspected his shoes.

"Who, Mr. Gelphert?"

"Otto Barassi."

Castañada had Gelphert taken away after assurances that, for now at least, he would be going to the sheriff's office, not jail.

"Where do you keep these guys at the sheriff's office?" I asked.

"In lockup." He smiled. "Who's next?"

"Trainor's right next door."

"Okay. We're gonna need a bigger boat."

We strode out to the owner's suite next door. Castañada took the lead with one of his remaining deputies. Maggie Nettles was standing outside the door.

"You didn't get in?" I asked.

"Oh, no, I got in. He wasn't too happy to see me," she said with an evil grin.

"Well, it's gonna get better. He's about to get arrested. When he comes out, you should have your phone ready for a nice picture. Maybe you can ask your questions again, get a nice additional *no comment*."

"I do know how to do my job, Jones."

I followed Sergeant Castañada into the suite, and we made a

beeline for Trainor. He was at his tall table again, watching the remaining fans below.

"Why are they smoothing out the ice?" he asked the guy with him. "They should be calling it off. It's dangerous or something—"

"Mr. Trainor," said Castañada. "Palm Beach Sheriff. I wonder if you wouldn't mind stepping outside with me for a moment."

Trainor frowned then caught sight of me. He attracted the attention of an older guy at another table, who came over to him.

"I am Mr. Trainor's attorney, and you are?"

"Sergeant Castañada, Palm Beach Sheriff's Office."

"Well, Sergeant, whatever it is, you can call my office tomorrow during business hours to ask any questions you may have of my client, and we'll decide whether we care to respond."

"It won't wait."

"Oh, Sergeant, unless my client is under arrest, he is free to enjoy his time without harassment from the likes of you."

"That's true," said Castañada.

"I'm glad you agree."

"John Trainor, as per the wishes of your attorney, you are under arrest."

The lawyer almost foamed at the mouth. He tried protesting, but Castañada shut him down. He read Trainor his rights and cuffed him.

"The cuffs are not necessary," said the lawyer.

"They weren't," said Castañada. "But you wanted it done this way, so here you are. You can call our office tomorrow to arrange for time with your client, and we'll decide whether we care to respond." Castañada looked at Trainor, who had gone purple with rage. "If he still is your client tomorrow."

Castañada pushed Trainor out of the suite, past the gaping mouths of all the suits. As they strode toward the elevator, Maggie Nettles shouted her questions and shot pictures with her phone.

When the elevator arrived, Maggie got in first and Castañada handed Trainor to his deputy, who made no attempt to remove her. A free and open press was the foundation of every democracy, especially when it was in your ear as you were led away in cuffs.

"Anyone left?" asked Castañada, who seemed to be enjoying himself.

"Barassi."

"Where's he?"

"This way."

I led the sergeant to another suite. I hadn't been in through the door—my previous visit was after having jumped the balustrade between the stands in front of the suites—but I was fairly confident my math was right.

Castañada led the way inside. He drew every eye as he burst into the box, and I searched the room for Otto Barassi. I didn't find him. But I did find his enforcer. The big unit came at me like a wounded bull.

"You're asking for it," he spat.

"Stop where you are," said Castañada.

"You want some?" said the big unit. It seemed to be a rhetorical question as he wound up to lay a haymaker on Castañada or me or maybe both.

"Do you want some?" said Castañada, pulling his sidearm out and pointing it at the big unit's head.

The guy stopped but didn't submit.

"Palm Beach Sheriff," Castañada said loudly. "Get on the floor."

The big thug slowly dropped to his knees, and Castañada urged him to lie down on his stomach.

"Where is Otto Barassi?" I said to the room.

No one said anything, but a couple of heads turned to the stands out through the floor-to-ceiling windows. I dashed out there and found no one. Castañada had drawn everyone inside. Except one. Otto Barassi had climbed over the balustrade and was running up into the next suite. I vaulted over the steel railing and chased him up the steps.

Barassi was running out the door into the elevator lobby as I reached the windows, and I sprinted across the room. I launched out into the foyer: no sign of Barassi. The elevator hadn't returned yet, so I scanned the area and noticed the door to the fire stairs closing. I took off in that direction and down the stairs, two or three at a time.

I had a couple of decades and an athletic build over Barassi, so despite not laying eyes on him, I knew I had to be gaining. I pushed the door open to the public concourse. Again there was no sign of him, but there were no other people around either. Those that were leaving had left, and the rest were in their seats waiting for the hockey game to resume.

But Barassi wasn't invisible, so I went back to the stairs and raced down to the maintenance level. I ran out into the concourse and looked one way then the other. That's when I saw him. He had gotten farther away than I thought, but it had cost him. He was stumbling. He clearly didn't get dragged out onto the beach for a jog by his wife on a regular basis.

I chased after him. He reached the gap that led out to the playing surface, and I saw him pause. Then he jumped into a golf cart. He took off and disappeared.

I ran harder until I reached the gap and looked up toward the rink. Past the line of players waiting to retake the ice, Barassi zoomed away in the cart, not fast but certainly quicker than I could run.

The end boards of the rink were open like a gate. Barassi drove right through and onto the ice, almost running head-on into the Zamboni that was leaving.

The remains of the crowd cheered as they saw the golf cart zoom to where the goal was about to be replaced. I ran to the edge of the ice and stopped. I couldn't catch up on foot, so I grabbed the closest vehicle I could find. It happened to be the Zamboni.

I climbed up and told the driver I needed to borrow his vehicle. I was prepared to pull him out of his seat if it came to that, but discretion was the better part of valor, and the driver simply jumped down.

I had never driven a Zamboni before, but I had ridden a tractor once or twice, and it felt similar. I made a wide turn and headed off in pursuit.

It was then I saw the folly of my decision.

The Zamboni wasn't built for comfort, but it also wasn't built for speed—I could have outrun the damned thing. It was like a car chase in slow motion. I saw Barassi at about center ice as I passed the goal line. I headed after him at a glacial pace and couldn't catch up at all. It started to feel pointless.

Then I saw the folly of *his* decision.

The side boards at the other end of the ice were closed. Both teams left the ice at the end where we had entered, as did the Zamboni, so there was no other way off the rink. Barassi was trapped. He must have realized that as he headed toward the goal line because he yanked hard on the wheel to turn around, but he obviously miscalculated the available surface friction. The cart turned but slid onward toward the boards at the end of the rink.

He slammed into the boards hard with a sickening crunch like a defender body-checking a winger. The Plexiglass windshield popped out and dropped onto the ice, and the crowd gasped. I headed straight at the cart. Barassi saw me coming, and I noticed the fear in his eyes.

Then he took off again, *sans* windshield, in the opposite direction. His wheels spun hard, and he fishtailed back and forth but got moving in the general direction of the exit.

I pulled the Zamboni around. It was designed not to skid and slide, and the tires offered more grip than those on a golf cart, but it fishtailed slightly as I swung a wide arc back after Barassi.

Then it all happened again, just in the opposite direction. We chugged across the ice like a circus act. The players started taking the ice, splitting left and right around the golf cart like a synchronized skating troupe.

Number eight, the winger, skated up beside me and nodded.

"All right?" he asked.

"Not bad."

"We got a game going on here, you know?"

"That's why I'm after this knucklehead. He's trying to kill the game. He's the saboteur."

"He is, is he?"

Barassi reached the center ice more or less heading forward, still not completely in control but just enough, and as the rear of the cart swung away, I saw Barassi turn and glare at me. Then he gave that mirthless shark's smile that said he was getting away and there was nothing I could do about it.

He was right. But I wasn't the one he needed to be worried about.

Number eight pushed off strong and within a second was flying across the ice ahead of me. He skated out wide, down the wing he knew so well, and along the boards to the back of the rink toward the open gate. Then he cut hard and headed right down the middle of the ice. Right at me.

And right at Otto Barassi. Barassi hunched over the wheel like they were playing chicken. At the last moment, number eight cut around the golf cart to pass him by, but as he did he hung his hockey stick out like a lazy jouster and, with a deft touch, hooked the blade around Barassi's neck and pulled him from the cart.

Barassi went spinning across the ice on his belly, leaving a trail of blood from the teeth he lost as his face hit the ice. When he came to a stop, the players started circling him like wagons in a western. I stopped the Zamboni, jumped down, and skated on my shoes across to him.

The players didn't look too concerned about Barassi—blood and expelled teeth were not strange sights on a hockey rink. Sergeant Castañada attempted to slide out to us but landed on his butt before he got two feet, the product of a Florida upbringing, no doubt. Two of the players hooked their sticks under Barassi's armpits and dragged him to the side, where Castañada placed him under arrest.

The crowd went wild.

CHAPTER FIFTY-SIX

MAGGIE NETTLES RECOUNTED THE WHOLE THING IN A THREE-PART front-page series over the next few days. Ron sat on his stool at Longboard Kelly's, regaling us with tales of financial shenanigans and public mismanagement. Trainor's loan was called in, and his passport was confiscated as a condition of his bail. Maggie's report claimed that the league would declare bankruptcy before the week's end, with Miami's team owner suggesting liquidators would recover the assets before Christmas.

"Not great for Florida," said Danielle. "I wonder what happens to the arena."

"Maggie says it's likely that Trainor's bankruptcy team will sell his share for pennies on the dollar."

"Will it survive though?"

"She says hockey will be gone but basketball will remain, and what else, I don't know."

We sipped our drinks in the twilight as the party lights across the courtyard took over. The air grew cool, enough for long pants but not a jacket. I was still feeling off-kilter. I couldn't shake the feeling that we had achieved the goal of saving our insurance client their money at a greater cost than I was comfortable with. The team was gone, and with it the livelihoods of the players and coaches and staff. It didn't feel great to have contributed to that outcome.

Then my day got better as my wife's ex-husband sauntered in. Eric, still in an expensive suit, looked well out of place at Longboard's. The breeze seemed to buffet him as if he didn't have the heft to stand straight in a draft.

"Evening all," he said as he approached the bar.

He received nods all around, and Muriel asked what he would like to drink.

"A beer would be great, thank you." I would have pegged him for a chardonnay man.

"Congratulations on your election to the state Senate," said Danielle, clinking glasses with him.

"Thank you."

"Yes, congratulations," I said, offering a nod but keeping my glass to myself.

"I appreciate that, Jones, even if you didn't vote."

"I did vote, as it happens."

"You did?" said Danielle.

"Of course. It's not just our right, it's our responsibility." I felt the piousness swell inside as I said it.

"Well, good for you, Jones. I admire your civic participation, even if it was at my cost," he said with a smile.

"It wasn't at your cost, Eric."

"When you vote for the other guy, it's kind of at my cost."

"I didn't vote for the other guy. I voted for you."

I felt every eyeball on both sides of the bar on me. I watched Eric, waiting for the punch line. But there wasn't one.

"So what brings you to Longboard's?" I asked.

"I thought you might like an update on my last official act as state attorney."

"Which is?"

"To build a case against half the world. You really did sweep up everyone this time, didn't you?"

"I had a Zamboni at my disposal, so . . ."

"What will happen?" asked Danielle.

"A lot of plea deals, testimonies, depositions, and legal fees. Some fines will be issued, the unions will be booting out some deadwood, and the power company will jettison some employees who don't quite fit their corporate culture."

"And former Senator Vargas?"

"Once a senator, always a senator, Jones. There's no case against him. But he'll lose his directorship of the league and the consulting fees his wife would have earned."

"And Trainor?"

"He'll plea and probably get fined. Might do a little time at a minimum-security farm, but that's a stretch and will depend on how aggressively my successor wants to go at it."

"So scot-free, basically."

"He'll lose his team, his league, a lot of money, and any prestige he's built up, and that sort of thing means a lot to these guys."

"It seems like a real fall from grace," said Danielle.

"It is, but then, these guys always have money squirreled away somewhere. He'll bounce back, just maybe not all the way."

"And what about the arena, Senator?" I asked.

"Senator-elect," he said. "I'll do all I can to make sure the county and state get the best out of it. The private side of the deal will probably be sold off, and the county will want to restructure the agreement to ensure their controlling interest. Losing the hockey league means the arena is a tenant down, but I'm told Kenny Chesney's promoter has shown interest in holding a concert there, so that will attract other events."

"So when are you moving to Tallahassee?" I asked.

"I'm not moving to Tallahassee. I'm only required there for sixty session days a year, so I'll be staying here. I'm sure we'll see each other around the traps."

"Awesome," I said.

Eric finished his drink and said his goodbyes.

After he walked out of the courtyard, Danielle turned to me. "That's not the worst result."

"Not the best either. I'm glad the county won't lose its shirt, but I don't feel great about it. The bad guys didn't win, but they didn't exactly lose, did they? And what about the players and the coaches? They lose their chance. For many it will be the end of a dream. What will they do?"

"Get real jobs," said Mick as he picked up the empty glasses and turned away into the darkness behind the bar.

CHAPTER FIFTY-SEVEN

We enjoyed one more beer, and I started to get restless again. I wanted to stay, but I had to leave. I couldn't take advantage of Ron and Cassandra's hospitality anymore, and we lived a couple hours away. A long, boring drive that I didn't want to do with too many beers under my belt.

"We should head out," I said. "Want to get back to Miami at a reasonable hour."

"We're not going back to Miami," said Danielle.

"I'm not sure Ron and Cassandra can put up with much more of us."

"We're more than happy to have you," said Ron.

"We're not going to Ron and Cassandra's," said Danielle. "We're going camping."

I shot Ron a look of confusion that was returned tenfold. Danielle eased off her stool and reached across the bar. Muriel handed her a cooler bag with a couple of wine bottles sticking out the top.

"Follow me," said Danielle with that half smile that does all sorts of things to me.

I waved goodbye to Muriel and Ron and followed Danielle out

into the parking lot. She put the wine in her car and told me again to follow her.

"Have you ever pitched a tent in the dark?" I asked.

"No," she said, getting into her car.

I followed her out onto Route 1 heading north. I had no idea where we were going, so I watched her taillights closely. We passed the port, and I waited for us to turn west toward the Everglades. I figured most of the camping in Florida was in the Everglades, as foolhardy as that sounded—*darkness* and *Everglades* didn't grab me as words that easily sat together.

But we didn't turn west. Danielle turned east onto Blue Heron Boulevard, past Phil Foster Park, and continued onto Singer Island. I wasn't sure what her thinking was, but my heart sank. She led me down into our old subdivision and toward the rubble of our house. I didn't want to see it. I had no idea why she wanted me to.

Danielle pulled into the driveway. The leased car that had burned was gone. I parked behind her and looked at what her headlights lit up. It wasn't a dream, and there hadn't been some kind of miracle. The house was still rubble and ash.

Danielle killed the lights. I got out and met her at the trunk of her car.

"What are we doing?"

She collected a backpack and hefted it onto her shoulder. Then she picked up the bag Muriel had given her.

"Bring the cooler," she said and walked away.

I grabbed the cooler and slammed the trunk shut. I followed Danielle around the side of the darkened shell of our house.

In the middle of the back lawn was a pitched tent. Lanterns hung from the front of it, throwing a soft glow across the lawn toward the water. I slowed, unsure of what I was seeing. When I reached the tent, I dropped the cooler. Danielle set her bags down as if arriving home from work.

I looked inside the tent and found a queen mattress topped with large pillows and two sleeping bags, illuminated by battery-operated candles. I turned back and noticed the two canvas camp chairs facing the intracoastal. The lights from Riviera Beach twinkled across the Intracoastal, washed out like a watercolor.

She pulled out some paper sacks and set them on the small table between the chairs.

"We've got some hummus and pita, and Mick made some smoked fish dip."

I nodded but said nothing.

"Will you open the wine?" she asked, sitting in a chair with her back to me.

I moved like a ghost to the cooler bag and opened a bottle of wine, then found two glasses wrapped in towels in the bag. I poured the wine and sat beside Danielle. I handed her a glass, and she took it with a smile.

"Cheers," she said.

"What are we doing here?" I asked.

She glanced around as if she couldn't possibly know what I meant. "We're home."

"The house is gone."

"Doesn't matter," she said. "This place is your mooring. I could see you were floating, a little lost. I wanted to bring you back."

She held out her glass and tapped mine.

"I thought you were my mooring," I said.

"I like to think I'm the wind in your sails, but, no, this place is your mooring. Hell, what am I saying? It's our mooring. Sometimes you have to leave to know what you had. Sometimes you never get it back, but sometimes you do."

She held up her glass and then took a sip, so I did the same. Then I looked out at the dark water and smelled the briny scent of home.

Danielle opened the hummus and fish dip and a packet of pita bread. She pulled off a piece and dipped it in the hummus. I watched her eat as she watched the water. Then she turned to me.

"What do you think you'll do?" she asked.

"About what?"

"The house." She smiled. "Build a nice big mansion like the neighbors? Now's your chance."

I turned in the direction of the wedding cake next door and then back.

"What would you like to do?" I asked.

Danielle sipped her wine. "I'd build it back the exact way it was."

I sipped my wine and looked at the lights on the water, and for the first time in too long I felt a smile creep onto my lips.

"Exactly what I was thinking."

IF YOU ENJOYED THIS BOOK

One of the most powerful things a reader can do is recommend a writer's work to a friend. So if you have friends you think will enjoy the capers of Miami Jones and his buddies, please tell them.

Your honest reviews help other readers discover Miami and his friends, so if you enjoyed this book and would like to spread the word, just take one minute to leave a short review. I'd be eternally grateful, and I hope new readers will be too.

ALSO BY A.J. STEWART

Miami Jones series

Stiff Arm Steal

Offside Trap

High Lie

Dead Fast

Crash Tack

Deep Rough

King Tide

No Right Turn

Cruise Control

Red Shirt

Half Court Press

Past The Post

The Ninth Inning

Big Thaw

Three Strikes

John Flynn series

The Compound (novella)
The Final Tour
Burned Bridges
One for One
The Rotten State
Lost Luggage

Lenny & Lucas series

Temple of Gold

Danielle Castle novella

Little Packages

ACKNOWLEDGMENTS

Thanks for Lisa Kaitz for the stellar work, and Stacey for her eagle eye. The scoundrels in South Florida (you know who you are) and of course all the readers.

ABOUT THE AUTHOR

A.J. Stewart is the USA Today bestselling author of the Miami Jones mystery series and the John Flynn thriller series.

He has lived and worked in Australia, Japan, UK, Norway, and South Africa, as well as San Francisco, Connecticut and of course Florida. He currently resides in Los Angeles with his two favorite people, his wife and son.

AJ is working on a screenplay that he never plans to produce, but it gives him something to talk about at parties in LA.

You can find AJ online at www.ajstewartbooks.com.

Made in the USA
Las Vegas, NV
13 December 2022